THE
DRAGON RIDGE
TOMBS

ALSO BY TIANXIA BACHANG

The City of Sand

THE
DRAGON RIDGE
TOMBS

TIANXIA BACHANG

TRANSLATED FROM THE CHINESE
BY JEREMY TIANG

DELACORTE PRESS

Translation copyright © 2018 by Jeremy Tiang
Text copyright © 2006 by Shanghai Xuanting Entertainment Information Technology Co., Ltd.
Jacket art copyright © 2018 by Michael-Paul Terranova

All rights reserved. Published in the United States by Delacorte Press, an imprint of Random House Children's Books, a division of Penguin Random House LLC, New York. Originally published in Chinese and in paperback by Anhui Arts Publishing House, Hefei City, Anhui Province, China, in 2006.

Delacorte Press is a registered trademark and the colophon is a trademark of Penguin Random House LLC.

Visit us on the Web! GetUnderlined.com

Educators and librarians, for a variety of teaching tools, visit us at RHTeachersLibrarians.com

Library of Congress Cataloging-in-Publication Data
Names: Tianxia Bachang, author. | Tiang, Jeremy, translator.
Title: The Dragon Ridge tombs / Tianxia Bachang; translated from the Chinese by Jeremy Tiang.
Other titles: Gui chui deng zhi long ling mi ku. English
Description: Trade hardcover edition, first American edition. | New York : Delacorte Press, [2018] | Companion to: City of sand. | Originally published: Hefei City, China : Anhui Arts Publishing House, 2006. | Summary: Teenaged best friends Tianyi and Kai journey deep below a mountain range, where ancient tombs are certain to contain riches but are rumored to be guarded by merciless supernatural forces.
Identifiers: LCCN 2017052668 (print) | LCCN 2018000177 (ebook) | ISBN 978-0-553-52415-4 (ebook) | ISBN 978-0-553-52414-7 (trade hardcover) | ISBN 978-0-553-52417-8 (library binding)
Subjects: | CYAC: Adventure and adventurers—Fiction. | Best friends—Fiction. | Friendship—Fiction. | Supernatural—Fiction. | Grave robbing—Fiction. | Feng shui—Fiction. | China—Fiction.
Classification: LCC PZ7.1B265 (ebook) | LCC PZ7.1.B265 Dr 2018 (print) | DDC [Fic]—dc23

The text of this book is set in 13-point Perpetua.
Interior design by Ken Crossland
Printed in the United States of America
10 9 8 7 6 5 4 3 2 1
First American Edition

THE
DRAGON RIDGE
TOMBS

CHAPTER ONE

AFTER OUR LAST ADVENTURE IN CHINA'S TAKLIMAKAN Desert, I didn't see Julie Yang for a while. She was busy arranging medical treatment for Professor Chen and dealing with the police about the members of our expedition who hadn't made it back—sadly, our mission had ended with the professor's assistant and three of his students falling victim to the curse of the Jingjue queen; they would now lie forever beneath the shifting desert sands. When the authorities questioned us, I was worried they'd find out my best friend, Kai, and I were gold hunters, so I said as little as possible. Archaeological expeditions are always risky, but four deaths and a professor who'd lost his mind raised serious suspicions.

Kai and I had rented a tiny apartment in Beijing and were

trying to decide whether we could make a living from gold-hunting work. We were seventeen, neither of us headed to college. One night, as I lay in bed, there was a sharp knock on the door. Kai was out on the town, but I'd decided to stay home—I'd had bad dreams the night before, and my head was throbbing. I called out that I was coming, hoping it wasn't another surprise visit from the cops.

I opened the door. It wasn't anyone in uniform. It was Julie. I told her to come in quick and asked how she'd found me. She said Gold Tooth, an antiques dealer who had a stall at Pan Market, had given her our address.

"You know Gold Tooth?" I was startled.

"Not very well. My father used to collect artifacts and did some business with him. But Gold Tooth is friends with Professor Chen. I went to see him to track you and Kai down—I still owe you money. I'm leaving the country with the professor in a couple of days to get him medical help in America, so I probably won't see you for a while."

Finally, Kai and I were getting paid! I thought it might be politer to refuse, though. "You're going home? Is the professor any better?" I asked. "I'd just been thinking of visiting him. Don't worry about the money for now. We didn't do that much, after all."

Julie plonked the cash on the table. "I'm paying you. That was our arrangement. But there's something I hope you'll agree to.

"Our ancestors were in the same line of work. My grandfather washed his hands of gold hunting because it brings terrible karma, and no matter how good your destiny is to start with, sooner or later you come to a bad end. I hope you'll find something else to do. If there's a way I could get you guys to the States, I could help arrange—"

"Thanks for the offer, but you only know half the story," I interrupted, losing my temper. "There are two sides to every issue. Good things can turn bad, and bad things can turn good. That's called dialectical materialism. You already know I'm a reverse dipper, so I might as well tell you the rest. I have principles. I'd never touch an ancient tomb that's already been discovered and preserved. But deep in the forests and mountains are other graves no one knows about, all of them stuffed with valuables. These graves are impossible to find, except by people like me who know the secrets of feng shui. I'm gifted at reading the earth and the sky. If I didn't look for these graves, they'd probably stay hidden underground forever. Don't forget, I'm the one who found the lost city of Jingjue in the desert for you. But I would never damage any of these places, and it offends me when you imply that I don't show the proper respect."

Seeing that I was prepared to go on for quite a while, Julie held up a hand. "All right. I was just trying to give you some good advice, but you're clearly not going to listen to what I say. I don't think anyone in the world would defend reverse dipping the way you just did. Forget I said anything. I guess you won't be wanting this money either."

I hastily snatched the money she'd placed on the table. "A deal is a deal. Thanks for this. But let's call it a loan. I'll pay you back with interest, how about that?" She nodded curtly and stormed out, and I wondered if I'd gone too far. What would Kai make of this?

Later that evening, I sat watching as Kai counted the cash.

Or rather, he tried to count it a few times but couldn't reach a total. I didn't blame him. It was a staggering amount, more than we'd ever seen.

Finally, Kai tossed the bundle of bills onto the table. "Tianyi, I thought you were the clever one," he grumbled. "Why did you have to go and say this was a loan? Tell you what, let's just spend it all, and then we'll go stay with my relatives down south. Julie will never be able to find us there."

"You're useless," I snorted. "Who cares about the money? Once we go reverse dipping, the treasures we find will be more than enough to pay Julie back. Plus, we can buy all the equipment we need, not to mention stop worrying about where our next meal is coming from. Starting now, we're on a mission. Let's get ready for a big haul."

We began planning right away. The remote tombs I had in mind wouldn't be easy to find—who knew how long it would take us? This was a good sum of money, but it would run out eventually.

Kai was more pragmatic. He reckoned Gold Tooth was doing well with his antiques business—especially since a lot of his clients were foreigners. The tourists were better informed and harder to cheat these days, but as long as you had high-quality stuff, they were definitely willing to empty their wallets.

"How about if we opened our own shop?" said Kai. "Get some old things to sell, and if it goes well we won't need to do any reverse dipping. Breaking into tombs might be quick money, but it's a lot of hard work."

I nodded. "Not a bad idea, Kai. Turns out your brain does work sometimes. We've got the capital, after all. Let's start small, and we can learn the antiques trade as we go."

4

The next day, we went off to find a shop to rent, but we couldn't find anything suitable. Then we realized we might have aimed too high and decided a stall in Pan Market would do just as well.

Pan Market was famous for the sheer variety of goods on offer. Extremely valuable antiques weren't common, however; they tended to sell in private deals, rather than being displayed in the street for everyone to gawk at.

Following Gold Tooth's advice, we went out into the suburbs in search of early Qing dynasty pots and bowls, old coins, snuffboxes, pocket watches, and other small items to sell. Unluckily, I kept seizing on things that turned out to be worthless, and when I did find something special, I let it go for far too low a price. We ended our days with a loss.

At least we hadn't spent too much money collecting the knickknacks, so we didn't put much of a dent in our capital. The main thing was to train ourselves to see the true value of things. People spent years acquiring this knowledge, which I was starting to realize might be more complex than feng shui. We certainly weren't going to get there overnight, but Gold Tooth said I was a natural.

A few weeks went by, which we spent mostly helping out at Gold Tooth's stall. He finally suggested that we close our stall and join him in his. We were thrilled to accept. One slow morning, when hardly any customers had shown up, Kai, Gold Tooth, and I sat on the ground playing cards.

Halfway through a round, someone started pacing in front of our stall. Kai thought the man was a customer and called out to him, "Sir, can I help you? Is there something you'd like to see?"

5

"No—no, nothing, but do you take old things?" the man stammered.

I looked up. The man had purplish-red skin from long hours in the sun. Probably a farmer of some sort. His clothes definitely pegged him as someone from outside the city, and he had a hillbilly Shaanxi accent. He was clutching a tattered leather bag.

Wondering what sort of antiques this guy could have, I glanced at Gold Tooth. He didn't hesitate. "Join us," he told the farmer. "Sit. You must be tired from your trip. Allow me to offer you some tea."

The farmer clearly hadn't seen much of the world and didn't quite know how to make conversation. Perching on the folding stool I'd brought out, he clutched his bag tightly and kept his mouth shut.

I stared at the bag and suddenly wondered if he might be a reverse dipper too. Probably not, but he did seem guilty of something. Maybe he really did have a precious item in there. I made my voice as friendly as possible and said, "Yes, please enjoy your tea, sir. It's the very best. May I ask your name?"

"I'm called Li Chunlai," said the farmer. Unable to get comfortable on the stool, he shoved it aside and squatted on the ground, suddenly looking more relaxed.

Gold Tooth and Kai pretended to continue the card game. In our line of business, it's important not to crowd the customer. The ones who turn up with items to sell are usually jumpy, worried someone will snatch their treasure from them.

I kept a smile plastered on my face. "Mr. Li, you were saying something earlier about old things. Do you have antiquities we can take off your hands?"

"Anti-what?"

So he was a real bumpkin. I broke it down for him. "Antiques—you know, valuable things from the past. Could you let me take a look?"

Li Chunlai looked around to make sure no one was eavesdropping. "I only have one shoe," he whispered. "How much can you give me for it?"

I bit back a snide comment. All that trouble for an old shoe? But maybe there was something more to the story. "What kind of shoe?" I probed.

Apparently finding me approachable, Li Chunlai grew bolder. Unzipping his bag, he let me peer inside. His tattered satchel contained a finely embroidered satin shoe, no more than three inches long. It was exquisite and could have fit only onto a lady's bound foot. I recalled that this was known as lotus feet.

Before I could get a proper look, he'd zipped the bag shut again, as if afraid the shoe would fly out of his possession.

"Wait!" I said hastily. "I wasn't done looking. Where in the world did you get that?"

Li Chunlai shook his head. "All you have to do is name a price. I don't care about the rest."

"Mr. Li," I said, "you have to let me have another look. How else do you expect me to give you a price?" Lowering my voice, I added, "Are there too many prying eyes around here, is that it? Tell you what, let me treat you to a snack. There's a restaurant nearby that has excellent mutton dumplings. It's clean and quiet, and we can talk business there. If your shoe is as valuable as I suspect, we'll need to discuss fair compensation. What do you say?"

The farmer was drooling at the thought of mutton dumplings. "That's a great idea. Better than sitting beneath the hot sun. Nothing like a good meal before getting down to business."

Nodding to Kai and Gold Tooth, I escorted Mr. Li down the block to the restaurant. The place was starting to get a bit of a reputation—the couple who ran it were excellent cooks. Their dumplings were delicious and generously stuffed, and the restaurant was always spick-and-span.

It was almost lunchtime, and already the place was starting to fill with customers. I was becoming a regular here, and the couple knew me well. They called out a greeting, and when I raised an eyebrow to indicate we'd appreciate some privacy, the wife bustled over to set up a table in their storeroom at the back. She got us bowls and chopsticks, then hurried out to fill more orders.

The storeroom was where I usually brought people when we needed to talk. Only the sacks of flour could overhear us. And I always told the owners to keep the change from lunch—a fee for use of the room.

"I hope this is all right," I said to Mr. Li. "We're alone now, so you can show me the shoe."

Li Chunlai looked bewitched by the enticing aroma of dumplings. He didn't react to my words, probably thinking only of the meal to come.

There was nothing I could do but force a smile and nudge him playfully. "Don't worry, they'll bring the food in as soon as it's ready. If I can offer you a good price for that shoe, you'll be able to eat mutton dumplings every day of your life."

This seemed to bring him to his senses, and he started

hastily shaking his head. "No way, no way. When I sell this shoe, I'm using the cash to find a wife."

I laughed. "For sure! What lady could resist you, with some money in your pocket?"

Li Chunlai loosened up. "That's right, maybe someone from Mizhi. They say Mizhi girls are the prettiest."

As he chatted away, the wife came back in with a steaming plate of dumplings. Mr. Li immediately stopped talking and began shoveling them into his mouth.

Seeing the rate at which he was going, I quickly ordered another large bowl, then put a saucer of vinegar in front of him. "Mr. Li, we don't serve dumplings in sour soup the way you like it in Shaanxi, but try dipping them in this."

Mr. Li got through a dozen dumplings without pausing for breath, head lowered over his plate. I waited patiently till he was done, then mentioned the shoe again.

I seemed to have earned his trust. He brought the shoe out of his satchel without hesitation.

Studying the shoe from all angles, I noted its tip pointed like a bamboo shoot, its green satin insole, the peonies embroidered in gold, blue, and red silk thread, and the sandalwood sole with a slot where fragrance could be inserted.

From the shape and pattern, I guessed it dated back to the Ming dynasty. Not many Shaanxi women had bound feet, unless they were from aristocratic families, which explained why the handiwork was so exquisite.

If Gold Tooth had been with us, a mere sniff of the shoe would have told him exactly where it was from, but I wasn't that advanced yet. Still, I was certain from the coloring and materials that this was the genuine article, not a copy.

Three-inch lotus shoes like these were popular with collectors, and this one would definitely fetch a high price.

I asked Mr. Li where he'd found it, and he told me the whole story.

He was from a drought-stricken part of Shaanxi, where things had been particularly bad that year. Without a drop of rain to water their crops, the villagers were driven to try all sorts of crazy remedies. When a blind fortune-teller said this was the work of a drought demon, they immediately clamored to know its name. Then a goatherd boy piped up that while leading his goats through an abandoned graveyard to the east, he'd seen a small child with green skin scurrying into an unmarked coffin. This was bizarre, particularly as no one had been buried there for a long time—and no one knew of a coffin still aboveground.

The blind fortune-teller insisted that this coffin must be where the demon was hiding. The villagers wanted to break it open to see what was inside, but the village elder disagreed—he thought the blind man was talking nonsense. In a rage, the fortune-teller led the others to the graveyard, determined to prove he was right. Sure enough, there was the coffin. Working together, the villagers ripped the lid off.

Right away, an awful stench hit them, a bit like a pile of fish left to rot in the sun, but worse.

The more fearless among them pinched their noses shut and went closer to have a look. They gasped—a female corpse lay in the coffin, her clothes and gold jewelry perfectly preserved, even though they were clearly centuries old. The body was dried out, the skin like fossilized wood.

By the dead woman's head lay a tiny creature like a monkey, covered in green fur. It was alive, curled up in a ball as if asleep.

The villagers argued about what they had discovered and what should be done. Only the fortune-teller spoke with authority.

"Kill it!" he said. "The green creature is the drought demon, and it must be killed before it wakes up at nightfall. If you wait, you will never catch it. Beat it to death; then give it a good whipping to tear the corpse apart and ensure it doesn't come back to life."

A few bold souls grabbed the creature and bashed its head in with a hammer. The strange thing was, it didn't bleed. Instead, when they whipped it, each lash released a puff of black smoke. When the body was destroyed, it burst into flames and was instantly reduced to ashes.

The sun was now beginning to set. The villagers asked the fortune-teller what they should do with the corpse, and he replied that leaving her where she was would bring disaster, and to put the coffin lid back on and burn her along with all her possessions.

They hesitated at first. This was an ancient corpse, and the jewelry she'd been buried with was surely worth a great deal.

As they were debating what to do, dark clouds rolled over them and thunder started rumbling. Finally, the village elder put Li Chunlai in charge of setting the fire. The rest of them ran off. Mr. Li was the sort of man who always did what he was told, and though he was terrified, he steeled himself to follow instructions.

Hoping to get the job done before the rain started, he quickly scraped together some twigs for kindling, piled them around the coffin, and lit a match.

As he waited for the coffin to catch fire, Li Chunlai started thinking that it was a shame not to take a bit of the gold for himself. He'd waited a second too long, though, because the flames suddenly blazed up.

As regret swallowed him, he was blinded by a flash of light, and four thunderclaps sounded in quick succession. The rain came down in buckets, drenching him and dousing the fire.

Dripping wet, he stared at the smoldering coffin, his heart thumping. The heavens were giving him an opportunity. The contents of the coffin were still intact. If he was going to grab them, it had to be now.

The other villagers were long gone. After having waited forever for the sky to open up with rain, they weren't about to let a drop go to waste. Li Chunlai was all alone in the desolate graveyard with the dead woman. He was still terrified, but then he thought of how much money he could get. Enough to marry a nice plump lady and put an end to his bachelorhood. He grabbed a nearby shovel and pushed the lid, which had already been pried open and weakened by the flames, aside.

The first time around, he'd been squashed in the crowd and had only managed a quick glimpse of what was in there. Now he had to brace himself to take a proper look at his spoils.

Most of the original foul smell had dissipated, replaced by an equally repellent mixture of acrid burning, dampness, and mustiness. Even as the rain continued, this strange odor assaulted him.

Li Chunlai gritted his teeth, held his nose, and peered into the coffin. He couldn't believe his eyes. It was as the others had said—there was jewelry aplenty. No time to think about demons.

The storm was growing more violent, and it would soon be pitch-dark. Li Chunlai pulled himself together and fixed his sights on a gold bracelet. His hand had just closed around it when someone slapped him hard.

He cried out, thinking the lightning must have reanimated one of the other corpses buried here. The region was famous for its living dead, though he'd never expected to actually encounter any himself.

But when he looked behind him, he recognized his neighbor Ma Shun. The man was a sturdy, barrel-chested fellow, famous in the village for his courage. There was nothing that scared him, and when he was in a temper, he could pound anyone around him to a pulp. No one dared make him angry.

Ma Shun had also noticed the dead lady's valuables and decided to grab them for himself—but with so many people around, he hadn't had a chance. When the village elder put Li Chunlai in charge of setting the fire, Ma Shun had given up on the idea—but then the rain came, and he'd figured there hadn't been time for the coffin to burn entirely, so he sneaked back to see what he could salvage.

Mr. Ma couldn't be bothered talking to a weakling like Li Chunlai. Brushing him aside, he pulled every garment and accessory off the corpse, then rolled them into a bundle. He was about to take off when he noticed Li Chunlai staring at him.

"Don't think of saying a word to anyone or I'll tie you up in a ditch as food for the wolves," he threatened. Then he looked through his loot and pulled out one of the corpse's shoes.

"Here. Call it hush money." He growled and threw the shoe at Li Chunlai.

Li Chunlai caught it and stood there with the sad little shoe in his hand. He didn't dare offend Ma Shun, so he grudgingly agreed to stay quiet. There was no way the sodden coffin could be burned completely now, so they got rid of the evidence by digging a hole and chucking it in.

Back in the village, Mr. Li told the elder and fortune-teller that he'd done as he was told, and nothing but ashes was left. The blind man nodded in satisfaction. "That's good. My old master used to tell me that people buried in the wrong place easily turn into walking corpses, which in turn become drought demons. I might not be able to see, but I'm certain in my heart that's why it hardly ever rained here. I bet this woman was buried with a child in her belly, and her corpse gave birth to it. How could a baby live underground? It would have quickly died too. Drought demons sprung from children are particularly vicious, and working with its undead mother, no wonder it was such a terror. Only burning them both to ashes could save us."

Li Chunlai quaked to hear this, but there was no way he could confess the truth without being severely punished, so he stuttered something and went home to sleep.

That night, he tossed and turned in bed. Every time he fell asleep, he saw the corpse and her child reaching out to throttle him, and he woke in a cold sweat. The rain was still pounding, and there was nothing to do but try to sleep again. Just before dawn, hearing a commotion outside, he threw on his clothes and rushed out to see what was happening.

Ma Shun's house had been struck by lightning and burned to ashes. He, his wife, and their two daughters had died in the fire.

Li Chunlai knew this was a bad sign. Already a coward, he felt his courage shrivel even further, chills running down his spine.

Searching the remains of the Ma dwelling, the villagers found the valuables from the coffin. When the village elder sought out Li Chunlai for an explanation, he'd had no choice but to confess the truth.

The village elder spent quite a while bawling out Li Chunlai in private, then warned him not to say a word to the rest of the village. Mr. Li nodded, keeping his wits about him enough to not mention the shoe he'd kept for himself. Ma Shun might as well take the blame—he was dead, after all. Li Chunlai told the elder that this was all Ma Shun's idea, which was easy to believe, given how spineless Mr. Li usually was. The elder didn't ask any more questions but announced publicly that the Ma family had died because of Mr. Ma's greed.

Uncultured as he was, even Li Chunlai could tell that the shoe now in his possession was likely to be valuable enough that he might finally be able to afford to get married. Shaanxi was a hotbed of tomb raiding, and outsiders often turned up in the village to ask if anyone had artifacts to sell. He never dared show the embroidered shoe to any of them, though, afraid that word of what he'd done would get out.

Finally, a distant relative from the next village had to deliver some goods to Beijing, and Li Chunlai asked if he could hitch a ride. Once he got to the big city, he asked around until someone told him Pan Market was the best place to sell an antique. It was practically destiny that the first person he spoke to happened to be me.

Although Li Chunlai looked feeble, there was steely cunning buried deep within him. I sensed that there were details he had left out, and moments when he didn't seem to be telling the whole truth. Still, listening carefully, I was able to piece together most of the story.

"That's a convoluted tale," I said when he concluded. "From what I've seen, this sandalwood-soled shoe isn't in bad condition—not many specimens make it through hundreds of years intact. I've seen a few pairs, but the embroidery was so discolored they might as well have been tree bark. But—"

"How much is it worth?" Mr. Li broke in anxiously.

I shrugged. "If you had the pair, then we'd be talking real money. But just one shoe . . . Is there any way for you to get hold of the other? This one seems a bit lonely on its own," I pressed. "The antiques trade is all about completeness."

Li Chunlai frowned. He had no idea where the other shoe might be, and he'd had to keep this one hidden for months before he'd managed to get it to Beijing.

"All right," I said. "I'll make a deal with you. I've always had a soft spot for you rural folk—back when my grandfather fought in the Civil War, it was the villagers who kept him alive. So you see, I'd never try to trick you. I reckon I could get seven hundred yuan for this shoe at our market stall. So how about this—I'll give you six hundred for it. That means hardly any profit for me, but we'll call that a finder's fee. Now that we're friends, the next time you get your hands on something similar, you bring it straight to me."

"Six hundred?" Li Chunlai's mouth was agape. "Are you sure?"

"Too little? I'll throw in another fifty."

"That's plenty. I thought I'd get three hundred at most."

I gave him six hundred and fifty yuan in cash, and he counted the notes more than ten times before putting them away, hiding them somewhere in his layers of clothing. I told him to be careful with the money, as there were always pickpockets about.

Afterward, we chatted about his village, which lay on the Ganyuan Gully of the Yellow River, in Shaanxi's very poorest county. It turned out they were next to Dragon County, which I'd heard a lot about. A hilly region, it was rumored to be a national burial site, full of too many tombs to count.

Any of the fine-glazed Tang dynasty ceramics from these tombs would sell for tens of thousands, which was how many farmers in these regions made their fortunes. They'd dig them up from their fields, and just like that would be rich. From the early twentieth century onward, collectors had descended on the area, which was now more or less picked clean.

To the south, the Qin Mountain Range were even more full of tombs, but these tended to be hidden away. The low-hanging fruit had all been plucked. One prominent Han dynasty grave had more than two hundred and eighty tunnels dug into it, left by burglars dating all the way back to ancient times.

Artifacts from this district were also rumored to be worth a mint, but Li Chunlai couldn't give me specifics—it was all just gossip he'd heard.

It was getting late, so I cut Mr. Li off and stood to leave. As we parted, he urged me again and again to come visit, and

I had to be polite for quite a long time before he finally said goodbye.

Back at the market, Kai and Gold Tooth were waiting impatiently for me. They leaped to their feet when I showed up, demanding to know what the mysterious object was.

I produced the embroidered shoe. "That farmer was guarding this like a gold nugget," Kai griped. "And it's nothing but an old shoe."

"It's an old shoe worth big money," Gold Tooth said. "A rare and fine specimen. Tianyi, how much did you pay for it?"

I told him, and he smiled. "Excellent bargaining—we'll get two thousand for this, no problem."

"Really?" I hesitated. "If I'd known, I'd have offered him more. I thought it was worth seven hundred tops."

"It's Monday," said Gold Tooth. "I don't think business is going to improve. Let's pack up and get something to eat. It's been quite a while since we've had mutton hotpot. How about it?"

Kai was in disbelief. He couldn't wrap his head around the worth of the old shoe. But he quickly recovered. "Great minds think alike—that's just what I was hungry for."

And so we went back to the restaurant where we'd first eaten with Gold Tooth. It was four in the afternoon, so there weren't many customers around. We got our usual corner table, and the waiter lit the flame under our tureen of broth. The dishes of raw meat and vegetables quickly arrived, and we dunked them into the boiling liquid to cook.

"Gold Tooth, could you explain to us why this shoe is so valuable?" I asked.

He turned the shoe over in his hands. "This is no regular

artifact. Didn't you notice what's embroidered on it?" he began. "Since the Tang dynasty, we've regarded peonies as the most precious of flowers, and while regular folk might have had peonies on their shoes too, they wouldn't have been as exquisitely rendered as this here. Besides, look in the center of the blossom—six little pearls. Not the best quality, but they raise the value of the shoe immensely. The most important thing is who the owner was. This farmer came from Shaanxi, which has always been a down-to-earth region—the peasants never bound their feet. Which means this was likely the property of a minister's wife from another province, or else some wealthy merchant's out-of-town bride. Either way, it must have been someone with money. The more I look at it, the more I think I was being too cautious when I said two thousand. We're looking at six grand at least. And if we had a *pair,* well, the value would increase four or five times."

My mouth fell open. I immediately made up my mind to stop by Shaanxi as soon as I could, to give Li Chunlai some more cash. I'd feel like I had ripped him off otherwise.

We kept chatting as we ate, and the conversation moved on to the ancient tombs in Shaanxi.

"I've never been there myself," said Gold Tooth, "but colleagues who have tell me the area around the Qin River is absolutely packed with treasure—more than you can count. Dragon County alone must have a hundred thousand graves. In some places, one ancient tomb is built on top of another, like a layer cake of dynasties. I reckon we ought to make a trip and see if we can pick up anything good. Even if we don't, it's always nice to see a bit more of the world. I'd have done it sooner if I were in better shape."

"I was just thinking about going there too," I said. "Why don't we take a road trip? We'll do some business along the way, and with Kai and me along, we'll look out for you."

We shook on it, and started making plans. I'd heard that there were all kinds of long mountain ridges there, the sort we called "dragon spines," and anyone going deep enough into them was sure to be rewarded. I was keen to get a big haul soon. The money we owed Julie was hanging over my head. I hated being in debt.

Gold Tooth was also eager to start on the journey. "If we want to get anything valuable, our best bet is to go to the more remote areas," he said.

Kai suddenly thought of something. "Should we bring some extra black donkey hooves for luck? There might be a lot of walking corpses there."

"Good thinking," I said breezily. "We may not encounter any dumplings, but better to be ready."

It was a good thing we were.

CHAPTER TWO

I SHOULD EXPLAIN THAT I WASN'T TALKING ABOUT THE KIND OF dumplings Li Chunlai had devoured, but rather a trade term used among reverse dippers. We refer to the undead, people unable to rest peacefully in their coffins, as "dumplings."

Finding a good burial place is a matter of good feng shui. The right spot not only ensures the dead will remain asleep, but also protects their descendants and keeps their clan prosperous and safe.

Burying someone in the wrong place can go badly in a couple of ways: the entire family of the deceased might have unspeakable ill luck, such as ending up in prison and losing all their property, with the whole clan eventually dying out; or the dead person, unable to rest easy, will never decompose and end up as an undead creature. To be clear, this has nothing to do with embalming techniques and everything to do with bad feng shui.

Of course, after more than five thousand years of Chinese civilization, many of the places with good feng shui have been taken. There are only so many dragon meridians, after all, and even with all the varieties—flying dragons, crouching dragons, hidden dragons, and so on—we're stuck, at least until the landscape itself changes by way of earthquakes, floods, or landslides.

I explained all this to Kai and Gold Tooth, and we ended up chatting in the restaurant for hours. By the time we were done, we'd made arrangements to close the market stall for a few days while we headed off to Shaanxi to see what we could find.

Although this involved a trek from Beijing, it wasn't like we were going to some remote location in the middle of the desert, so we wouldn't require much equipment. We caught the train to the Central Plains, where we had initially decided to visit Li Chunlai at his home. At our destination, however, we heard that there had been an unusual amount of rainfall that year, and the resulting floods from the Yellow River had washed up quite a few ancient tombs. This seemed like an opportunity too good to miss, so we changed our plans and decided to go west along the river instead.

This involved a long bus ride to Gulan, our nearest crossing point. The bus broke down halfway, delaying us another four or five hours. Our driver took us a little farther after that, then said, "It'll be dark by the time we get to Gulan, and the ferry will have stopped running. Why don't you get off here?

The river's narrow at this bend, and you can usually get a boat to bring you across, though it isn't an official crossing place."

This sounded like a better plan, and we'd save a day that way. So the three of us got off the bus, a decision we regretted almost instantly when we saw how remote the place was. There wasn't a soul in sight. With the bus gone, however, we had no choice but to walk to the river and hope for the best.

We heard the roar of rushing water some distance away, and when we actually got to the bank, our eyes widened. So much for the river narrowing! Maybe because of the flooding, the waves were high, the water full of churning yellow mud, rampaging along at high speed. If there had been a dock here, it had certainly washed away.

As we waited, dark clouds rolled overhead and it started to drizzle. We were lightly dressed, and while Kai and I weren't doing too badly, Gold Tooth was starting to shiver. He cursed the bus driver under his breath.

The rain grew heavier as the day dragged on, and soon everything around us was gray. Rain blurring the outlines of the landscape, and the river raged away. I screamed into the emptiness. It felt good to let out all the frustration, and there was no one around to bother anyway.

Still more time passed. Gold Tooth, Kai, and I huddled together for warmth, though it didn't do much good. I had begun to think we might freeze to death, when the blast of a horn cut through the air. We turned to see a boat rocking its way toward us. Leaping to our feet, we waved frantically, but the boatman shook his head just as vehemently.

We weren't about to let this boat go by after all that time— who knew when the next one would come along? Kai got out our wad of money and waved it at the boatman, and that seemed to do the trick. He tacked to a spot a little ways ahead, where the water was calm enough for him to dock safely.

Kai went over and began negotiating. It turned out the boatman was on an urgent mission to deliver spare mechanical parts to a larger vessel marooned downriver. He had only been sent out in these conditions because the situation was so dire.

The crew consisted of the boatman and his young son. We agreed to pay them double their usual fee if they brought us to Gulan on the opposite shore.

The cabin was completely taken up with mechanical gear, so we had to stand on deck. At least we had gotten a ride, and could look forward to finding a hotel in Gulan where we'd thaw out under a warm shower and grab a bowl of the local specialty: piping-hot buckwheat noodles.

With the river going as fast as it was, we made good progress. Then, just as we were discussing what else we might do for dinner, there was a tremendous jolt, as if we'd hit something underwater. I almost bit my tongue off.

Rain was still pelting down, and lightning sliced through the dark clouds. The boatman rushed toward the bow to see what had happened. The water was so deep here it was unlikely to be a rock, and any floating debris would have been carried along by the river at the same speed as us, so we couldn't have crashed into it. Before he got there, the boat swayed again, and we clutched the nearest railing, terrified of being plunged into the water. A wave splashed over us, and we all got a mouthful of yellow mud.

I'd been getting drowsy, but this woke me up. I looked up

front to see the boatman crouched against the side. He looked panicked. Who was steering? I rushed over and tried to pull him to his feet, calling out, "What's wrong? What did you see?"

"Old Man River," he whimpered, pointing at the water. "He's come for us. He's going to take the boat."

The boat was shaking more violently than ever, and Kai and I struggled to the bow to see for ourselves what the boatman was talking about.

Suddenly, water sluiced across the boat again, spinning it horizontally across the river and flinging Kai to the deck. Lucky for us, this was a modern motorboat—if we'd been on an old-fashioned wooden one, it would have fallen apart by now.

Grabbing hold of Gold Tooth, I yelled to ask Kai what the boatman could have seen in the water.

"No idea!" he yelled back. "Something big and dark, maybe the size of a truck."

"Get your shovel!" I shouted. "Whatever this thing is, we have to stop it. If it keeps ramming us, we'll capsize for sure!"

Kai wound a rope around his waist and then around mine so we wouldn't fall overboard. When the boat stabilized, we hurried to the side that seemed to be under attack and peered over the edge. It was pretty dark by then, and the rain was still pouring down, so we only caught glimpses of the murky water when lightning brightened the sky. There was definitely something there, but only a little mound protruded above the surface. Was it some sort of aquatic creature? The next time it charged, I took aim and swiped at it with my shovel, but the handle wasn't anywhere near long enough.

The impact sent me over the railing, my shovel flying into the river. Luckily, Kai grabbed hold of the rope and pulled me back, or I'd have plunged into the water.

Stumbling to my feet, I bumped into the boatman, who was still crouched in a ball of fear. I shook him by the shoulders. "Turn the boat around!" I shouted. "If we don't get out of here, we'll all get killed—you and your son too."

The boatman was superstitious and had got it into his head that if Old Man River was attacking us, then we had no choice but to wait quietly for death. But mentioning his son propelled him into action—he would have accepted his own doom, but his son was worth fighting for. Shakily, he rose to his feet, then yelled, "It's coming back!"

I looked to where he was pointing. The boat's lights happened to illuminate the creature now, and I saw it clearly for the first time. It was dark green, plunging in and out of the water, at least as big as a truck, rampaging around the boat in a bid to sink us.

With no time to look more closely. I shoved the boatman into the cabin, and as he made for the wheel, I noticed a pile of long metal pipes. Calling Kai over, I handed him an armful and took some myself. Hurrying back out, we flung them like javelins at the creature. I had no idea how many direct hits we scored, but after a dozen or so poles had disappeared into the water, the creature seemed to take the hint and glided away.

The rain started to let up. Gold Tooth had tied himself to a post, though he'd been flung about as the boat moved. He still clutched his travel bag for dear life, which was fortunate, as it contained all our cash. I told him to hang in there, that we'd soon be at a hotel with nice warm showers and a hot meal.

The boatman's son was lying in a corner, bleeding from the head. Fortunately, we were almost at Gulan and could send him to the hospital as soon as we docked. Already pinpricks of light from the town were appearing in the distance.

Just when we thought the disturbance was over, something else hit the boat, with several times more force than before. Unprepared, we once again ended up on the deck. Kai grabbed a rope, while Gold Tooth and I caught hold of his belt and legs. "Don't rip my pants!" Kai cried as the boat careened wildly to one side.

I wanted to go back to the cabin for more metal pipes, but we were shaking so violently it was all I could do to keep from being flung overboard. I'd be lucky if I made it through without getting my head smashed in.

As we rose and fell, water flooded the deck, and we got another drenching. Frantic to get his son to the hospital, the boatman was pressing his vessel full steam ahead, never mind if Old Man River or the Dragon King had other plans.

The Yellow River is full of turns. After passing the Dragon Gate, it zigzags all the way to Gulan, where the waterway straightens a little. As we came around the final bend, whatever was pursuing us suddenly gave up, and we shot away from it.

The lights of the town were brighter now, right up ahead. We moored by the dock and finally found ourselves on solid ground again. Kai paid the boatman the agreed price, with a little extra for what we'd been through, and the dock workers helped get the boatman's son to a hospital as quickly as possible.

CHAPTER THREE

GULAN'S HISTORY CAN BE TRACED BACK TO THE SHANG period, while its city walls are from the Ming dynasty. Despite its long history, the town doesn't have much of a reputation, and few people ever visit. The three of us looked like drowned rats as we wandered around until we found an inn. We got lucky—they had only an hour of hot water each day, and there was still thirty minutes of it left.

After we each took a good shower, we felt restored. We went down to the inn's dining hall and ordered bowls of spicy noodles that warmed us from the inside. Halfway through our meal, the cook came over to ask if we'd come from Beijing.

I could tell right away that he didn't have a southwestern accent. He told us that his surname was Liu, and he was originally from Beijing, though he'd been in Gulan for some decades now.

Mr. Liu said he'd seen us come in and wanted to know how we'd ended up in such a state. I told him about our encounter with the giant underwater creature, and he replied, "I've seen it too. The water level is high this year, and when that happens, these creatures appear. I can show you a spot to get a closer look, if you like."

"What on earth was it? Some sort of turtle spirit?" Gold Tooth asked.

Mr. Liu shook his head. "It's a type of big fish, that's all. Folk around here call them iron-headed dragons. Sailors say they only show up when the water's high. That's why they call them Old Man River—they think they're transformed from the river itself."

"That's quite a story," Kai said skeptically. "How big is this fish, anyway?"

"Big! Let me tell you, the time I saw one of these, there was a flash flood, but then the water retreated just as fast. The iron-headed dragon was marooned in the shallows. Lots of superstitious people around here said it was the Dragon King and we had to return him to his home, but before we could move it, the fish died. People were burning incense and praying on the riverbank, hordes of them. I saw the body when I came along to join the villagers."

"Could you describe the fish?" I asked.

"Huge. Seven layers of green scales. Its head was black, and harder than iron."

"Sounds like a small whale," Kai said. "How could something like that exist in a river? Really bizarre."

"What happened next? Was the iron-headed dragon buried, or did it get eaten?" I asked.

Mr. Liu chuckled. "Not eaten. It was so ancient its flesh was practically fossilized. It was just left on the side of the bank in boiling-hot weather and began to rot in less than a day. You could smell the stench miles away. It was awful. So eventually we decided to hack the flesh off and burn it, then tossed the bones in the mud."

"That's a shame," Gold Tooth said with a sigh. "If you could have gotten it to a museum, plenty of people would have wanted a look at it."

"True! But no one dared—we were too afraid the Dragon King would swamp us with a flood, or worse."

"Mr. Liu," I said, "would the bones still be scattered on the riverbank after so many years?"

"You can still see them, but not on the riverbank. After we burned the flesh and organs, we were discussing what to do with the bones when a visitor arrived from a distant province. He looked like a merchant of some kind, a spiritual man. He handed us a bunch of money and said we should build a Fish Bone Temple at Dragon Ridge, not far from here."

"Fish Bone Temple?" said Gold Tooth. "There's one in Tianjin—fish bones as rafters, the fish head as the door. It's used to worship the Dragon King."

"In Tianjin?" I repeated. I hadn't heard about it.

"That's right," Mr. Liu said. "The merchant often traveled over water, and he thought he could keep himself safe at sea by paying for this temple. It wasn't large, didn't even have a courtyard, just the same as any old Dragon King temple. So we used the bones for the structure, and its skull became the door.

An altar with a statue of the Dragon King, and we were done. Whenever someone got sick or there was a drought, people would go there to pray. The funny thing is, if you prayed for rain, you'd end up wishing you hadn't—it would just get drier instead. So after a while, people stopped bothering. As for the merchant who paid for the whole thing, he never showed up again."

"And the temple's still there?" I asked.

"Yes, but it's been neglected for some time. The Dragon King statue crumbled away after a couple of years. People said the merchant must have had an impure heart, or else he'd committed some awful sin, so the Dragon King wouldn't accept his offering. Besides, the temple's right in the heart of Dragon Ridge, and it's such a troublesome trek that no one wants to go all the way out there. You should go have a look."

"What's there to look at?" Kai asked with a smirk. "The three of us almost became fish food. I think I'd rather stay away."

Gold Tooth caught my eye, and after a quick discussion, we agreed to spend a day or two resting, then go see this Fish Bone Temple at Dragon Ridge. A giant fish skeleton had to be worth something. At worst we could get some museum to buy it, which would cover the expenses of our trip.

Seeing how Mr. Liu was the talkative sort, I suggested that he sit with us for a bit. It was a chance to ask if he happened to know of any old tombs around these parts. He told us that old graves kept being uncovered by the floods, mostly from the Song dynasty. There wasn't much worth taking, though, just moldering bones and broken jars.

The most precious object found was during a drought

year when the Yellow River was so low you could almost see the riverbed. While clearing silt from the banks, some townspeople came upon three monkeys made of metal, each weighing hundreds of pounds. They scrubbed them clean and found them to be gold-plated and covered with exquisite patterns. To this day, no one had any idea what purpose they served. Some people said they were Tang dynasty demon catchers, others that they were sacrifices to the river. They had been carted off to a museum.

"And what of the tombs themselves?" I pressed him.

"Oh, you're into old things like that," Mr. Liu said thoughtfully. "It's a shame you weren't here a few years ago; there were plenty then. Almost all gone now. Not just regular collectors—the government turned up too, more than ten times." He leaned forward and lowered his voice. "Speaking of which, an old man once told me that Dragon Ridge has a Tang dynasty tomb, a pretty big one. In the last year or two, plenty of grave robbers have shown up, but no one's been able to find it. Too many hills around Dragon Ridge, and the tomb's hidden too deep. Hard to say if it even exists. Just rumor, maybe. Anyway, no one's ever set eyes on it."

CHAPTER FOUR

SOME OF THE THINGS MR. LIU TOLD US STRUCK ME AS STRANGE. Why was the Fish Bone Temple, a temple dedicated to the Dragon King, in the hills? Surely it ought to be by the riverbank, where the Dragon King lived.

And he'd said the temple wasn't large—which was odder still. Was it worth going to so much trouble to build something small? Could there really be a spot on Dragon Ridge with such good feng shui?

When he mentioned the big Tang dynasty tomb, I was even more intrigued. Then something clicked in my brain, and I laughed silently. What if the real objective of all this was the tomb? In other words, was this "merchant" actually a reverse dipper who had built the temple as the perfect cover for secretly tunneling into an underground burial place?

That didn't make sense, though. Dragon Ridge was deserted—you could go there and probably not run into a single person. But if this tomb was buried so far down that you couldn't get to it in a single day, then the villagers would have grown suspicious to see the merchant hanging around the hills. Hence the ruse with the temple. It all fit.

I had to see this for myself. It was the only way to be sure if this reverse dipper, this predecessor of mine, had found this rumored Tang dynasty tomb. I asked Mr. Liu for detailed directions.

"Fish Bone Temple's on the side of Dragon Ridge," he said. "It's fine to have a look at it, but definitely don't walk any farther into the hills. It's dangerous there. Lots of sinkholes covered in a thin layer of earth. Take one step and you'll plunge in so deep you'll never get out. That's because it's full of limestone caves, a whole warren of them. People talk about getting lost in the Dragon Ridge tombs—and just like the sinkholes, if you get stuck in one of those caves, it'll be your grave. And they say to beware of ghosts too. Just take my word for it and stay away."

He continued: "Five surveyors went to look at a Dragon Ridge cave and were never seen again. The townspeople say they must have gotten trapped in a ghost-wall—when spirits build an enclosure around you and you can't get out. This was more than two years ago."

I thanked Mr. Liu profusely for his help. "We'd love to look at this Fish Bone Temple. It sounds really unusual. But don't worry, we'll just look at the fish skeleton—what reason would we have to go into the wilderness like that?"

Mr. Liu got up and bid us good night. As soon as he returned to the kitchen, the three of us started making plans. Even if it turned out that this ancient tomb had been picked clean, we'd probably still be able to find some of its artifacts in the surrounding villages. In any case, this trip to Shaanxi wouldn't be a wasted one.

"This isn't going to be like Wild Man Valley, is it?" Kai piped up anxiously. He was thinking back to the time I first took him gold hunting. "All that running around, not to mention we almost died—all for a couple of broken bits of stone that weren't even real jade."

"I can't promise you anything—we only just heard about this big tomb," I told him. "Maybe this is a sign from fate that we're about to have a hefty windfall. We'll be able to pay Julie back everything we owe her. Wouldn't you like that?"

I told him and Gold Tooth my theory about the temple being a cover-up for reverse dipping, which got Gold Tooth excited. He'd always admired people in this line of work, but because he suffered terribly from spring fever and asthma, he'd never been able to go after treasure himself. As a result, he had to make do with the spoils from inferior grave robbers, who just dug anywhere and brought in any old junk. It was late summer now, so Gold Tooth's allergies wouldn't be a problem, and because he was with two reasonably experienced gold hunters, he might actually get to go on an expedition!

Still, I warned that he should probably keep watch aboveground rather than following me and Kai, just in case anything went wrong.

I'd been hoping for a big heist on this trip—and now this opportunity had fallen into our laps. We didn't have a lot of tools with us, but our shovels would do for both digging and self-defense. Or our one shovel, since we only had Kai's left— mine was now at the bottom of the Yellow River.

The most important thing was illumination. We had three powerful flashlights, whose beams were so bright that if you shined it straight into someone or something's eyes, they'd be temporarily blinded.

The biggest problem was that we didn't have proper gas masks, only simple ones. Gulan was unlikely to sell the real thing, and every gold hunter knows to beware of poisoned air. Never mind. I made a list of items for Kai to find. If he couldn't get them around here, he'd have to find some other way to get his hands on them.

We needed two large birds (I made sure to emphasize they should be alive, otherwise Kai would surely have turned up with a platter of roast goose), candles, ropes, gloves, and canned food. Maybe some chocolate. I said to also look into the post office for a map of the area.

"What about rifles?" Kai asked. "I don't feel as brave without one in my hand."

"There aren't many wild animals around here," I said. "You don't need a rifle; just use your shovel to whack whatever turns up. Anyway, this may be all for nothing."

Gold Tooth nodded. "That's right. This sort of limestone landscape is prone to earthquakes. Even if there really is a Tang grave, anything could have happened to it over the centuries. Let's not get our hopes up."

I vaguely remembered that Shaanxi was known for having lots of undead corpses. What if we encountered a dumpling? This reminded me how close we'd come to dying on our last expedition—even though Gold Tooth had given us gold-hunting charms that were supposed to protect us.

When I asked him about them, he smiled sheepishly. "Don't be angry, Tianyi. Those charms might not have been exactly genuine, but I didn't know that when I handed them over. Anyway, I'm sure there was a psychological advantage—you two had never seen the real thing, so you must have been filled with confidence. I'll get you some proper ones, if I can."

I laughed. "We'll count on you, then. You need charms to ward off evil when you go reverse dipping. Our black donkey hooves will help. But you're right, if you don't feel protected—well, not having confidence might be more dangerous than anything else."

Exhausted from the day, we fell asleep quickly and didn't wake up till the next afternoon. While Kai and Gold Tooth went in search of supplies, I sought out Mr. Liu to press him for more information about Dragon Ridge. Disappointingly, he didn't have much to add to what he'd said the night before. I tried a few other people, but it was all the same—there was a lot of talk about the hills in these parts, mostly legends and superstitions, without much useful information. The rumors of ghosts and evil spirits were enough to keep people away, so few villagers had spent much time there.

After another day's rest, we set off for Fish Bone Temple along the route laid out by Mr. Liu. Kai carried two geese in a bamboo cage on his back.

CHAPTER FIVE

DRAGON RIDGE WAS PART OF THE LARGER QIN MOUNTAIN Range, a constellation of hills spread over a large area. Over the centuries, wind and rain had chopped these up, widening the gullies between the peaks and hollowing some out, leaving just a thin shell of earth that your foot would go right through. As a result, although some hills appeared close together, it often took more than half a day to get from one to the other.

There wasn't even any agreement about what the place was called. While the Gulan townspeople called it Dragon Ridge, nearby villagers preferred the name Coiled Snake Hill—a less majestic name, but a more accurate description of the landscape.

At nine in the morning, the three of us left Gulan, taking

buses where we could, and walking where there was no other way of getting through, asking everyone we met if they had any more information to share. It was dusk by the time we got to the small village at the foot of Dragon Ridge, a hamlet of just twenty families. Not wanting to risk falling into a gully in the dark, we decided to spend the night here.

Choosing a house near the village gate, we knocked and explained that we were weary travelers in need of shelter, and asked the elderly couple if they could put us up for the night. We offered payment, of course.

The homeowners looked dubiously at us. With our many bags and live geese in a cage, it wasn't surprising that they wondered what we were up to.

"Uncle, Auntie," Kai said with respect. "We're on our way to visit some old friends, but we got lost and can't find an inn. We're far from home, and there's really nowhere else we can turn. If you'll just give us a roof for the night, there's twenty yuan in it for you." Without waiting for them to say yes, he was already thrusting a banknote at them.

Seeing that we didn't seem like bad people, the couple agreed and started clearing out a room for us—one that looked as if it hadn't been occupied for many years.

Pointing at the buckets on a carrying pole in the yard, Kai said, "Tianyi, go get some water from the well."

"What for? Isn't your water bottle still full?"

"It's something I learned from my dad. When he was in the army, whenever they were housed with a civilian, they'd make sure to fill the water tanks, then sweep out the yard and mend the roof if it needed mending."

"Do we really have to?" I grumbled. "I don't know where

the village well is, and I'll probably get lost in the dark. Anyway, I need to stick around so I can ask them about the area. Don't say too much—we don't need to frighten them with your nonsense."

The old couple came in to say they'd fried us some eggs, which they served us along with thick buckwheat pancakes. I quickly thanked them. As we ate, I asked who this room had belonged to.

Unexpectedly, they began weeping. Once the husband had calmed down, he spoke. "Our only son once lived in this room, but ten years ago, he decided to go up Coiled Snake Hill in search of a missing goat and never returned. The villagers spent four days looking for him, but there was no sign of him. We had to accept that he had probably fallen through an earth crust, crashing to his death in the cavern below."

"Now we have no one to take care of us in our old age," the wife cried. She sniffled and wiped tears away. "Our neighbors do what they can to help us."

Our hearts ached to hear their tale, and we gave them a little more money. The couple thanked us over and over, saying how happy they were to have met some good people.

I asked a little more about the area, but the couple said there weren't any ancient tombs in this district, though the older generation had spoken of a great mausoleum from the Western Zhou period. Apparently there had been lots of spooky incidents around there, with people encountering ghost-walls even in the daytime. Those unlucky enough to fall into such a trap would end up wandering at the bottom of the gully, where, if they were fortunate, they eventually ran into someone who helped them out. Otherwise they died.

The ruins of Fish Bone Temple were still around but had been abandoned for decades. They were at the far end of a gully, two hills past the village. The merchant who'd paid for its construction said this was a good feng shui spot, and a temple here would surely win the Dragon King's favor. When they were finished, though, nothing changed, and the sky still rained when it wanted to, rather than on demand, no matter how much incense was burned. After a while, everyone stopped bothering, and the temple fell into disuse.

"When we were crossing the Yellow River," I said, "our boat was almost overturned by the Dragon King. I'm curious to see these fish bones for myself."

The couple said it would be fine for us to see the temple, but to stay away from the rest of Coiled Snake Hill. Even people who'd been here all their lives got lost in its tangled roads, let alone strangers like us.

I nodded in thanks. We'd finished eating by then, and started clearing our plates and chopsticks. Outside, Gold Tooth whispered, "Tianyi, look at that!" He was pointing at a rock in the center of the courtyard. "This stone tablet looks really old."

I said nothing but bobbed my head to show I'd understood. The old couple had gone off to bed, so we pretended to need fresh air and sneaked out to have a closer look at the artifact.

If not for Gold Tooth's sharp eyes, I would have walked right past the rock. The lozenge of stone had been severely damaged, with several deep gouges right down the middle, as if it had been used as a cattle post. Half of it appeared to be missing—even the carved animal head at what would have been the center was split down the middle. Any words had long been worn away, and this half head was the only thing that showed it was a stone tablet rather than any old rock.

"You think this is worth something?" Kai asked dubiously. "Maybe long ago, but look at it now. All the carvings are gone. It's practically the ghost of itself."

"I didn't say it was worth anything," said Gold Tooth. "It's obviously not—a shame, but there you are. Don't forget, though, that my family were reverse dippers too. Looking at this animal head, I can guarantee that there's a Tang dynasty tomb in Dragon Ridge. As to where exactly it is, we'll have to rely on Tianyi's feng shui skills."

I touched the stone head. "You think this was a burial plaque?"

"I'm pretty sure," Gold Tooth said. "Even from this crumbling bit of a head, I can see what sort of creature it was—a celestial lynx. At the height of the Tang dynasty, they built all their tombs in the hills, with some sort of marker aboveground— a camel, lion, or other animal, carved out of stone. The idea was that these beasts would guard your eternal rest. The celestial lynx is said to be an animal from the Western Paradise, with a voice like a heavenly choir. This must have been a plaque that spoke to the virtues of the dead person. There'd have been one every li for eighteen li before the grave, and the celestial lynx would usually be the marker for the second li."

"Wow," I marveled. "Gold Tooth, you might not know any feng shui, but with your grasp of history, you're still leaving me far behind. Let's go back to the room—we shouldn't be discussing this in the open air."

We continued making our plans with renewed confidence. It seemed we'd definitely be rewarded for our trip. The only puzzling thing was, why were the locals talking about a Western Zhou tomb, when this was clearly a relic from the Tang dynasty?

"Could there be more than one grave, on the same feng shui meridian?" Gold Tooth asked.

"It's possible," I said, "but not every spot on the meridian is equally auspicious. There'll be good and bad spots, and even the very best location is only big enough to hold a single tomb. Of course, two dynasties centuries apart might well have picked the same spot."

Time for bed. The next morning, we'd take a good look at Dragon Ridge or Coiled Snake Hill, whatever it was called. And maybe other homes in this village also had similar artifacts— we'd have to snoop into a few more houses on our way back.

CHAPTER SIX

First thing the next day, we packed our bags and set off. The old couple's directions—go past two hills—had sounded simple, and while it wasn't too much distance as the crow flies, we spent so much time going up and down that it was almost dark by the time we'd traveled that far. In the waning light, the land spread below us. The earth here was shot through with yellow, carved by the scalpel of the wind and the crisscross of gullies and canyons, some of the crevasses startlingly deep.

These harsh surroundings were inhospitable to life, and there was no one else to be seen. The wind howled over the bleak hills, sounding like the anguished cries of a thousand ghosts. Dotted here and there were what looked like bottomless pits, pitch-black spots in the scarred landscape.

We camped in the shelter of a rock outcropping and set off again the next morning.

It was a three-hour walk before we managed to find Fish Bone Temple. And it was in even worse condition than I'd imagined. Knowing it had been abandoned for decades, I'd expected to find it looking run-down, but the structure seemed as if it might collapse at any moment.

The temple consisted of just a single room, without the usual side chambers. The door was nowhere to be seen, though at least that made it easier to see that the entrance was indeed through the mouth of an iron-headed dragon whose bones we could clearly see holding up what was left of the place.

Kai got out his shovel and struck one of the beams. It rang out clearly—they were still strong. Looking closely, we could tell these were no ordinary fish bones. Even without flesh on them, they were sinister, hideous. We'd never seen anything like this. It was different from a whale, or any type of fish. It was gigantic, so big we wanted to avert our eyes.

Inside, the floor was covered in cobwebs, and the fish bones were no longer visible—they were hidden behind the tiles that covered the ceiling.

The walls hadn't crumbled away entirely, and we could still make out writing on one of them: "May the wind and rain be obedient." A few rat nests occupied part of the room, and the creatures scurried away squeaking when we showed up.

We didn't dare spend too long inside—it seemed like a strong gust of wind could bring the whole place crashing down on top of us.

Back outside, Gold Tooth told us there were a fair number of Dragon King temples in seafaring areas of China, but hardly any in the interior. The one in Tianjin had been built after a giant fish got washed up on shore and died there, in similar circumstances to the one in Gulan.

Looking around the gully that the temple rested in, I chuckled. "If this is a good feng shui spot, I'll go home and burn my copy of *The Sixteen Mysteries of Yin-Yang Feng Shui*," I said.

"What's wrong with this place?" Kai wanted to know. "Plenty of wind, listen to it! Ah, but you need water for it to be truly auspicious, don't you? If only there were a brook or something."

"There are even more rules governing temples than there are for graves," I said. "Temples are meant to bring good fortune—you can't just plonk them down anywhere. Even the stars have to be in alignment. Have you seen a single other temple in a gully? Not even a lowly Earth God temple would be somewhere so deep. The rule is that the valley's darkness has no heart to be pierced."

Kai looked puzzled. "What does that mean?"

"It means that this isn't a good spot for a temple. Look at these gullies, like snakes slithering along the ground, dwarfed by the hills around them. Absolutely no force to them. Besides, dark energy gathers around mountains and crevasses. If this were a verdant hill covered in trees, it might help mitigate things, because plants have a power of their own. But look at this barren, cracked place. Going by feng shui principles, you'd never build a temple here, much less bury a person. Now that I've seen it, I'm certain it's the handiwork of a gold hunter covering up a reverse dip."

"But why make such a big production of it?" Kai said, shaking his head. "He could just have said he wanted to build a straw hut or something. Besides, no one ever comes up here, except maybe an occasional goatherd. The Dragon Ridge caverns over that ridge sound terrifying—no wonder the villagers stay away."

"He probably wanted to win the trust of the locals. Putting all that money into the temple was supposed to guarantee an end to droughts, so of course the villagers thought well of him. If he'd just shown up and started construction, they'd definitely have found his behavior strange. Why put a perfectly good building in a gully? And you know they'd have found out—even if no one ever passes this way, they seem to know everything that goes on. So why not say this is a good feng shui spot, and build a temple? That's a proper scam."

Kai and Gold Tooth nodded—my explanation was the most plausible one.

Before now, I'd had two main worries. First, was there even a grave here in the first place? It seemed like a definite yes. Second, had this fake merchant managed to find the tomb and make off with any spoils? Looking at the temple, I could tell he was certainly a man who got what he wanted. Yet I thought it would still be worth our while to visit the tomb. If the merchant had been a gold hunter, the rules said he could take only one or two objects, so there'd be something left for us. Whoever he was, he must've been a true master of the craft to have found this tomb when so many others had failed. And a true master would surely value our rules more than his own life. Such honor is hard to find these days.

We walked around the temple a few times but didn't see any sign of a tunnel. Either it was well hidden or my predecessor had sealed it after he finished the job. Gold Tooth asked if there was any way to pinpoint the location through feng shui, and I said not while we were stuck in the valley—I'd need to be looking down from a height in order to know the lay of the land.

Gold Tooth blanched at the thought of climbing up another hill. His life normally consisted of indulgence and no exercise, and he was already half-dead from the trek here. So I told him and Kai to stay close to the temple and keep searching for an entrance, while I went off to gain some perspective.

I climbed up the nearest peak—it was so steep I had to use my hands as well as my feet. Before long, I was atop the ridge, gazing down at a piece of land that looked as if someone had scrunched it up, leaving it wrinkled and full of complex patterns.

Shaanxi had high plains to the north and became hilly to the south, where Dragon Ridge lay. This area was relatively low-lying, and even this ridge wasn't particularly high. If I were flying overhead, it would probably appear as no more than a scar on the earth.

Holding up a rod to gauge the level, I analyzed my surroundings. Sure enough, this place was worthy of its name—there was the power of a dragon in this meridian, arising from a deeply buried "dragon palace." This wasn't the sort of power that ran through places where, say, emperors got buried—those were magnificent, sweeping vistas, whereas this was much quieter and stiller, buried far beneath the surface. Once upon a time, Dragon Ridge might well have been a suitable site for a royal tomb—but nature had ruptured that majesty, slicing it up, leveling mountains with earthquakes. With such severe damage, the place was no longer as potent as it once was.

Even so, I could tell at a glance that the dragon palace still rested far below the ridge I was now standing on—and no doubt so did the Tang dynasty tomb. Calculating the length and angle of the meridian as it wound through the hills, I made a careful note of the probable sites of the grave.

Gold Tooth and Kai were still scrabbling about the temple. I blew the whistle around my neck. They looked up at me and shrugged to say they hadn't found anything, then went back to circling the building.

It's always easier to get up a hill than down. The way I'd come was too steep to return by, so I looked around, and a little to my left I spotted a shallower slope scraped out of the hill by wind and rain, or perhaps something like a mudslide. It would be easier to get down from there.

Starting my descent on that path, I found so much loose shale underfoot that I was sliding more than walking. Noticing a slightly more level patch nearby, I hopped over to it. Barely two steps later, I found it crumbling beneath me, and suddenly my body was halfway beneath the surface. This wasn't good—I'd stepped onto a hidden cavern.

The villagers had mentioned these deadly traps, but I'd assumed the area around the temple would be safe, and had gotten careless. Up to my waist in the dirt, I had enough presence of mind not to struggle—as with quicksand, the loose soil here would suck me down faster the more I moved. The best thing to do was wait for help, keeping as still as possible. I didn't dare breathe too deeply, for fear even that would pull me lower. If I got in past my chest, I'd be in real trouble.

With both arms outstretched, I tried to keep my body in

balance. When half a minute passed without my sinking any further, I gingerly reached for the whistle.

I blew loud and hard, sending ripples through my chest and belly, and slid another few inches in. Breathing was getting difficult. I had to fight the impulse to push with my arms.

Each minute felt endless. Where were Kai and Gold Tooth? If they hadn't heard the whistle, then I really was doomed.

Just as I was gasping for air and my thoughts were starting to break up, they finally appeared, strolling casually over the ridge, laughing and joking.

As soon as they saw me, they ran over. Kai unfastened the rope coiled at his waist. He had the bamboo cage on his back, and the two geese squawked in alarm at the sudden motion.

They stopped ten paces away, afraid of getting sucked in too, and threw the rope over. I grasped at this salvation, winding it tightly around my wrists. The two of them pulled hard, and I slowly rose from the dirt that held me captive. As my legs kicked free, the entire crust caved in, and just like that there was a huge hole in the side of the hill, growing by the second as more dirt funneled in.

Panting hard, I wrenched open my water bottle and took a few big gulps. Then I poured the rest over my head, wiping my face clean. As I looked at the gaping cavern behind me, I realized I'd lost count of how many times I'd escaped death. It never stopped being terrifying, and this instance was much worse because I'd had time to process what was happening. There could be no worse mental torture than that realization. It was a full twenty minutes before I was calm enough to think again.

Seeing how pale I was, Kai and Gold Tooth waited awhile

before asking how I was. "Better," I told them as I got to my feet.

We went over to the edge of the giant hole and looked into the void. "Could this lead to the tomb?" asked Gold Tooth.

I shook my head. "No way. Gold-hunter tunnels wouldn't be this loose. This is a mountain cave that's gradually eroded from the inside, leaving only a thin bit of soil over it."

Then I filled them in on what I'd discovered earlier—the tomb being one kilometer from Fish Bone Temple, which was consistent with the tunnel starting at the temple itself. A kilometer-long route would be no sweat for an expert, though it would take more than a day to dig.

"This guy had too much time on his hands!" exclaimed Kai. "Why not just build the temple directly over the tomb?"

"My guess is he wanted to enter the tomb from below," I said.

"From below?" Gold Tooth seemed puzzled. "Do you mean because the walls and ceiling would be too secure, so the floor's the only vulnerable point?"

"I would guess so. This was at the height of the Tang dynasty, and with all their resources, I'd expect a mountain tomb to be especially secure. The underground vault would be solid rock reinforced with metal bars. But even the most airtight ancient grave must have at least one point that's permeable, in order to allow some air to circulate. If not, that'd be bad for feng shui."

"So there's a back door?" Kai asked.

"Not exactly. It's only a way for air to move around. It wouldn't be an actual opening, just an area that's not as solid as the rest."

We discussed it a bit more, then decided it was worth the effort to pay the Dragon Ridge tomb a visit. The Fish Bone Temple tunnel would be our point of entry. It had only been a few decades, so its position shouldn't have shifted too much, and even if parts of it had collapsed, we'd just dig our way around—that would still be easier than finding our own way in, and far safer, given the likelihood of tumbling into another hidden cavern.

Having made our decision, we headed back to the temple. Kai and Gold Tooth had searched for a long time with no luck. Feng shui wouldn't help us here—this wasn't a real temple and hadn't been built along those principles. What had this gold-hunting predecessor of mine been up to?

Then a lightbulb went on in my head. "Let's have a look at the Dragon King statue. If there's a tunnel, I bet it's hidden under the altar itself."

CHAPTER SEVEN

THE ROOF OF FISH BONE TEMPLE TREMBLED IN THE MOUNTAIN winds, letting out alarmingly creaky noises. After studying it for a while, we realized that despite its dilapidated appearance, the place was surprisingly solid, perhaps because of the sturdy fish bones.

Only the bottom fifth of the clay Dragon King statue was left, with no sign of the rest. Before the altar was an imitation coral mound, also made of clay, once brightly painted but its color now rubbed off.

According to my theory, if there was a tunnel, it would be beneath the mound of earth. Kai asked what I was basing this on, but I ignored him, not wanting to reveal that I'd been inspired by a martial arts thriller I'd read recently.

I put down everything I was carrying and rolled up my sleeves, and we shifted the altar together. Some of the little clods of dirt got trampled, but most of it remained in place. Could this be the mechanism?

Kai was in a bad mood now and decided brute force would be simpler. Bringing his shovel down hard on the altar, he found the packed earth surprisingly sturdy. He was drenched in sweat by the time he'd demolished half of it, revealing the pale stone surface beneath. So there was no tunnel there—all that work for nothing.

Gold Tooth, who'd been standing some distance off to avoid the flying dirt, suddenly shouted, "Tianyi, Kai, look— isn't there something behind the altar?"

I crouched down and peered at the back of the altar, which was about half my size. I'd assumed it was built into the wall, but now I realized there was just enough room behind it for one person to pass. When I knocked on this area, it sounded hollow.

A couple of kicks and the altar split apart. It was a layer of clay over wooden boards, and behind them was a hole in the ground. So it was under there after all, but we could never have guessed that by looking at the front portion, which was solid clay.

"Nice work, Gold Tooth," I called. "We're in. Maybe we'll still be able to get a big haul."

This thought buoyed us up, and we quickly grabbed our things and hurried over to the hole. Shining my flashlight in- side, I saw it was about average size, large enough that even someone chubby like Kai could enter without much difficulty.

"What great craftsmanship," I said. "Look at it—the shovel marks on the walls are evenly spaced, and these curves are so perfectly round they might have used a compass."

Gold Tooth was equally appreciative, but Kai couldn't see anything special about it. He waddled over with his two geese in tow and said, "All right, let's shove these birds in first to see if it's safe."

"Hang on," I protested. "The tunnel's been sealed up for years. Give it a chance to air out before you send the geese in. We could do with a break anyway."

Kai put the geese back in their cage and got out some beef jerky. This was a fake temple, so we weren't worried about desecrating it, and we happily sat on the altar to have our breakfast.

As we chatted about how best to enter the tunnel, Gold Tooth came up with a question: If this ridge was hollow, why bother digging a tunnel through Fish Bone Temple? Why not just find a cave and enter from there?

I'd been thinking about this and reasoned that these hollow veins would actually be hard to come upon. After all, wasn't that what the names Coiled Snake Hill and Dragon Ridge implied? That this place was a tangle of pathways? Everyone who'd been through said these limestone caves were a maze, and it wasn't like there was just one big hollow inside the ridge. Anyone wandering in might not easily find their way out.

The gold hunter who built Fish Bone Temple must have had great abilities to pinpoint the location of the tomb within this confusion.

The tunnel sloped as it went down, at an angle I was sure

had been carefully chosen to lead straight to the tomb. Even if it broke through into a cave, as long as we continued in the same direction, we wouldn't get lost.

I really did admire whoever made this tunnel. If only I'd been alive back then, I'd have been glad to pay my respects to this predecessor of mine.

"There's a good chance we'll enter a cave on the way," I said to the other two. "They're everywhere around here. We just need to remember that every time we take a breath, we'll be releasing carbon dioxide into the air, so——"

"That sounds dangerous," Gold Tooth interrupted. "Now that we've found the tunnel, why not cover it up and come back when we're fully prepared? It's not like the tomb is going to sprout legs and run away."

"We don't need to worry about that. I'll have a gas mask on, and I'll light candles along the way. If they go out, that'll mean there isn't enough oxygen, and we'll double back. Besides, we'll make the geese go first, and if they start to get sluggish, that'll also be a warning sign. Our gas masks might not be top quality, but they'll be enough to get us out safely."

Gold Tooth seemed reassured by my explanation—perhaps too reassured, because now he was insisting on going down himself. I'd initially thought it would be just me and Kai, but that's the trouble with this line of work: once you know where the grave is, it's hard not to want to see it for yourself. I understood how Gold Tooth felt—after all, he worked with antiques, and his reputation in the market would surely go up if he could brag he'd been right to the source.

I tried to talk him out of it, but when he remained stubborn, I gave him a mask and told Kai to lead the way with his geese. I followed closely behind, and Gold Tooth brought up the rear. Slowly we crawled forward. There were wooden reinforcements every so often along the tunnel, so we didn't need to worry about it collapsing, but it still felt like the darkness was pressing down on us. I lit my candle every so often, and it burned brightly.

It still felt like something was squeezing us, though. Gold Tooth tapped my leg from behind, and when I looked back, he was covered in sweat, panting hard. I told Kai to stop for a rest, then placed the lit candle on the ground. Before I could ask Gold Tooth what the matter was, the candle suddenly flickered out.

"Do you think it's a ghost?" Gold Tooth asked in a whisper.

"Not sure," I answered.

We were still some distance from the tomb, so I really didn't think so. I put my hand to my mask, wondering if enough of my breath had escaped to blow out the candle. Not a chance. I pulled off my gloves to see if there was any kind of breeze. Nothing.

Thinking I'd try lighting the candle again, I struck a match, but I saw that the candle had vanished. How could that be? It should have been easy to retrace someone else's route down a tunnel they had carved out, but now it looked like this place was haunted.

I reached out to feel the spot where the candle had been and touched something cold and hard—a paving stone. Ripping off my mask, I tapped Kai's leg. "Let's go back. Something's wrong here."

Hearing this, Gold Tooth immediately turned and started frantically crawling back the way we'd come. This was hard on

Kai, who fit so snugly into the tunnel he wasn't able to turn around. He was forced to move backward now, still holding on to the two geese.

We'd barely traveled five meters when Gold Tooth suddenly stopped. "Keep going," I called. "Just a little farther. We can rest when we're out."

Gold Tooth looked back, the blood drained from his face. "The tunnel's blocked. We're trapped."

I shined the flashlight up ahead and made out an enormous stone slab closing off the path. I'd examined our surroundings every step of the way, and there had been no sign of any mechanism that could have done this. The entire tunnel was made of dirt, so where could a giant rock have emerged from?

There was no option but to try the other way again. I gestured to Gold Tooth to turn around and nudged Kai to start moving forward again.

Not knowing what was going on, Kai lost his temper. "Tianyi, are you trying to torture me? Pushing me this way and that. I can't move another inch. If you want to go forward, you'll have to crawl over me."

I had no idea what we were up against, but this was definitely not a good situation, and staying put wasn't an option. "Stop talking and keep moving," I snapped at him. "Go on, just do it."

Sensing the urgency in my tone, Kai stopped complaining and started shooing the geese ahead of him. We quickly crawled more than two hundred meters before he stopped again. I thought he had run out of steam, but then his voice came back to me: "Hey, Tianyi, there are three openings up ahead. Which way should I go?"

"Three openings?" These sorts of tomb tunnels usually only went one way. What kind of reverse dipper would have time to make a three-pronged fork? I couldn't figure out what was going on.

I told Kai to get into the center tunnel so I could get far enough forward to study the three branches. Behind me, Gold Tooth was too exhausted to speak. I shouted back that he should have a rest while I took a look at the situation.

The three tunnels ahead, along with the one we were presently on, formed a perfect crossroads. The one going forward had smooth walls and good construction. As for the other two, they'd clearly been dug in a hurry. There were heaps of dirt at the junction, probably dumped there when the two side tunnels were dug.

Could this have been the work of the same person who built Fish Bone Temple? Had his escape route been blocked by a stone slab, forcing him to dig these other tunnels in an attempt to escape?

But speculating about that wouldn't help us get out. I tied a rope around my waist and started crawling down the left-hand branch, telling the other two that if I ran into trouble, I'd whistle and they should pull me back right away.

Gold Tooth plucked a golden Buddha charm from around his neck and handed it to me. "Tianyi, put this on," he said. "It's been blessed, and if there's anything nasty in there, it will keep you safe."

"It's too precious—you should keep it for your own protection," I told him. "This place seems dangerous, but I don't think it's spirits, just some sort of man-made trap we haven't seen before. I'll be fine, don't worry."

Gold Tooth grinned, reaching into his pocket to pull out twenty or so other charms, some Buddhist, some Taoist, made of gold, ivory, or jade, all different sizes. "I've got a whole arsenal here, and they've all been blessed by monks. I'm not scared of anything."

Now I realized why he'd been so insistent on following us—he had a hoard of charms to keep him safe. "You're right," I said, "reverse dippers aren't afraid of ghosts. What I'm worried about is that this situation is like nothing I've seen before. I want to make sure it's all right before we continue."

I took the gold Buddha and hung it around my neck. I'd handled enough antiques by this point to know this was definitely the real thing.

The left-hand branch had a strong breeze coming through it, so I knew it must open out somewhere. At least I didn't need to worry about breathing. Still, I pulled on my gas mask as a precaution, then went in with my flashlight trained on the path ahead. This tunnel was much narrower, probably because it had been made in a hurry. It felt a bit like being buried alive, and I was glad I didn't suffer from claustrophobia.

I moved quickly, afraid there might be something dangerous in the air—after all, the gas mask wouldn't protect my eyes and ears. The tight crawl space took away my sense of distance, so I had no idea how far I'd gone before I found another stone slab blocking the way. This looked like part of the structure, and it was so well embedded I couldn't tell its size. There was definitely no getting around it. The tunnel expanded dramatically at this point, as if the digger had tried to find a way around the stone but had not managed to find its edges.

I tried not to feel disheartened at being blocked a second

time, but I went back the way I came and told the other two what I'd seen. We couldn't understand it. Did there just happen to be a big chunk of rock smack in the path of the tunnel?

And there was still no explaining the piece of stone that had sprung up out of nowhere, keeping us from going back. Ancient tombs are full of all sorts of intricate mechanisms, but this went beyond intricate to downright bizarre.

There were only two paths left unexplored. I didn't have high hopes about the right-hand branch, but it seemed like bad luck to admit it. Besides, as the saying goes, don't shed tears until you see the coffin. Hopefully we'd actually get to see a coffin—by making it through to the burial chamber.

No point scaring myself. After a few minutes' rest, I climbed into the right-hand tunnel, and as I'd expected, a bit farther in, there was a giant piece of rock blocking the way forward. I yelled in frustration, then stopped abruptly when I noticed that something was different.

CHAPTER EIGHT

As I shined my flashlight at the rock face in front of me, I saw that someone had tried to dig upward.

Fish Bone Temple was in a gully, and this passage sloped down toward the natural limestone caves. To tunnel upward was surely the longest possible way out, and also the most complicated, because the mountains here were riddled with holes and might easily collapse. This was a last resort.

It only took a single glance upward for me to know there was no hope here. This little offshoot went on barely ten meters before reaching another dead end. Where were these rocks springing up from? It was as if we were in a giant stone sarcophagus, sealing us in tight.

Back at the junction, I told the other two the bad news.

Kai and I had been in many sticky situations before, so he wasn't really worried. Seeing that we weren't panicking, Gold Tooth settled down too. That's the strange thing about human beings—fear spreads like wildfire, but if you can get enough people in a group to remain calm, it creates a firewall from the emotion.

Being frightened impairs your judgment, so the most important thing in these situations is to avoid scaring yourself. The way I saw it, we just needed to figure out where all these stone slabs were coming from. Once we knew that, we'd be able to find a way out.

"This is my fault," lamented Gold Tooth. "I should have stayed up above in case you didn't come back. Now there's no way we can summon help."

"Don't worry," I consoled him. "We're not desperate yet. Besides, I don't know what good you could have done from the outside—these rocks must weigh a ton, and you'd need dynamite to get them out of the way."

"Do you have a plan?" Gold Tooth asked hopefully.

"A plan?" I laughed. "I'm taking it one step at a time. We could have died crossing the Yellow River and didn't. So I guess we've got luck on our side. We'll find a way out."

"I'd rather have drowned in the river than die here like a trapped rat," Kai said with a moan.

"Listen," I said, "both of you. Three of these tunnels are blocked, but the fourth one should lead us into the Tang dynasty tomb. Focus on that. The gold hunter who built Fish Bone Temple came this way too, and we haven't seen his skeleton anywhere, which means he managed to escape. So let's keep going and see what happens when we've found the grave."

This made sense to them. Once again, Kai led the way with his geese. As we crawled ahead, I thought how rushing into things has always been my downfall. It's not a good trait in a gold hunter, who needs to be prepared to survive any strange situation that comes up.

If Julie Yang had been with us, she'd never have let us enter the tunnel together. I wondered how she was doing in America and whether she'd found help for Professor Chen yet.

"Tianyi!" Kai's voice cut through my tangled thoughts. "Cave up ahead!"

I heard water dripping, which made me crawl faster. Kai was already through into the larger space. I shined the flashlight around and saw heaps of dirt underfoot, debris from the tunnel we'd just passed through.

Gold Tooth emerged behind me, and we explored our new surroundings. This wasn't a limestone cave, just a little hollow within the mountain. The water was coming from the far side, probably where the legendary Dragon Ridge caverns began.

The tunnel continued at the other side of the cavern at exactly the same angle. "Listen," said Gold Tooth. "Doesn't that dripping sound like it's from a larger cave? So why didn't the Fish Bone Temple guy get out that way, rather than digging these side tunnels?"

"Everyone around here says these caves are a maze," I replied. "It's easy to get disoriented. So how would he find a way out so easily? All we know is that this path leads to the tomb. As to how we get out, well, that's another question."

"Stop talking and let's keep moving," Kai urged. "We can come back here if there's no other way out, but we should see the tomb before deciding."

"I've never seen you so keen to find an exit," I retorted. "You're just after the treasure in the tomb, aren't you? As long as you know those jewels won't help you if we're stuck down here."

"I'm being strategic," Kai said. "Think about it. Is there a way out? We have no idea. Are there precious artifacts in the tomb? Definitely. So let's go with what we know for certain, stick the treasure in our pockets, then deal with the maybes. If we really are trapped, at least we won't die poor. And——"

"Enough," I said, cutting him off. "Save your energy. You'll need it."

Kai pushed the geese into the next stretch of tunnel and made to follow them. I yanked him back and pulled his gas mask on first. Although the passage to the limestone cave should be fine, we might find it harder to breathe as we drew closer to the burial chamber. Better to be prepared.

Masks on, we dampened towels from our water bottles and slung them around our necks. Gold Tooth gave Kai a jade Goddess of Mercy charm as additional protection.

Now we were ready to tackle the second stretch. It was very short—just fifty meters before it started sloping upward, then another ten meters before we hit brick.

These green clay bricks usually sat right underneath the coffin and would only be a foot deep, easy to break through with a shovel. Every other surface of the tomb would be built of thick stone and iron bars, with molten metal poured into any cracks to seal them tight. The bricks composed the one area that was vulnerable.

On the whole, Tang dynasty graves were among the most solid and magnificent structures in Chinese history, and they were often built into mountains, surrounded on all sides by heavy rock fortifications. Their weak spots were protected by traps that kicked into action once the bricks were disturbed. These could be anything from a deluge of sand, flying arrows, or an avalanche of crushing stones to gates slamming down and sealing the place shut. These small patches of porous brick were part of the design so some air could get in, but the imperial families who'd built these tombs had clearly decided they'd rather lose that airflow than allow a single thief to find their way in.

Another gold hunter had come before us and would already have dealt with these traps, which at least saved us some trouble.

Kai pushed the geese up against the end of the tunnel so they could sample the air. As we crouched down below, I couldn't stop thinking about the stone walls that had just appeared out of thin air behind us. I didn't know of a single mechanism that could do that. Were they ghost-walls? Somehow they seemed pretty solid to me. What strange creatures awaited us? Whose tomb was it? Had my gold-hunting predecessor managed to escape?

The geese seemed fine, so Kai smashed through the green bricks, and the three of us climbed up into the tomb. The burial chamber was quite large, at least two hundred square meters. I shined my flashlight around and gasped. "This is the tomb," I said. "But where's the coffin?"

CHAPTER NINE

Ever since ancient times, burial chambers have contained coffins. *The Book of Burial,* a centuries-old book, recorded that these chambers were also known as "the halls of merciful peace" and were at the very heart of every tomb. Whether these were family mausoleums or individual graves, the deceased would be dressed in formal robes and laid to rest in the coffin, the lid firmly closed. If the body was unavailable for one reason or another, a set of clothes belonging to the departed would be buried in his or her place. The coffin is the one essential component. Gold-hunting rules are strict about this, and no practitioner would ever remove the coffin along with the other treasures. Besides, the coffin in this tomb never would have fit through the narrow tunnel.

Once again, my world felt like it had been upended. None of this made sense. Could the coffin have evaporated?

We stared for a while, our mouths open. Gold Tooth's brain was the quickest—he nudged me and murmured, "Tianyi, it's not just the coffin. Look around—what else is wrong?"

I shined my flashlight around the room again. He was right: the chamber had been stripped. The floor was completely bare. Never mind the absence of grave goods, there wasn't so much as a pebble.

Everything about this structure suggested it was meant for an aristocrat. The perfect right angles of the floor slowly gave way to an exquisitely constructed dome. An orderly earth and a circular heaven, exactly as the ancients conceived of our universe.

There were six stone racks on the ground, standing empty. Gold Tooth and I recognized them at once—they ought to have held six varieties of jade, representing the sky, the earth, and the four cardinal directions. Only a member of the royal household would receive such an honor.

The walls weren't exactly bare, but rather than proper murals, they had only basic sketches with no colors, mostly depicting thirteen ladies of the court beneath the heavens. These women had ample, soft curves, which would have been considered the epitome of beauty at the time. Some were holding embroidered boxes, some jade teapots, and some musical instruments.

I'd never seen anything like this. "What do you make of it?" I asked, turning to Gold Tooth.

He shook his head. "Very strange. This is obviously the

tomb of an important person, almost certainly a woman—perhaps a concubine or princess. But these pictures . . ."

"They're unfinished?" I ventured.

"Yes. That's not just unusual—it makes no sense at all."

I knew he was right. You never see half-finished tombs. Even in the case of someone falling out of favor at court, they'd still receive a proper burial with all the available pomp. That was because every emperor knew that appearances had to be maintained, and conflicts had to be kept within the palace grounds. Even if someone was assassinated or put to death, they'd still receive a grave befitting their station.

I got out a candle and placed it in the southeast corner of the room. The flame was weak, but it remained firmly upright and didn't show any sign of wanting to go out. Relieved, I called the other two over to show them. To save batteries, we shared one flashlight between us. Luckily, there was nothing around for us to trip over. With the two geese in tow, we passed through the stone doorway into the front chamber.

Right up to the Qing dynasty, the front chamber of every tomb was known as the "life room," because everything in it had to be set up according to the way the deceased had lived. If they'd been at court, then that was what the chamber had to look like. For the rest of the aristocracy, with the exception of the emperor, this representation had to largely be symbolic; otherwise grand palaces would be springing up all over the place belowground. Instead, miniature versions of their earthly homes were created to serve as their tombs.

A perverse destiny had given us a ready-made tunnel into this tomb, only for us to find it empty and ourselves sealed inside. Our only hope was the front chamber. There we were in for another shock: the front chamber was even bigger, but the perfect replica of an ancient palace was only half finished. The basic structure was in place, but whoever built it seemed to have given up and sealed the stone walls with iron bars and molten metal, leaving only the floor still permeable. In one corner was a pool with a little fountain still burbling away.

I pointed this out to Gold Tooth. "Look at that. This is what's known as a coffin-stream. In feng shui terms, that's a highly auspicious feature. Looking at this place from the outside, I'd noticed how the weather had damaged the hills—in feng shui terms, we'd call this 'crippling the dragon,' because the altered landscape wouldn't have as much good energy. Yet inside, we have this rare feature that's neither flooded nor dried up over the years but still works just fine. If a woman had been buried here, her descendants would have enjoyed great fortune because of this."

"A coffin-stream?" Gold Tooth repeated. "I've heard of them, but I've never seen one for myself. So this is good feng shui? That's odd, then. Why would they only build half a tomb and not even bury the dead person?"

"Strange things happen all the time," I said. "We're just encountering an unusual number of them today."

"That's not so weird," Kai said, butting in. "Maybe they were rushing off to war, or they spent too much money and couldn't afford to finish the job."

Gold Tooth and I shook our heads. "No way. Changing locations halfway through a burial is the most inauspicious thing you can do," I said. "And this place is perfect in feng shui terms, not to mention practicality: it's so hard to spot from the outside, keeping it safe from grave robbers. If there had been a war or some other great disaster, they wouldn't have bothered to seal up the place."

Gold Tooth nodded in agreement. "Yes, and judging by the condition of the walls and door, they didn't stop work in a hurry; instead they took their time with the final closing of the tomb. They weren't postponing either—it would've been too much work to get that door open again. Not just that one, there'd be at least four similar doors beyond it."

Why had they walked away, then? Surely for some un-avoidable reason, but it was impossible to imagine what that might have been.

My gold-hunting predecessor must have fallen for the same ruse and ended up in an empty tomb. Again I reminded myself that his corpse was nowhere to be seen, so he must have gotten out.

There was nothing that could help us here, so we beat a retreat into the main chamber, quickly checking out the back room and side chambers. There was nothing there either, and finally we decided that we might as well go back the way we came.

As we headed through the main chamber, we all agreed that this whole situation was impossible to explain. "There are such things as false tombs. General Cao Cao and Emperor Hongwu both used them as decoys," I said. "But this definitely isn't one of those, because—"

Before we reached the tunnel, Kai suddenly smacked me to be quiet, and Gold Tooth raised his finger to his lips at the same moment. Looking up, I saw something in the southeast corner of the tomb, right behind the candle.

The candle was flickering, throwing uncertain light into every corner. In the shadows was a large, terrifyingly pale face, its body hidden beyond the circle of light.

We were by the stone doorway, too far away for our flashlights to reach the figure. It was just a blurry, eerie mass.

I'd looked into every corner when we first got to this point, and there definitely hadn't been anything at all like that. None of the court ladies in the murals had such an enormous, alarming face.

We waited in silence for the intruder to move, but it didn't stir. "Tianyi, we should get out of here," Kai whispered.

"Not yet. Let's see if it's a human or a ghost."

I couldn't even tell if the face was male or female, old or young. Without a coffin, this couldn't be a dumpling, so whatever it was must have crept out of the tunnel while we were in the other rooms. No regular person would dare dive into this tunnel, though—could we have met another gold hunter?

This made me remember the so-called merchant who'd built Fish Bone Temple. Could it be that he'd never died? Or never found his way out and gotten trapped here? Was this his vengeful spirit?

If this was just a ghost, it wouldn't be a big deal. We had gold Buddhas and jade Goddesses of Mercy to keep us safe. And if this was a gold-hunter's spirit, well, we were related, so maybe they'd even be able to point us toward the way out.

In any case, we had to break the stalemate. It wouldn't do any good just staring at each other. Cupping my hands around my mouth, I called out, "Seeking baubles in the dark dragon turns, the hill shifts and the sky is seen. The stars move aside, and northern dippers cluster around the southern light."

This was exceedingly polite, in the lingo of reverse dipping. It roughly meant that we didn't mean to step on anyone's toes and had come along this path just because it was there—we'd hoped to make a living for ourselves, that's all.

Reverse dipping isn't an accepted profession—we're not builders or farmers, merchants or scholars—and it has rules all its own. For instance, a gold hunter can enter and leave a tomb only once—repeat trips are forbidden. After all, we're talking about someone's final resting place, and it would be disrespectful to have people traipsing in and out all the time.

Another rule is that within the profession, when two people choose the same target, they're free to be there at the same time, but whoever enters first gets first pick of the treasure. Gold hunters have an ironclad rule that you can take only one or two items from each tomb—partly to avoid attracting unwanted attention, and partly because it would be unfair not to leave some things for the people who come after you. Given how much stuff tends to accumulate in ancient burial places, it's not that difficult to share the spoils. This is where we differ from common grave robbers, who regularly get into fights over their loot because they don't have the skills to find major tombs on a regular basis and don't understand that grave goods come with negative energy, so helping yourself to too much leads to trouble.

There's a particular set of values that makes up the order of gold hunters, and anyone with the right skills and vocabulary is considered to have joined the ranks. I learned some of this from my grandfather and heard the rest from Julie during our expedition into the desert.

So if this figure facing us was indeed a fellow gold hunter, then we'd surely be able to come to an agreement. That was presuming it was alive, of course, though we'd probably be able to work something out with a ghost too—they usually just want you to give their corpse a proper burial.

Having said my piece, I waited for a response. The language I'd used had been formal enough that a fellow gold hunter would definitely know we meant well. A long time went by, though, and the face remained impassive. Even as half the candle burned away, the figure stared at us, as if carved out of stone.

Not a gold hunter, then. I repeated my words in regular Chinese, but there was still no reaction.

We were getting uneasy now. The worst thing in these situations is silence, when you don't know what the other party has up their sleeve. The exit was in the center of the room—but with that face staring at us, who knew what it had planned? Without knowing its intentions, we didn't dare get any closer.

I had another thought: What if this was in fact the owner of the tomb? That would be awkward. "Honored individual, could we ask who you are?" I called out. "We were just passing through, and when we saw that tunnel, we wanted to see where it led. We mean no harm!"

Getting anxious, Kai chimed in. "We're going back where we came from now," he said loudly. "If you don't say anything, we'll assume you're all right with that. Deal?"

Gold Tooth frowned. "Guys, are we sure this isn't just a picture on the wall? The candlelight might be playing tricks on our eyes."

Could he be right?

Somehow this whole place felt evil. First a giant stone appeared out of nowhere to block our way back; then this ghost, human, or demon materialized out of nowhere too. Or was Gold Tooth right, and were we just spooking ourselves?

The candle was almost out, and we didn't dare linger anymore. I stealthily reached into my pocket and pulled out my trusty penknife, holding it in one hand and a gold Buddha charm in the other, then signaled to the other two that we should cross the room and confront this apparition head-on, whatever it might be. Kai nodded and picked up his shovel, handing the geese to Gold Tooth.

We moved in a triangle formation, Kai and me in front. With every step, my palm grew sweatier around the knife handle. I was frightened and tense. I even started hoping this was a dumpling, something I could get into a proper fight with. This spooky figure in the dark was more terrifying than any undead creature could ever be.

When we were almost there, the candle finally winked out with a final puff of smoke. And just like that, the face vanished too.

CHAPTER TEN

INSTINCT SENT A SHIVER DOWN MY SPINE AS WE PLUNGED INTO darkness. *This is nothing to be scared of; it's just physics,* I told myself. *If the candle kept burning forever, that would mean the place was haunted.*

There was a crash behind us. Kai spun around in a fighting stance, but it was just Gold Tooth. He'd collapsed from shock. I helped him up and tried to soothe him.

"Are you all right? Don't worry, you're perfectly safe with Kai and me here."

Gold Tooth let out a shaky breath. "Silly of me. I thought . . ."

I waved away his fears and quickly lit another candle. Once again, the person dipped into view, only it was clear that this was no human being, but just a face, and what was more, a face carved out of stone.

The stone face was atop a massive sarcophagus that I was absolutely certain had not been there when we'd first come in—there was no way we could have missed it. Baffled, we could only draw closer. It was three and a half meters long and about my height. It was made entirely of stone, gray and heavy, and there was a face carved into every surface. The ears were a little too large, and the eyes stared straight ahead expressionlessly, but they were unquestionably human—yet there was something stark and frightening about them.

"What is this?" Kai blurted out. "Did a ghost make it appear?"

I shushed him and turned my flashlight onto its base. "Gold Tooth, can you tell us anything about these carvings?"

"Probably from the Shang dynasty. Look, you can see the thundercloud markings from the Western Zhou period. I'd bet my life on it—these didn't exist during the Tang dynasty."

My experience with antiques was mostly with the more recent Ming and Qing dynasties. I'd never seen anything from as far back as the Shang. Gold Tooth's words were even more confusing. What was a Shang coffin doing here? Everything about this place indicated it was from the Tang.

"Never mind which dynasty it's from," Kai yelped. "I'm getting freaked out just looking at it! Let's just go. Whatever it is, it has nothing to do with us."

"Not true," I said. "It's made of the same type of stone as the slab that blocked our path. If we want to find our way out, we'll have to figure out what this is."

"No," said Gold Tooth. "I'd rather take my chances in the

Dragon Ridge maze. We have a compass, so we won't get too lost."

I nodded. "All right. We have ropes to leave a trail behind us. But do you really think we're going to get out, when whatever's keeping us here can make rocks appear out of nowhere?"

As I spoke, I had a sudden memory of the old guy in the village who'd said there weren't any Tang tombs in these hills, only Western Zhou ones. And now here was this coffin—but then how to explain the unmistakably Tang wall paintings and design?

My head was spinning with confusion. Even the most experienced reverse dipper would have found this impossible to understand. And of course Gold Tooth had no interest in solving the mystery—his focus was on money; there was clearly no treasure to be had here.

"If we're staying," Kai said, "then let's get on with it. No point in standing around. Come on, I'll help you with the lid."

I put a hand cautiously onto the stone surface. It felt solid enough that our chisels might not be able to pry it open. And if there was a dumpling inside, it wouldn't turn out well for us. Something about those impassive stone faces told me to proceed carefully.

Turning to the other two, I said I'd changed my mind, and we should just go back the way we'd come. Perhaps the tunnel had changed again, and we'd find our way out this time. Gold Tooth didn't need to be asked twice. He gathered the geese and was already halfway down the hole. I went last, taking one last look at the candle still burning in the southeast corner before jumping down after the other two.

Right away, we could tell something was wrong. We'd

climbed up here along a forty-five-degree angle. So why were we on level ground now? Shining our flashlights around, we gasped—this was another burial chamber, and carvings of that strange face were all around us. Where had the tunnel gone? We stared at each other.

"What's going on, Tianyi?" Kai growled.

"How do you expect me to know?" I answered. We went back down the same hole we entered from, and ended up somewhere completely different!

"It must be ghosts!" Gold Tooth exclaimed. "They're trying to confuse us."

I hushed him. There was no point getting all jumpy now. Maybe this was the real tomb, the Western Zhou one. Was that where the faces came from? They were exactly the same as the ones on the stone sarcophagus.

Once again, we kept only one flashlight on to save batteries, and I lit another candle as we studied our surroundings. This was a sort of burial passage, with paintings on either side of us, the bright red of blood. How had the color been preserved for thousands of years? Here and there, gray stone broke through the surface.

The corridor was several meters wide and perfectly straight. It disappeared in either direction, paved with rough-hewn stone. Everything about this felt crudely done and heavy, unlike the exquisite craftsmanship of Tang dynasty construction. We'd entered another era, a heavier one.

"Those faces," Gold Tooth said with a shudder. "I'll never forget them. So creepy, smiling but not smiling, absolutely cold-blooded."

"I know what you mean," I said thoughtfully. "The ones on

the stone coffin were blank-faced, but these have different expressions." I shined the torch around, and sure enough, they were displaying joy, sadness, anger, shock—but there was a coldness to all these emotions.

Kai held the candle up for a closer look. "They all seem . . ."

"Fake," I said, pinpointing the word he seemed to be searching for. "They look like bad actors making faces, not people with real feelings."

"That's right!" said Kai. "That's exactly what they look like."

"You can see through them," Gold Tooth added. "Look, there's treachery in the happiness, mockery in the rage. At the market stall, I have to act sincere with the customers, but I'm sure I look fake to some of them. But this is another level. Something that's not human, trying to look like us."

A chill swept across my heart. "But what does this mean?"

Although I'd studied what I could of *The Sixteen Mysteries of Yin-Yang Feng Shui,* there were still many things I didn't know, such as the finer points of history and culture. These faces now told me nothing at all. Gold Tooth might not be an expert, but his decades of experience were worth more than my knowledge at this point.

"We need to think up a strategy," I said to the other two. "Barging around with no plan is obviously not working."

"I'm scared," Kai said softly. "Just tell me what's going on, Tianyi."

Kai was usually fearless, so I had to admit that things looked bad. "We've been ambushed by whatever's happening," I said. "We need to figure it out."

"Next time I'm bringing dynamite," Kai said. "Then we'll just blast our way out."

"Let's get aboveground first, before we start talking about next time." I turned to Gold Tooth. "Can you tell us anything about these faces? Anything at all?"

Gold Tooth shook his head. "All I know is that a Western Zhou artifact like this is worth a fortune—though you might struggle to find a buyer. I've seen enough to be dead certain that the coffin is from the Western Zhou. And the fashion for decorating burial goods with human faces is from the Shang period."

"Hang on, wasn't the Shang before the Western Zhou?"

"Yes, but the trend continued all the way to the time of the Three Kingdoms. So that's consistent with this being a Western Zhou artifact. There is one detail that isn't quite right, though. Did you notice what it was?"

CHAPTER ELEVEN

"You're the expert," I said impatiently. "Just tell us!"

"Sorry, occupational hazard. In the market, I'm so used to spouting enigmatic questions and intoxicating customers with my air of mystery. It's hard to be straightforward."

"This isn't the time," Kai snapped. "We're in a tight spot here. Just come out with it."

Gold Tooth nodded. "I'm no archaeologist, and I wouldn't dare be this certain with most things, but I distinctly remember seeing a coffin just like that one in Luoyang Museum. Western Zhou faces are very distinctive. It left quite an impression on me. That's why I'm so sure."

It's true that Western Zhou artifacts have certain distinctive characteristics: fluid lines, genderless and ageless figures with large earlobes. Besides, it was the only dynasty that featured lightning patterns, so the lightning design surrounding the base of the coffin seemed conclusive.

Human figures before and after the Western Zhou were more individualized, and it was only during that one period that they became generic, with no markers of age or sex. I asked Gold Tooth why that might be. He said only an expert would know—he was able to recognize these features on the coffin but could not explain their origin.

"And what's with the multiple faces?"

"There's a legend of the Western Zhou king having four faces, one facing each direction, so he could always see what was going on. In some versions, he has four ministers who do the looking for him."

"I see. But that doesn't have anything to do with the coffin, does it? There are five faces, including the one on the lid. Do you think this face has anything to do with its occupant?"

I knew even as I asked the question that it was pointless. We were all lost in the fog here, and Gold Tooth's guess was as good as mine.

None of this talk was helping us find a way out, and we were still confronted with two directions to choose from, as well as a hole above us leading to the coffin of many faces.

"We have no idea where we are," I said. "But if Gold Tooth is right and this passageway was built during the Western Zhou period, then I think I can make an educated guess. Shang tombs weren't as luxurious as Tang ones, but they were a whole lot bigger, built by creating giant stone halls, and often spanning many stories, rather than being all on one level. The tunnel we entered by got blocked by a stone slab, which might well be the outer perimeter wall of the Western Zhou tomb, some distance from the grave itself. Though I still don't understand how it suddenly popped out of nowhere. That's the bit that baffles me."

"Stop thinking about it," urged Kai. "You're not going to figure it out. Let's just work on getting out of here. No ancient tomb can defeat the three of us. You've got your feng shui skills, Gold Tooth has heaps of experience, and I've got strength—or I'm stronger than the two of you, at least."

"Feng shui, experience, and strength are all very well," Gold Tooth grumbled, "but what we need now are new brains."

Kai sighed. "Don't you know the saying 'Better three fools than one wise man'? Don't you think we're foolish enough?"

"Never mind all that," I said. "What we really need is luck. We've been really unlucky so far, and every step seems to get us into more trouble. If this place follows the structure of Western Zhou tombs, the level below us ought to be the burial pit, and there's no exiting from that. I say we go back up to the main chamber and try to find the tunnel out."

"Hang on," said Kai. "Isn't the burial pit where all the treasure would be? Why don't we see if we can grab a thing or two before looking for the way out? I'd rather not go home empty-handed. Why'd we go to all this trouble, otherwise?"

"Forget it," said Gold Tooth. "You might be young enough to keep going, but my old legs feel like lead. Let's not look for more trouble. We'll do as Tianyi says and find the way out. This place is weird, and who knows what other traps lie ahead."

Seeing that we were both set on going back up, Kai reluctantly picked up the geese and started to follow us, then suddenly halted. "Wait, wait, shouldn't we open that stone coffin and look at the dead guy's face, to see if it's as strange as the carvings? He might have a mask on, maybe even a gold one. That'd be worth something."

Gold Tooth and I ignored him—this was no time to get distracted. I gave Gold Tooth a leg up into the hole. Then we followed him back up into the chamber.

Nothing had changed. The eerie stone sarcophagus was still in its corner. We all got our flashlights out and shined them across the floor, looking for our tunnel.

Apart from the six empty plinths and the coffin, there was nothing at all in this room. It was an impossible situation, a Western Zhou sarcophagus in a Tang tomb.

Kai pointed at the hole we'd just come through. "That's the only opening. Wasn't that the original tunnel?"

I pointed my flashlight at it. Yes, that was definitely the hole we'd first entered by. So why did it now lead to a passageway, rather than our tunnel? As I tried to figure it out, Gold Tooth exclaimed, "Tianyi, Kai, look at the side of the coffin. There's a . . . staircase."

We went over, and sure enough, a wide staircase was suddenly visible, each step consisting of a single strip of stone. I pointed my flashlight up to see where it led, but the stairs continued into the darkness, more than ten meters up the wall.

"It feels like this place really is haunted," I said. "Tunnels turning into passageways, Tang graves sprouting Western Zhou coffins, staircases appearing out of nowhere. I say we've got little to lose by climbing the stairs and seeing where they go. If this is a Western Zhou tomb, they'll lead to the top level. Maybe then we'll be able to get out through the extraction tunnel."

"Okay, I'll go first. You two follow my lead!" Kai said with renewed spirit. He bounded up a few steps, then stopped. "Tianyi, what tunnel were you talking about? What does it do?"

"The extraction tunnel?" As I came up the stairs behind him, helping Gold Tooth, I explained, "These old tombs are carved out of mountains. So first you have to hollow out the rock—the extraction tunnel was how all the debris was brought up to the surface. It got sealed after the interment, and the slaves and craftsmen were usually buried alive inside. If we're lucky, the workers will have been clever enough to leave themselves a secret escape route, and maybe we can use that to get out of this godforsaken place too."

We'd been walking about five minutes now, and I was starting to feel something was wrong. Then I saw it. When we'd started climbing, I'd noticed the second step had a crescent-shaped notch in it, probably gouged out by mistake during construction. Twenty or thirty steps later, I'd noticed another one and thought nothing of it, but after that I started counting. And now it was clear—the crescent-shaped flaw appeared every twenty-three steps.

This was no coincidence; we were climbing in circles. I yelled at the other two to stop—there was no point; we'd never reach the top.

We beat a hasty retreat, but it seemed there was no downward way out either. Descending was easier, and we went a lot faster, but even after we'd been going back for longer than we'd spent coming up, there was still no sign of the ground. We'd lost our way back to the burial chamber.

We were all breathing hard by now, especially Gold Tooth, who sounded like a broken accordion. I called a halt, and Kai plonked himself down, mopping at the beads of sweat on his forehead. "Tianyi, a few more hours of this and we'll probably starve to death down here," he said.

Our backpacks had been full of food when we'd set out, but because we'd needed to make space for our equipment, not to mention the treasure we expected to bring back, we'd left all our rations at the temple. We had a bottle of water each, and that was it. Now that Kai reminded us, all our stomachs started rumbling violently.

This was more dangerous than ever. By blundering onto these stairs, we'd allowed ourselves to get caught by a ghost-wall and were now doomed to go in circles until we managed to break free. I cursed myself for being so impetuous.

"Don't blame yourself, Tianyi," said Kai. "If we weren't trapped here, we'd be trapped in the room downstairs. Let's just think how to get out of here."

"The stair with the crescent-shaped notch comes up every twenty-three steps, whether we're going up or down. So there's no way out in either direction."

"That's it, then." Kai flopped onto his back. "We're done for. We'll just lie here and die, and the next group of reverse dippers can find our bones."

A couple of tears trickled down Gold Tooth's face. "My poor eighty-year-old mother, and my little eighteen-year-old niece. I'll probably never see them again. If I make it out alive, I swear I'll leave this profession."

I remembered with a pang that I'd meant to call my parents earlier but never got around to it. We hadn't spoken in a while, and I wondered if they were worried about me.

Kai, meanwhile, took affront at Gold Tooth's words. "What are you whining about? At least die like a man. If you don't stop it, I'll rip out your gold tooth."

Gold Tooth valued his gold tooth more than anything else, so this threat made him clap his hands over his mouth. He protested in a muffled voice, "Kai, we're all dead men here. Kindly leave my corpse intact. No waiting till I'm weak with hunger to pounce on my tooth."

"Enough out of you two," I snapped. "No one's starving to death. If we have to die, let's at least go out in a blaze of glory."

"Easy for you to say," Kai retorted. "Where would you find glory in this place?"

"We could fling ourselves down the stairs. If they really are endless, we'll fall forever."

"I think what Tianyi means to say is that we're not doomed just yet, so we shouldn't give up hope." Gold Tooth peered anxiously at me. "Right, Tianyi? That's what you're driving at?"

"Be quiet and let me think," I said, exasperated. "Ever since we came in here, it's like we've hit ghost-wall after ghost-wall. No matter where we turn, something's blocking our path. Gold Tooth, do you know anything about ghost-walls?"

Gold Tooth shrugged. "Not much. There were a few cases around Di'anmen Road some years back. People got so worked up they didn't dare go outside after midnight. Otherwise you might get caught and have to wander up and down the same street until sunrise. And I've heard stories from other towns too. But is this really a ghost-wall? Normally they just make you walk in circles. I've never heard of anything this powerful. Besides, we're carrying so many charms and amulets, spirits shouldn't be able to affect us."

"Have you forgotten, Tianyi?" Kai butted in. "You always say places with good feng shui won't accumulate negative energy. So how could this be a ghost-wall?"

I shook my head. "I don't think it is one. I just wanted to rule it out as a possibility. In that case, I think I know what's going on. Just don't be frightened at what I'm about to tell you."

CHAPTER TWELVE

"IF THE GHOST-WALL DIDN'T SCARE US, I DON'T KNOW WHAT will," Kai said. "Come on, out with it. Even if we're going to die, I want to explain to people in the afterlife how it happened."

"I'm just worried this won't make sense to you. But I'll tell you what I think, and you can tell me if it sounds plausible."

They turned their full attention on me, but I was in no hurry to explain my theory. First, I had a question for Gold Tooth. "In the village near Coiled Snake Hill, you saw a damaged stone tablet. Then there were pictures of court ladies in the first room we came to, and a magnificent burial chamber. All those were in the Tang dynasty style, right?"

"Yes, I'm absolutely certain those were Tang. The craftsmanship, the design, the clothes in the painting—there's no way I'm mistaken."

"And yet in the middle of a Tang dynasty tomb we saw a Western Zhou sarcophagus. And we saw a passageway with Western Zhou murals. And back in the tunnel, the wall that came out of nowhere was Western Zhou too."

"That's right!" Gold Tooth exclaimed. "So that must mean ghosts are at work."

"I'd say a rather particular ghost."

"A particular ghost? Do you mean the ghost of whoever's buried in this tomb?" Gold Tooth asked. "But would that be a Tang or Western Zhou person?"

I waved that away. "Maybe I didn't express myself clearly— I shouldn't have used the word 'ghost.' Not something supernatural, but something that can be explained with physics. Plenty of scholars are researching this phenomenon, though there isn't a particular term for it yet. Let's just call them 'spirits' for now."

"What's the difference between ghosts and spirits?" Kai looked puzzled. "Tianyi, whose spirit are you talking about?"

"Not whose spirit. I'm talking about the spirit of the Western Zhou tomb, not the sort that gets left behind after a person dies. The Western Zhou tomb is itself a spirit. What we're faced with is a Western Zhou spirit grave in an abandoned Tang structure."

Gold Tooth was starting to understand and nodded vigorously. "There are stories about ghost houses and ghost ships, not to mention ghost towers and ghost cars. So it's possible that what we've encountered here is a ghost grave."

Kai looked bewildered. "Can either of you make sense?"

"Look, I've been in the antiques business for many years," said Gold Tooth, "and there's something I've come to believe deeply. Every exquisite artifact gathers the blood and sweat of countless artisans, and as time goes on, it starts to acquire a soul, or you could say a spirit. If it gets destroyed, and is no longer in the world, that spirit remains. That's why so many ships, long after they've been wrecked and sunk to the bottom of the sea, will still be visible on the surface, steaming along their old routes."

"Oh," said Kai. "When we saw the stone tablet, didn't I say it was the ghost of itself? It seems I had the answer all along, and you two idiots didn't pick up on it."

"This reminds me of something," said Gold Tooth. "A relative of mine came to Beijing on business. He checked into his hotel and was given the keys to room 303. He got back that night after twelve, so exhausted he could barely keep his eyes open. He stumbled up three flights of stairs. The door to 303 was ajar. He didn't think anything of it, just went in. There was a cup of warm water on the table, so he took a big sip, then crashed onto the bed. The next morning, the porter shook him awake. He'd been asleep on the third-floor landing."

"You think he saw a ghost building?" said Kai.

"Yes. At first he thought he'd been sleepwalking, but then they went to room 303, and the door was locked, nothing had been touched, and the bed hadn't been slept in at all. He left without understanding what on earth had happened. On his next visit, he ended up at the same hotel. Chatting with the receptionist, he learned that the hotel had burned down some years ago and been rebuilt unchanged, only a little larger. Everything else was exactly the same, down to the room numbers. Ever since, a few times every year, some guests go into their rooms at night, only to wake up in the corridor. No one really paid attention—it was just a bit weird. When my relative told me this story over dinner, I chalked it up to another funny story. And look at us now. In a ghost grave."

Gold Tooth turned to me. "That was impressive," I told him. "I would never have put two and two together like that."

"What else could explain one tomb being stacked on top of another?"

Two tombs, from different eras, jostling for space on the same desirable spot. That happened, of course. Really good feng shui locations are hard to come by.

This was the key point, and it explained everything else. Maybe the Western Zhou period was when this bit of the valley was first recognized for its importance. Feng shui wasn't as developed as it would be during the Tang dynasty, but humanity has always sought to better itself, and the very best minds of any era would definitely have discovered this place.

So some Western Zhou king died and was buried here, in a stone coffin carved with faces. The tomb was roughly as we'd seen it—tall external walls, three stories within. The lowest level was used for storing grave goods (probably a lot of livestock and pottery, going by other tombs of the period); the middle one would have held the stone coffin and nothing else (even if the deceased had precious personal items, they'd simply have gone into the coffin with him); and the topmost level would be connected to the extraction tunnel. And right now, we were stuck between the top and middle floors.

The owner of the stone coffin would have rested peacefully here for a thousand years, but then sometime before the Tang dynasty, for reasons we might never know—war, grave robbers, political intrigue—this tomb had been utterly destroyed.

Then the Tang dynasty came along, and the emperor's feng shui master identified this part of Dragon Ridge as a prime burial place, and so it was excavated to build a mausoleum for an important female member of his household.

Halfway through construction, the remnants of the first tomb were discovered. Abandoning a partly built royal tomb is extremely inauspicious, quite apart from the money, labor, and materials already expended. Then again, having two tombs in the same spot was also unlucky, even if one of them had been all but eradicated. In this situation, not even a feng shui master could resolve the impasse. More likely, the workers and feng shui expert worked together to fabricate some version of events that could fool the emperor, so he'd come up with more money to shift the tomb to another site.

The sarcophagus that had suddenly appeared and the stone wall blocking the tunnel—those things were the older tomb reasserting itself. The candle hadn't actually vanished—a wall had appeared on top of it.

Gold Tooth agreed, then creased his forehead. "There's one thing I still don't understand. So there's the spirit of a Western Zhou tomb—how come the Tang dynasty builders discovered this only when they were almost done? As soon as we stepped into the tunnel, that wall appeared out of nowhere. That's a bit of a coincidence."

He was right; that was something I couldn't explain. Surely this was more than bad luck—had the ghost grave somehow chosen us to appear to? Strictly speaking, although it could be seen and touched, this wasn't a physical object, only the spirit of the tomb stuck here on earth. It didn't exist in a permanent state, but appeared one portion at a time. Would the whole tomb eventually reveal itself, or would it only ever be partially present? We still had no idea.

"This is the head of the dragon meridian, a source of clear energy," I said to Gold Tooth. "The tomb would have soaked up all that energy, and even after it was destroyed, it would have remained within the meridian. There's nothing odd about that—the only peculiar thing is why the ghost grave appeared at this time. In other words, did we activate its appearance, or was there some other cause?"

"As far as we've seen," said Gold Tooth, "at least three groups of people have come in here since the original tomb was destroyed. Two of those groups—including us—were from the order of gold hunters, several decades apart, and both encountered this ghost grave, getting trapped inside in the process. The third group was the one that built this Tang dynasty tomb. The group must have been fairly large, since Tang tombs were huge projects. And it must have taken them a long time to finish. Yet they discovered the Western Zhou grave only toward the end of the process. Why?"

"That's right," I said, "so it must be a particular action that makes the Western Zhou tomb appear, rather than a question of time. But we weren't even halfway down the tunnel when that stone wall materialized and blocked our way back."

"I guess the original tomb was completely eliminated," mused Gold Tooth. "Not one brick was left—that's why the Tang dynasty crew thought they'd been lucky enough to find a large natural cavern at a good feng shui point. Then later, the ghost grave showed up. They, we, and this first gold hunter must have all done the same thing. But what?"

"At least we know what happened now," I said. "We also know that whatever it was, there must be a way to undo it. The people who came before us must have thought of this too, and they managed to get out. Now we just need to do whatever they did."

"Well, it has to be something ancient people could have done," Kai said.

"You're actually making sense, Kai. For once."

Kai grinned. "Hunger helps me think."

"We can narrow it further," said Gold Tooth. "It's something that happened only toward the end of the Tang construction, but it's also something we did almost right away when we entered."

"Which is?" Kai asked. "You two are supposed to be the smart ones. Let me give you another clue. What do we have in our supplies that the ancients would have had?" He looked from me to Gold Tooth. "Candles."

"Candles?" The thought had crossed my mind, but then I'd dismissed it. Surely the construction hadn't taken place in darkness—they must have worked by candlelight right from the start. Of course, we had no way of knowing the details of what people did back then—perhaps they really did have some weird superstition about not using candles at the start of a project. That seemed unlikely, though. And surely someone would have recorded that in a book somewhere.

As my mind whirred, the geese started squawking and fighting. "Be quiet!" Kai shouted at them. "Or I'll roast the two of you feathered idiots." The birds ignored him and kept gabbling at each other. "What a commotion!"

A lightbulb went off in my head. "Kai! Geese! The geese!" I yelled.

"Do you know what Tang dynasty workers did just before they finished building a tomb? They had an animal sacrifice—three types of livestock, three types of fowl. It was meant to appease all the lingering spirits so they'd leave the incoming dead person in peace."

"Ah!" yelled Gold Tooth. "So you're saying it was the geese that made the ancient tomb appear?"

"Yes! Why didn't I think of this before? The gold hunter who came before us would have brought ducks or chickens along to test the air quality—that's standard gold-hunting practice. That's why he got trapped in here too."

"Three types of livestock, three types of fowl," repeated Gold Tooth. "And geese are the most powerful species of fowl—according to legend, they're able to see spirits. Maybe we summoned the tomb faster because we happened to bring geese with us."

Grabbing one of the birds, I got out my pocketknife and held it to the creature's throat. The only way to be sure was to slaughter it and see if that made the walls disappear.

"No!" Gold Tooth yelled, grabbing my hand. "Tianyi, don't!"

CHAPTER THIRTEEN

"NOW WHAT?" SAID KAI. "WHAT'S THE PROBLEM?"

Gold Tooth motioned for me to put down the knife. "Tianyi, Kai, don't get upset, but something seems wrong to me."

"I'm not upset," I said. "You know me. When I have an idea, I want to act on it right away. But if you think something's wrong, feel free to tell us."

"It's like this," said Gold Tooth. "The way I see it, if we're right about the Western Zhou spirit grave appearing because we brought the geese . . ."

"Yes? What are you getting at?" Kai snapped.

"Give Gold Tooth a chance," I said.

Gold Tooth cleared his throat. "As I was saying, if we kill

these two geese, there'll be no more fowl, and the Western Zhou tomb might vanish. But have you thought about where we're standing right now? This endless staircase is part of the old tomb—it wasn't there originally but materialized after we'd been here awhile. So we might actually be in a natural cave, or else deep in the mountain itself."

I understood his point. "You mean if the ghost grave suddenly disappeared, then we'd end up outside the Tang tomb, which means we might still be trapped, or even buried alive."

"Yes, and what's more, the ghost grave doesn't seem to be the whole of the Western Zhou tomb, only part of it. These steps were at the boundary of the ghost grave, but there's no clear division. Or maybe this whole place is in a state of flux, but we don't know if it's expanding or contracting. If we kill the geese . . ."

He was right—this was a riskier position than we wanted to be in. "So we need to get back to the Tang dynasty tomb, into the burial chamber or the tunnel," I said. "We can kill the geese there, once we're in a safe place."

This was easier said than done. It didn't matter whether we went up or down; on every twenty-third step we encountered the crescent notch, with no end in sight. No matter how hard we tried, we were stumped. We couldn't just shut our eyes and jump—as Kai said, we'd keep falling until the end of time.

Then Gold Tooth thought of something, and we tried his plan for lack of a better one. I lit a candle and stayed put at the damaged step, while Gold Tooth and Kai went on. When Gold Tooth was no longer able to see the light from my candle, he stopped moving and lit his own, while Kai went on alone. The hope was that by creating a visual link, we'd prevent the stairs from looping and come back out into the Tang tomb.

Unfortunately, the candlelight wasn't able to reach more than five or six steps before getting swallowed. There was something unnaturally dense about this darkness—it reminded me of what we'd experienced in the cave in Xinjiang, the stuff of nightmares. As the memory came back to me, I started trembling all over, as if our companions who'd died in Xinjiang were lurking in the dark, watching my every move.

Even the powerful flashlight beam could extend a distance of only six steps before fading. So the three of us could visually cover only twelve steps, about half as far as we'd need to break out. Gold Tooth's idea had failed.

Giving up, we huddled together around a candle, turning off the flashlight. "Why don't we try that again, but this time I won't stop when I can't see the light anymore," Kai said. "I'll just keep running till I get out."

"No way!" I shouted. "Don't try to be a hero. There's no point—you'd just die. If we get separated, there's no chance any of us will get out of here alive."

"What choice do we have? We're not going to get out just by standing around."

"We need to think of a solution! This is just like you, Kai, wanting to use brute force instead—"

Seeing that we were starting to quarrel, Gold Tooth cut in. "Guys, we don't have time for this. Tianyi's right. We can't let ourselves get separated."

Sighing, I sank down onto a step. Something poked at me—the coil of rope I was wearing at my waist. "That's it!" I yelled. "Why didn't I think of this before? We've all got rope on us, at least a hundred meters altogether. That's how we'll stay connected to each other."

We quickly tied our ropes together, and then Kai stood on the damaged step, a candle in his hand and the rope firmly looped around his waist. Would this work? I had no idea, but we had no other options. Before I could set off, Kai grabbed my arm.

"What if the rope breaks? Tianyi, be careful."

"You be careful too. If the rope breaks, don't panic and pull at it. As long as you let it lie there, I'll be able to find the end. And whatever happens, don't move. If Gold Tooth and I get out into the Tang tomb, we'll pull on the rope and get you out too."

"Sure, and if you get into trouble, just blow your whistle and I'll pull you back."

There was definitely enough rope to get us beyond twenty-three steps. Would this finally break us out of the trap? Trying not to get our hopes up, Gold Tooth and I set out.

With every step we took, I turned back to make sure I could still see Kai's candle. At the sixth step, just before the light disappeared, I told Gold Tooth to stay put. He lit a candle, made sure the rope around his waist was secure, and handed me the slack.

"I'm going to keep walking now," I said. "If I get past the twenty-third step, I'll tug the rope three times, you do the same for Kai, and we'll all walk out together."

"Good luck," Gold Tooth said gravely. "I'll keep my fingers crossed."

Seeing that he seemed calm and steady, I nodded and set off, playing out a little rope for every step I took. At the twelfth step, I stopped and looked at the remaining rope. Even though there was enough, I couldn't help quickly calculating in my head how much farther I could go. Then I kept moving. Was it really that simple? Get past the twenty-third step and end up back in the Tang dynasty tomb? There was nothing but endless dark ahead of me. My heart beat faster, but I could only keep going, counting every step.

Twenty-one, twenty-two, twenty-three. Another stair with a crescent-shaped notch. This was spooky. I pressed on, determined to keep going until I ran out of rope.

As the coil of rope shrank in my hand, I felt my heart contract and prepared to turn back. Then I noticed a glimmer of light and cautiously took a few more steps. Someone was up ahead. The light I'd seen was the candle at his feet. As I drew closer, I recognized his broad back.

Kai ought to be behind me, yet there he was up ahead, rising on tiptoe, looking all around. So we'd failed once again. My hope turning to ashes, I tapped him on the shoulder. "It's me. Again."

Taken by surprise, Kai jumped away from my voice and pitched forward. I tried to catch him, but he was too large and I only managed to rip off a piece of his sleeve. Luckily, he was nimble enough to catch himself before tumbling more than a couple of steps. Looking back at me, he gibbered, "Tianyi, how did you get up there? And why didn't you make a sound? You scared me to death, you really did."

"Oh, don't be a big baby. You can take a little scare, can't you?" I sat down next to him and put down the rope. "But seriously, our hypothesis was right—we're in the chaotic zone at the border of the ghost grave, and there's no such thing as fixed space here. Call Gold Tooth back, and we'll come up with another plan."

Kai tugged the rope. Soon Gold Tooth stumbled up to us, and we explained what had happened. He sighed. "Well, let's come up with something else while we still can. In a few hours, we'll be too hungry to think straight, and then we really will be doomed."

At the thought of hunger, Kai's eyes grew wide and he grabbed one of the geese by the neck. "Now, hang on. If all else fails, we have two plump birds here. I know you said not to kill them, but it should be all right if we just eat one for now and leave the other alive till we get out of this maze."

"We don't have any firewood," I said, "so how are you going to cook it? Or were you planning to eat raw goose meat?"

"Didn't people eat raw meat in olden times?" Kai retorted. "When I get hungry enough, I won't care if it's raw or cooked."

"If you mean cavemen, sure, they ate raw meat and drank blood, but I think you'd better hang on a little longer. If we really can't get out, then you go ahead and enjoy your uncooked goose. Our last meal was at Fish Bone Temple, only six or seven hours ago."

Meanwhile, Gold Tooth had started sobbing. "Tianyi, are we really done for? We've thought of every possible plan, but we can't get past these steps. What terrible luck!"

I started to comfort him, but I couldn't get the words out. My mind was all jumbled too. These wretched steps. The number twenty-three kept floating in my mind. It was significant somehow. I touched the crescent-shaped notch, feeling as if I were struggling in the middle of a vast ocean. Suddenly, a piece of driftwood appeared.

Kai started to say something else about the geese, but I shushed him ferociously, afraid he'd break my train of thought. It was on the tip of my tongue—where had I heard it . . . ?

When it came to me, I slapped my thigh hard, startling the other two. "We've been tricked by these stairs! This isn't a ghost-wall or ghost-grave border zone or whatever; it's a regular trap. Just an ordinary cunning trap."

One of the chapters in *The Sixteen Mysteries of Yin-Yang Feng Shui* describes the various traps in ancient tombs, and I'd finally remembered that one of them involved a sequence of twenty-three steps. This was known as the "floating stair," and its design had been lost for a thousand years, though many mathematicians and scientists were absorbed in studying it. Some thought it was a form of hypnosis, which worked by placing some sort of marker or number on a stair and, through a complicated mathematical model, laying out a network of branching and combining staircases that appear, by an optical illusion, to be a single set of steps. The crescent-shaped notches were actually a trap, leading us farther and farther into the maze. The walls and ground were quite possibly coated with some sort of light-absorbing pigment, making it abnormally dark, which also diminished our sense of direction. By paying too much attention to those marked steps, we'd been fooled into thinking we were traveling in a straight line, whereas we'd actually been lured into turning here and there, going in a big circle around the many branching paths. That's probably why the stairs were so shallow, so it was easy for us to be confused about where we were going.

The floating stair was already in use during the Western Zhou period, and it made sense that it would be among the defenses of a royal tomb. Not every set was exactly twenty-three steps, but we could use that number to find our way out. Luckily, I'd remembered this in time. Not bothering to explain this to the other two, I told them to follow me, then quickly constructed an octagonal *bagua* symbol with pebbles on the ground, using what I remembered of the formula from the book to calculate our way out.

I went around and around a few times in my head but felt my brain turning to mush. No point asking the other two—Kai was only good at counting money, and Gold Tooth's math expertise was restricted to business.

"The main thing you need to understand is that this trap relies on optical illusions based on the slightly different heights of the stairs. I think brute force might be the answer after all. Let's just roll our way out."

"I said we should roll down earlier," Kai said, "but what if we never get to the end? Can you guarantee this will work?"

"Just do as I say—start rolling."

The candle winked out at that moment. Gold Tooth was afraid of the dark and quickly got another one out, but he hesitated before lighting it. "Tianyi, I've just thought of something."

"Not again," Kai said. "Out with it, then."

"My brain's working slowly because I'm scared, but my grandpa used to talk about a trap that went in straight lines, like a maze. When you stood inside, you only ever saw a single passageway, but it was actually dozens of twisting paths. I once saw a copy of the *Heavenly Manual* from the Sui dynasty. It mentioned these sorts of mazes, and there was a picture of staircases going around each other like the number eight. Is that where we are?"

"That's the basic idea. But every trap is going to have a different design, and you have to calculate your path according to a formula—but I can't make it work."

"I've heard of the floating stair too," said Gold Tooth. "But not many people used that trick after the Zhou dynasty because it was too easy to break out of."

Kai and I gaped at him. "Too easy?" we both said.

"Seriously, it's simple," Gold Tooth went on. "These traps all rely on some sort of misleading marker, and once you start paying attention to it, you'll never make your way out. So the answer is to walk with your eyes shut."

"That's right!" Kai shouted. "If we just stopped looking at that mark, and stopped counting stairs, we could just walk right out of here."

I didn't think it could be that simple. We'd spent so much time on this staircase already, who knew how far we'd traveled from our starting point? If we just started walking blindly, where would we end up? I struck my fist against the wall in frustration, and then it hit me. This trap was designed with solo reverse dippers in mind. There were three of us, and while we hadn't been able to stretch ourselves out over the length of the staircase, we could use width to our advantage.

When the other two heard my plan, they nodded excitedly. The stairs were more than ten meters wide, and one person, walking down the center of the stairs and looking out for crescent-shaped marks, wouldn't be able to keep an eye on the walls on either side and therefore wouldn't notice subtle shifts in direction. Hugging the wall wouldn't do any good either— you'd just move in a figure eight.

Instead, the three of us each held a candle and walked side

by side, checking in with one another at every stair. After a few steps, we noticed a second staircase branching off to one side, and made a mark there, as well as on a piece of paper. Soon, our map showed a tangle of pathways, shaped like an enormous pair of butterfly wings.

This floating stair made use of the natural shape of the cavern, and it actually wasn't all that large. It wouldn't have fooled a big group of people, but just one or two would be bamboozled by the width of these stairs if they didn't check the sides closely for deviations—unless they lit a candle on every single step. By the time we'd mapped out about two-thirds of the maze, we finally stepped onto level ground. We were back in the burial chamber, and the stone sarcophagus with its five faces glowered at us from the southeast corner.

I glanced at my watch—we'd spent four and a half hours on the floating stair, and it was now three in the afternoon. Our last meal had been at nine in the morning. So much for grabbing a few treasures and leaving. Instead we were trapped in a ghost grave.

I had promised myself we'd never venture into a situation unprepared again. Reverse dipping doesn't suit improvisation, but rather requires clear minds, plentiful experience, virtuoso techniques, well-chosen equipment, and meticulous preparation—not one element of which can be missing.

There was still a pile of floor tiles in the center of the room, revealing the hole that we'd climbed through—but it now led to the Western Zhou passageway, not our tunnel out.

The chamber was completely dark. Out of habit, I lit a candle in the southeast corner, though this was our final one. The little flame rose straight up, adding a faint glimmer of light to the otherwise eerie room. This tiny amount of illumination was all it took to make us feel a lot better.

Looking at the flame, we let out deep breaths. We were finally out of that deadly trap, and couldn't help laughing at the sheer relief of it. "You see?" I said to Gold Tooth. "In the end it was still up to Hu Tianyi to save the day. This place couldn't keep us down."

"Gold Tooth and I helped too," Kai said. "You'd never have gotten out on your own."

"I'm a vine winding itself round a tree, and you two are melons on the vine. The vine holds up the melons, and they rely on it for sustenance."

"What kind of gibberish is that?" Gold Tooth said, laughing.

I chuckled too, but a sudden thought sobered me up quickly.

Where were the geese? In our hurry to get out of the floating stair, I hadn't thought about them in a while. Turning to Kai, I asked, "Weren't you leading the birds? Where did they go? You didn't leave them on the staircase, did you?"

Kai raised his hand. "I swear, I brought them down to the burial chamber with us. I let go of them when we were celebrating." He looked one way, then the other. "I just turned around for a minute. They must be nearby. Quick, let's go search for them before they have a chance to get too far away."

Two loose geese wouldn't be easy to find in a vast darkened chamber. And if we couldn't find them, we wouldn't be able to break the spell. Where could they have gotten to? Just as we were about to split up and search for them, a terrifying screech pierced the silence. It was coming from the stone sarcophagus.

CHAPTER FOURTEEN

OUR HAIR STOOD ON END.

The three of us had thought we were almost done with this place, and now our geese were gone and this strange sound chilled our hearts. I held my pocketknife, Gold Tooth another of his golden Buddhas and a black donkey hoof, which was a potent charm against the undead. Kai had a big shovel. Step by step, we slowly approached the sarcophagus.

Kai led the way, speaking loudly to bolster his courage. "It's probably just the geese making trouble. When I get hold of them, I'll teach them a lesson."

Our hearts in our throats, we surrounded the coffin, only to find nothing behind it. The sound abruptly stopped.

Kai slapped the coffin lid. "It couldn't be coming from

inside, could it? Maybe the ghost grave came with a ghost dumpling."

"Don't say that," said Gold Tooth. "You're scaring me. May the Goddess of Mercy protect us." He held up a charm, only to realize he'd picked up the wrong one and was invoking the wrong deity—this was Buddha, not the Goddess of Mercy. He hastily repeated his prayer with the right name.

"The sound wasn't coming from inside the coffin," I said to Kai. "It was definitely coming from behind."

Before I could go on, there was a burst of white in front of me, and something landed on the sarcophagus. I jumped back in fright, then looked closely. It was one of the missing geese, looking fine and uninjured, spreading its large wings and waddling contentedly from one end of the stone coffin to the other. How had it suddenly dropped down from the roof? How had it gotten up there in the first place?"

We must have had the same thought at once, and now each of us shined our flashlights at the ceiling.

The round dome of a Tang dynasty tomb represents the heavens, and it is usually decorated with an array of auspicious constellations. That was more or less what we saw, although one side of the dome was also sprouting a stone wall—that Western Zhou tomb asserting itself again. We were probably the only three people living who'd seen this bizarre sight, two tombs fighting to occupy the same space.

Seeing nothing too alarming up there, we turned our attention back to the goose. Still no sign of the other one, so we continued our search, but it was no use. This tomb was so enormous—the burial chamber alone was more than a hundred square meters, though it wasn't actually finished. This was just the outer chamber, where the grave goods would have been stored. There would also have been an inner chamber, which would normally have held the coffin itself—this coffin was probably out here because the half-finished tomb didn't have a proper space for it. The side and rear chambers hadn't been built either, and the front one, which was also large, had a sunken room with a lake, and it would probably have been landscaped into some sort of garden.

How were the three of us going to find the missing goose in all this?

"At least we've got one of them. Be sure not to let it get away," I warned the other two.

I directed my flashlight down the hole, and sure enough, the tiled passageway was gone. In its place was a dirt floor— the tunnel we'd first come here by.

Somehow or other, despite all our blundering, we'd gotten our escape route back. No time to celebrate, though. Our flashlights were all flickering, and the replacement batteries we put in now were the last ones we had.

We jumped into the hole. I led the way, yelling to the other two. "Let's keep going no matter what. Gold Tooth, follow me, and Kai, bring up the rear. If you see that Gold Tooth slows down, push him along."

"What's the rush?" grumbled Kai. "The tunnel is back, after all."

"If the other goose wanders back, the Western Zhou tomb might materialize around us again. We have to get out while we can."

With that, I dove into the tunnel, the other two behind me, keeping a safe distance of two meters between us. After a short while, I turned to see how Gold Tooth was doing. He was panting heavily, but he soldiered on, as eager to get out as I was.

The tunnel looked exactly as it did when we'd first come through it. That struck me as odd—the ghost grave had appeared bit by bit, and I'd expected it to disappear the same way. After another twenty or so meters, I started hearing dripping water. I figured we must be halfway there, and yes, a little farther along was the cave. I started to crawl over and jumped into it, and when Gold Tooth appeared at the entrance, I lifted him down.

Sweat was pouring off the poor guy like rain, and he was breathing in quick gulps. "I . . . can't . . . I . . . really . . . can't . . . I'm . . . so weak. . . ."

Seeing that he really was exhausted, I told him to sit and rest. "Take deep breaths," I said. "When Kai shows up, we'll have to carry on. When we're outside, you can rest as long as you like, but this isn't the time. In a minute, you'll have to start moving again."

Gold Tooth could no longer speak. His mouth hung wide open, and he barely managed to nod. I looked back into the tunnel to see how Kai was doing, but he was still a fair distance away. His bulk made climbing through this confined space particularly difficult.

Seeing that he'd be a while, I went over to the opposite side and shined my flashlight into the tunnel. The limestone caves here were joined, all the way down to the very depths of the mountain. If the stone wall was still blocking our path up ahead, we'd have to find our way out here.

As I stared into the depths, I heard Kai's voice. "What are

you looking at, Tianyi? Has Gold Tooth gone on ahead? Let's go after him, quick."

I turned around to see Kai standing alone. "Where's Gold Tooth? You didn't see him?"

"You were the only one here when I arrived."

There was a peculiar sound from elsewhere in the cave. I quickly shined my flashlight in that direction, and froze. Looming out of a dark corner was a face similar to the ones on the sarcophagus. It looked completely inhuman, about the size of a sink. Its body was invisible.

The only difference was, this was no stone carving, nor was it a wall painting. Kai and I were both pointing our beams at the face when it started to move, its lips curling upward, its eyes shutting into half-moon slits. I'd never in my life seen a more terrifying smile.

Kai and I involuntarily took a couple of steps back, but then we stopped. Where was Gold Tooth? We had to help him instead of running off. His disappearance surely had something to do with the strange apparition.

Moving at the same time, Kai and I got out our weapons and slowly advanced on the ghostly face. Then, abruptly, a strange sound rose from the ground.

CHAPTER FIFTEEN

THE DARK CAVE WAS SHAPED LIKE A BOTTLE. WE HAD COME IN through the neck, and the noise was deep in the body, as was that eerie face. I pointed my flashlight at the sounds, which turned out to be coming from Gold Tooth, who was slumped on the floor, lengths of white silk binding his hands, feet, and mouth, which prevented him from speaking. He still seemed able to breathe, though. And he looked absolutely petrified.

Seeing us rush over, he struggled to cry for help, but all he managed was a muffled scream.

I didn't have time to think how he'd gotten into this state, just dashed over to cut him free. Before we reached him, there was a sudden creaking overhead, and he was abruptly hoisted into the air.

I pointed my flashlight up, and once again it caught the strange face, which was now hovering overhead, smiling coldly down at us.

Gold Tooth was jerked a little higher off the ground.

What on earth could be happening? The cavern roof rose high enough into the air that I couldn't make it out clearly. I signaled to Kai, and without hesitating, he dropped his shovel and got out his knife, reaching up to slice Gold Tooth's bonds. Luckily, the old man was still within reach, and he fell to the ground. I quickly helped him up.

"Are you all right? Can you walk?" I asked.

He'd been so badly throttled that he could barely shake his head. His limbs were like jelly.

Kai glared at the strange creature above us. "What is that face?" he shouted. "And why is this silk so sticky?" At the same time, he'd picked up his shovel and was pulling his arm back, and now he took careful aim and let it rip.

The pointy head of the shovel jabbed right into the ghostly face, at which point two rows of red lights lit up underneath it, four big ones and four little ones, like eight blood-red eyes.

A giant black creature dropped down from the roof. Quickly, I dragged Gold Tooth to one side, just before the thing landed where we'd been standing a second ago. I was close enough to see it clearly now.

It was a giant spider with a human face. Its body was soot-black, with white markings that had formed themselves into a humanlike face on its back, all the features exactly where they should be. Eight huge, hairy legs hung from its body.

I'd heard stories about these giant spiders from my dad, who'd encountered his share of them in the Kunlun hills. When he was in the army, his platoon had been searching for a missing comrade when they encountered a nest of such spiders. Thanks to their training, they managed not to panic and killed the three huge spiders in the nest with their rifles and bayonets. At the back of the nest, they found the man they were looking for. He'd been wrapped in silk, tight as a mummy, and all the fluids had been drained from his body.

From what I'd read, these creatures injected their victims with a paralyzing poison that left them fully conscious. The spiders then gorged on the live victim as they pleased. It was a slow, awful death. I shuddered to think of it.

All this flashed into my head in an instant, with the monster just half a meter from me, every one of its black hairs standing out in my flashlight beam. Before it could make a move, I stuck my pocketknife into its side. The blade was too short to do it any real harm, but it startled the spider. When it was close enough, I quickly sliced across one of its front legs.

Immediately, the creature scuttled a few paces back.

The shovel Kai had lodged in its back now worked free and clattered to the ground. Kai ran over to grab it. "Tianyi!" he yelled. "We must be in the spider's lair." He started hacking at the monster's body, driving the spider into the far corner of the cave.

Kai was about to go after it, when I shouted, "Leave it! Pick up Gold Tooth and let's get out of here."

Kai rushed back and scooped up Gold Tooth, who was still on the floor. He took a step and stopped suddenly—there was something soft underfoot. He looked down. "Hey, it's our missing goose!" he yelled. "It looks like the spider sucked it dry."

I hurried over to help with Gold Tooth. "Forget the goose. Quick, get him on your back. I thought there were more caves beyond this one, but it looks like they're all part of the spider's nest. Let's just get out through the tunnel. If we go into the caves, we'll never—"

Before I could finish, something tightened around my legs. I could no longer stand. The same thing happened to Kai and Gold Tooth. Just like that, the three of us were pulled downward, a force dragging us deeper into the cave. I struggled but couldn't get to my feet. A skein of silk the thickness of my forearm had wrapped itself around my calves. The spider Kai had scared off definitely couldn't produce anything that thick. Could there be an even larger specimen in the cave?

I struggled harder. I grabbed my pocketknife, planning to cut myself free, but when I looked up again, the roof of the cavern was rushing toward me, and I smashed face-first into it, almost breaking my nose—the creature must have swung me upward with a twitch of the silk. Blood streamed from my nostrils, and I could only whimper, feeling increasingly helpless.

We were rattled along for quite some distance, which ripped the backs of our shirts to ribbons, and soon our skin was left covered in long cuts. Were we heading back to the nest, where we'd be paralyzed and slowly eaten at the monster's leisure? I felt a chill all the way up my spine.

Kai had been stunned, but he managed to gather his wits. I hadn't found anything to cling to that might halt our movement, but he reached out and grabbed a stalagmite as we passed it, and this allowed him to hold himself stationary long enough to slice through the silk ropes around his leg. Ignoring the agony he must have been in, he sprinted over and caught up with me, cutting me free too. I cursed as I sat up, wiping the blood off my nose with my sleeve, then cutting the rest of my bonds off myself. Meanwhile, Kai turned to rescue Gold Tooth, only to find him farther ahead, shouting and waving his arms.

Gritting our teeth against the pain, we sprinted toward him. We only had a single flashlight between us, and its light wobbled as we ran, winking out just as we caught up with Gold Tooth. That was the last of our batteries, and now we were in borderless darkness. We had to move fast—if Gold Tooth got dragged away from us again, we wouldn't be able to find him in the dark, and then he'd suffer a torture worse than hell. I reached out blindly but only managed to grab hold of his liquor flask as he was wrenched away again.

No time to think. My shirt was so badly ripped that I was able to pull it off my body with a few tugs. Tearing it into shreds, I emptied Gold Tooth's flask over them and held a lighter to the makeshift torch, which flared up brightly. I flung it away from me, and as the fireball arced over the cave, we saw Gold Tooth about to disappear into a triangular opening in the wall. I made a note of the location before the fire could go out, and we ran toward it. Kai ripped off his shirt and tossed it onto the flames to keep them going. I caught hold of Gold Tooth's arm while Kai sliced through the silk.

Gold Tooth's face was bruised and battered, his body covered in wounds, but he was still conscious and alert. The spider's nest was no doubt through that opening, and we had to get out of here as quickly as possible, before the next attack came. Who knew how far into the cave we'd been dragged? I was completely disoriented, but that didn't matter; we just needed to get as far away as possible. By now we'd had to burn our trousers to keep the flames going, and we were standing in only our underpants, but we still needed to flee, even if it meant groping our way through pitch darkness.

Before we could get Gold Tooth to his feet, a few strands of spider silk came flying out of the triangular opening and looped into a lasso that wrapped around us before we had time to move. Kai tried to slice through the silk with his shovel this time, but it was pulled from his grasp. He tried to bend and pick it up, but he was stuck too firmly to do even that.

It wouldn't have been so bad if we'd been fully dressed, but in our half-naked state, the webbing clung directly to our skin, and there was no way to break free. The ropes drew together, dragging the three of us into a clump and hauling us toward the opening.

The nest must be on the other side—how many spiders would we find there? How big would they be? Actually, the answers didn't matter—as long as we wound up in the hole, this wouldn't end well for us.

There must have been seven or eight thick, sticky strands woven together, and more were spewing from the hole. It looked like the spider was going to wrap us up like human dumplings right where we were.

My mind was fizzing with panic, but I remembered that I still had a lighter, and I hastily got it out. The silk caught fire easily, and I was able to burn my way through the two or three ropes leading me toward the hole. Though the sticky stuff was still wrapped around my body, I was no longer being pulled into the lair.

Gold Tooth and Kai were being rapidly dragged toward the hole. I'd only have time to save one of them with the lighter.

Frantically, I pulled off Gold Tooth's trousers—his belt had been so badly frayed, they just slipped off—balled them up, and stuffed them into the hole. Then I held the lighter up to them, thinking I could burn off all the silk at once. As soon as the strands caught fire, a muffled explosion came from inside the nest, followed by giant tongues of fire shooting out.

In an instant, the cave was lit up bright as day by the inferno, and all the silk was going up in flames. I rushed to pull the other two aside, and we brushed the rest of the webbing off our bodies.

CHAPTER SIXTEEN

IT SEEMED AS IF HALF THE MOUNTAIN WAS NOW ON FIRE. AS THE flames crackled, I was finally able to see that the triangular opening was in a man-made wooden structure that had probably been sealed with some highly flammable substance like beef fat.

The wooden construction was about the size of seven or eight apartments. It wasn't clear what it had originally been built for, though from each pillar and beam hung corpses sucked dry by the giant spiders, both humans and animals, all reduced to desiccated husks. Even through the webbing wrapped around them we could see how they'd died horrible deaths—tormented expressions were etched on their faces.

As the room started to collapse, we saw three enormous

balls of fire writhing in the flames. Eventually they stopped moving, either burned to death or knocked out by the falling debris. Soon they'd be burned to mounds of charcoal.

The three of us stared, knowing we should get far away but unable to make our feet obey.

Kai suddenly pointed at the flames. "Tianyi, Gold Tooth, look—there's someone in there."

We looked where he was pointing, and sure enough, there was a human face—a giant one, several times bigger than the ones on the spiders' backs. In the flickering firelight, its already-disturbing features grew spookier, suspended as they were in the middle of the room. Finally, we could see that the face was carved into the side of a huge bronze urn.

Kai groaned. "Not that ghost grave again?"

I shook my head. "Nope. Probably the ancients thought these spiders were the gods come to earth and worshiped them. So this must have been a shrine, right where they nested. They kept slaves back then—many of those poor devils probably ended up as human sacrifices to these things. We've done a good deed today by destroying this lair."

The Western Zhou tomb must have had some connection to the spider altar. Maybe the latter survived when the former was destroyed, because it was hidden so deep in the caves. In any case, this was all the dust of the past, and no one would ever know what really happened—except perhaps a particularly determined historian.

"Let's not worry too much about all that. Are you injured?" I said to Kai. "Let's carry Gold Tooth out of here, and fast. There might still be spiders alive."

"It's a shame to go now," said Kai. "Why not wait till the fire dies down, then find a way to get that urn out? If we can get it to Beijing, it'll probably fetch enough to buy us a house each." He turned to Gold Tooth. "How are you doing? Better now?"

Gold Tooth was still in shock, dazed from fright and from being hit on the head. He stared into the flames, and Kai had to nudge him a couple of times to get an answer. "Ah, Kai, Tianyi, so the three of us . . . meet again in hell."

"What's wrong with you?" Kai said, shaking him. "We're not dead. And I have more good news for you—we're rich! See that bronze urn? Wait, is it getting scorched?" He made to go have a closer look.

From where I was lying on the ground, I yelled, "Stop! Leave it be! There's no way we could bring it back, anyway."

Kai had dollar signs in his eyes and wasn't about to listen to me, but the fire was too hot to get any closer, and he reluctantly had to retreat. As he stepped backward, he slipped on the dried husk of one of the spiders' victims, tumbling right on top of it.

Bold as Kai was, he still got scared out of his wits, shoving the corpse away with both hands as he struggled to his feet. As his fingers brushed the corpse's neck, they picked something up. He took a closer look—it was the claw of some animal, glistening in the firelight, translucent black, a gold wire threaded through it.

Kai held it up. "Tianyi, isn't this a gold-hunting charm?" He crouched down and ran his hands over the hollowed-out corpse. "Ah, and there's something else here."

He found a cloth bag, opened it, and placed the items inside on the ground one by one.

"Wait! Toss that charm over," I called to him.

He did as I asked, busily looking through the rest of his loot. I held the charm in my palm and studied it. It was sharp at one end and perfectly rounded on the other, the characters "mojin," meaning "gold hunting," inscribed on it in ancient script. Little chills shot through my hand as I looked at it. This was the real thing.

A genuine gold-hunting amulet, made from the sharpest of a pangolin's claws, had to be soaked in Sichuan paraffin for forty-nine days, then buried a hundred meters beneath a Dragon Tower for eight hundred days, in order to absorb the energy of the meridian. Only then was it fit to be inscribed with these characters. I'd only seen the real thing once—in Julie Yang's possession.

So was this the corpse of the gold hunter who built Fish Bone Temple and dug the tunnel we'd come here by? Had he gotten trapped in the ghost grave, worked out that he had to kill the creature he'd brought with him, but gotten ambushed by the spiders on his retreat? He was by himself, unlike us, and would have easily been defeated. It was sad to think of him dying here all by himself.

Kai came over with his treasure. "Look at all this, Tianyi— it's from the dead body."

I took the items from him and studied them carefully. Among the jumble of objects were seven or eight candles and two wadded-up paper lanterns. These were more valuable right now than any treasure—my lighter was our sole source of light. I told Kai to hang on to them carefully; they were our only hope for getting out of this place alive.

The sack also contained old-fashioned batteries, but no flashlight, and three little red pills. I blinked. Could these be the secret medicine made by the order of gold hunters back in the day? Generations of gold hunters had relied on these to ward off the effects of corpse breath—the toxic fumes given off by dead bodies. Modern gas masks protected our eyes, whereas my predecessors wouldn't have been so lucky. If a coffin was sealed tightly, the corpse breath would accumulate inside, and if it entered any of your orifices, you'd be in trouble. There were other methods of dealing with this—cutting vents in the coffin, sending large birds ahead to test the air—but the main defense had been these scarlet pills, made according to a secret formula, now lost to us, which held antitoxin properties.

There were a few other things in the sack: a basic compass and a chunk of saltpeter—also known as "northern pearl"—which could revive you with its strong aroma if you started feeling faint.

Last of all, there was a coil of thin steel wire at the bottom of the sack, along with a three-inch knife, a small bottle of Yunnan white medicine, and something I was thoroughly familiar with: a black donkey hoof with a string attached, used to prevent corpses from transforming.

"Are these things worth any money?" Kai asked.

I shook my head. "No, but we'll be able to make use of them. Looking at what's in this sack, I can imagine what it must have been like to be a gold hunter all that time ago. It's a shame my predecessor died here. Now that we've found him, I think we should give him a proper cremation, and hopefully his spirit will be freed and watch over us so we can get out safely. We'll burn his things along with him."

"Fine," said Kai. "I'll burn his corpse now. We killed the giant spiders, so we've avenged him. I reckon that means it's fine to take his stuff as a reward. I might be able to sell some of it at the market."

"All right," I said, "but don't expect to fetch a lot of money. I'm taking the mojin amulet, though. Don't think there's anything worth keeping in the rest, and those pills are probably past their expiration date."

Kai lost interest as soon as he heard there was nothing valuable. He wandered off with the sack in one hand and the body under the other arm. He got as close to the burning nest as he could, then flung the gold hunter and his possessions in.

I stretched my neck, aching from my cuts and bruises, though my limbs felt more mobile. I nudged Gold Tooth and asked if he was able to walk yet. He nodded blearily, though when he moved his jaw, he winced from the pain.

We huddled to come up with a plan to get out. We'd been dragged in such a zigzag by the spider that we had no idea where we might be. The local people had said this entire mountain was a network of limestone caves, but when we looked around, the walls were of compacted yellow earth, dry and friable. It seemed this landscape was composed of many different materials.

So the folklore was wrong. All the people who had disappeared from these parts, the goat herders and their flocks, hadn't fallen into deep caves as we'd been told. They were probably among the dried-out husks in this cavern.

We now had no clothes or food, and every minute we delayed increased the difficulty we'd face getting out. This Western Zhou urn was the sort commissioned to commemorate important events. Or else it was used in ancestor worship. Could the occupant of this tomb have been a devotee to the cult of human-faced spiders, and so insisted on being buried here? The human sacrifices would have been left by his descendants in his honor. Then, when the regime changed and the food stopped coming, the spiders would have started trapping prey again.

The fire was starting to weaken, and in the guttering light, we could see a dozen or so cave entrances surrounding us. We had to choose a way out—but which one? No time to think about it. Before more spiders could show up, we walked through the nearest exit.

CHAPTER SEVENTEEN

I TOLD KAI TO LIGHT A CANDLE, AND WHEN WE GOT TO THE next cave, we set it down at the entrance.

I watched as the flame rose straight up. "This is a dead end; the air isn't moving," I said. "Let's try the next one."

Gold Tooth and I started to leave, but Kai stayed put. "Aren't you coming?" I called.

He was pointing at the entrance. "Tianyi, smell. What's that? It's so strange."

"It's probably spider poop. Don't breathe too hard. It might be poisonous."

"No, come here! It's sweet, like, um, chocolate or something."

Chocolate? My stomach started rumbling at the word. How could there be chocolate deep beneath a mountain? I was too hungry to work it out. Gold Tooth, half-dead as he was, perked up and started tottering toward the cave entrance.

I sniffed. Nothing. "You're crazy," I said to Kai. "All I smell is burning."

"Get closer. It's strongest at the entrance. Thick and sweet. Maybe there's a cocoa tree?"

Now Gold Tooth nodded. "Yes, I smell it too, chocolate. Tianyi, it's coming from the cave."

I took a couple of steps forward, and at the entrance I also detected the most marvelous scent, sweet and milky. It filled my brain and made my injuries stop hurting at once. My sore muscles relaxed, leaving me soft and comfortable. "It's wonderful," I murmured. "Almost celestial."

We couldn't wait any longer and hurried into the dark cave with our candle. It was narrow, only two meters high, and maybe three or four wide. The rocks here were strangely shaped, twisted and gnarled like tree roots.

Kai darted ahead and sniffed vigorously, trying to find the source of the aroma. Suddenly, he pointed at a rock. "It's coming from there." He licked his lips, as if he'd have liked to take a bite out of it.

I put the candle next to the rock, and we studied it. Like a tree trunk, it was yellowish-brown and looked as if it was covered in a layer of gum. The few portions that stuck out were translucent, and its surface was covered in an irregular pattern. When the candlelight touched it, the lines seemed to grow fluid and move a little.

Kai couldn't help reaching out to touch it. Then he brought his finger up to his nose. "Hey, it's turned my finger into chocolate—smell it! Do you think we can eat it?"

I'd never seen anything like this. "Wait! Careful, Kai. Don't lick it."

Gold Tooth suddenly jerked to life. "Tianyi, this is our lucky day! Don't you think this might be fragrant jade?"

"What?" Kai gaped. "What's that?"

"It's a treasure, that's what! Fragrant jade, also known as golden jade."

"I've heard the name," I said. "So this is what it looks like? It's certainly fragrant, but why jade?"

Either this stone had miraculous healing powers or Gold Tooth was revived by the prospect of riches. Either way, he was positively animated as he said, "Some reverse dippers have found this in ancient tombs—it's an imperial treasure that was first discovered during the Qin or Han dynasties. Most people never got to see it, so no one really knew about it. Its smell is stronger in dry conditions. I had a little piece once, sold to me by a reverse dipper, but it was just a chip, nothing like this."

"How much would this be worth?" Kai asked.

"Large pieces of fragrant jade are very valuable. The outer skin is a much sought-after component in medicines. A chunk this size—and this looks like pretty good quality—would bring in enough to buy an imported car."

"We're not far from the temple with the bronze urn," I said. "Could this also be an offering of some sort?"

Gold Tooth considered. "I don't think so. It's in its natural state. If the skin hadn't been ripped, we wouldn't even have smelled it. This cave doesn't show any sign of having been disturbed—all these other rocks are probably natural formations too."

"If this doesn't belong to anyone," I said, "then we might as well take it. Funny how things work out. We had the bad luck of finding two empty graves, coming away without a single bit of treasure, and then this falls into our laps. At least this won't be a wasted trip."

Kai, who'd been waiting for me to give the go-ahead, immediately bent down to pick up the rock. Gold Tooth hastily stopped him. "Don't touch it like that. You need to wrap it in something first. If only we had a piece of cloth."

I looked at us—Kai and I were in our underpants, and the only spare bit of fabric we had between us was Gold Tooth's ragged shirt. We had to keep moving—there weren't many candles left, and our lack of food would soon become a real problem. No time to hang around and investigate the other rocks.

Noticing that the candle I held was halfway gone, I put it into one of the paper lanterns and told Gold Tooth to take off his shirt and wrap the rock in it. With Kai carrying the valuable burden, we hurried out of the cave.

Back in the main cavern, the bronze urn was nowhere to be seen, though there were little metallic glints in the embers like stars in the night sky.

Once again, it was too dark to see what was around us. "Just because no other spiders have appeared doesn't mean they're all dead," I said. "We need to leave right now."

Trying to reconstruct our route as best we could from memory, we felt our way along the wall until we came to a cave that seemed to be heading in the right direction. Again I told Kai and Gold Tooth to hold their breaths, took the candle out of the lantern, and placed it at the entrance.

The little flame immediately swayed in the opposite

direction. I put the candle back in the lantern and felt with my hand. I couldn't sense much of an air current, but the flame's movement meant that it wasn't a dead end, even if it didn't link directly to the outside. Could this be the path by which the spiders reached the surface to hunt for prey? We had to give it a try.

Holding up the lantern, I led the way. Kai and Gold Tooth followed, carrying the fragrant jade between them. We burrowed through this cave, and maybe because of that magical aroma, we felt full of energy and clearheaded, despite still being absolutely ravenous. We were bringing a valuable object home with us, and as long as we managed to get out, we'd have ample cause to celebrate.

This cavern was long and twisty, its ceiling rising and dipping, so narrow we had to go single file. Farther back, it started sloping upward at a forty-five-degree angle.

I climbed along until I felt a piercing gust of cold wind. It covered me with goose bumps. We were nearly outside. I shouted at the others to hurry as I saw a burst of light up ahead. There was a hole in the soil above. I stuck my head out and climbed to the surface. Back in the outside world!

Just as I was rejoicing, Kai popped his head aboveground and abruptly yelled, "Tianyi! Your back . . . there's a face on your back!"

CHAPTER EIGHTEEN

KAI'S WORDS FELL ON ME LIKE A BUCKET OF ICE WATER.

I twisted around but couldn't see my own back. "What are you talking about?" I shouted. "What face?"

Kai hoisted Gold Tooth out of the hole and they both gaped at me. "Tell him, Gold Tooth! Tell him he's got a face on his back. It's the truth."

Gold Tooth set down the fragrant jade. He rubbed his eyes, which were still bleary from being in the dark so long. "Between your shoulder blades, about the size of a palm, Tianyi. It's a bit like a birthmark—not very clear, but it's a face . . . or maybe an eye."

"What? I have an eye on my back?" My head felt like it was going to explode. I reached between my shoulder blades but couldn't feel anything on my skin. I urged Gold Tooth to describe in more detail what he saw, whether a face or an eye.

"It's round and dark red, not very clear—you have to look closely. Circles within circles, like the pupil of an eye. Yes, I should have said eyeball. It's not the whole eye—there are no eyelids or lashes."

"But, Kai, didn't you say it looked like a face? Why is Gold Tooth saying it's an eye?"

Kai stood behind me again. "I guess I was still thinking of those markings on the spiders, and then I looked at your back and thought it was the same. Actually, it reminds me of those eyes we saw back in the Taklimakan Desert."

I was starting to panic. This definitely wasn't a birthmark. I'd have known about it.

Then I heard Gold Tooth yelp. "Kai, there's one on your back too," he said. "Quick, look at my back—do I have one?"

I got them both to turn around. On Kai's left shoulder blade was a crimson spot the exact color of a birthmark, its lines blurry, about the size of a palm—and yes, shaped like an eyeball, though it was hard to be completely sure. The dark red blotch, like a bruise, was particularly striking in the setting sunlight.

Gold Tooth's back, by contrast, was smooth and unblemished, apart from where he'd been scraped by the rocks. "You're fine," I told him.

Meanwhile, Kai and I stared at each other in alarm. This couldn't be a coincidence. If we were the only two affected, it was likely the result of our last trip to the ghost-hole in Xinjiang. Had Julie Yang and Professor Chen come away with a curse too?

I tried to think. I'd seen Kai take off his shirt a couple of days ago, when he'd gotten drenched from the Yellow River. The mark hadn't been there then. So had it just appeared— could the Dragon Ridge tombs have been the cause? But then why didn't Gold Tooth have one as well?

"Don't worry too much, Tianyi," Kai said calmly. "It's no big deal. It doesn't hurt and doesn't itch. Give yours a good scrub next time you have a shower, and maybe it'll just wipe off. We have the fragrant jade, anyway. So glad we got something. Where do you think we are? It looks familiar."

I'd been too distracted by the strange marks on our backs to look at our surroundings. Now I looked up and couldn't help laughing. "After all that walking," I said, "we must have gone in one big circle. We're pretty much back where we started."

Earlier that day, I'd walked away from Fish Bone Temple to get a better look at the feng shui and stepped onto a crust of earth that crumbed away to reveal a hidden cavern; it was this opening that we'd just climbed out of. Quite a coincidence.

All our possessions were still at Fish Bone Temple, just ahead of us. We hurried over there—we needed to get dressed before it got cold.

Although we'd survived this expedition, the strange marks cast a pall over our victory. I made up my mind to visit a doctor as soon as we got back to town. Even though I didn't feel unwell, it was unsettling to have something like a tattoo appear out of nowhere on my body.

The wind roared through the gully, making us shiver as it hit our naked bodies. Carrying the fragrant jade, we made a dash for Fish Bone Temple. Luckily, everything was still safely tucked away behind the Dragon King altar. We pulled on clothes and gulped down some water, then gobbled the rest of our food. We'd made it! Now we could return to Beijing with an object worth a fair bit of money.

Gold Tooth stroked the fragrant jade, crooning a song about being rich. I wished I could share his joy, but whenever I thought about the red mark on my back, my enthusiasm dampened again.

Seeing I was down in the dumps, Gold Tooth said, "Tianyi, don't let the mark worry you. It doesn't look like it goes very deep. Maybe a doctor can get rid of it with medicine."

"This isn't a skin disease," Kai pointed out. "What's the use of seeing a doctor? Might as well light a fire and burn it off ourselves."

I sighed. "Forget it. You're right, it doesn't matter. Let's have a rest, and we can deal with everything else tomorrow."

Gold Tooth raised his flask to us, then gulped down the rest of the liquor. "After all that, I really feel like I've learned to treasure my life all over again. Whatever happens next, I'm going to make sure I enjoy it."

The sky was dark by the time we finished eating. We made our way down the hill to the village near Coiled Snake Hill, where we found another night's shelter, then headed for Gulan the next day. We'd planned to get back across the Yellow River but were told that after two days of heavy rain, the water was raging so dangerously that there would be no boats till the day after, at the earliest.

We discussed the possibility of finding another crossing, then decided we might as well spend a couple of days in Gulan, resting up after our adventures. Besides, maybe we'd find some good antiques in the village—it was worth scouting around.

And so we went back to the same inn we'd stayed at before, only to find it was full—lots of people were hanging around, waiting for the ferry to be operational again. Gulan was a small town without many accommodations to choose from, and so we ended up in the only place we could find, a hostel dormitory. There were eight beds in our room, and two were already claimed. We didn't dare leave the fragrant jade in a locker, so we wrapped it well and took turns keeping an eye on it. When we went out, it came with us.

That night, Kai and Gold Tooth stayed in the room with our loot while I went off to use the bathhouse at the inn. There I bumped into Mr. Liu. After some small talk, I asked if there was a doctor in town who was good with skin ailments. Mr. Liu said yes, there was one with superb skills who'd be able to restore anyone to health. There was no one better at treating psoriasis. Then he asked solicitously if I was all right.

I'd been on my way to take a bath, so I wasn't wearing much. I loosened my shirt and showed Mr. Liu my upper back, saying there was some kind of growth there I wanted looked at. He peered, then gasped in fright. "What on earth is that?" he said. "That's not a skin disease; that's some sort of bruise. It looks like a word, I vaguely remember that I've seen before."

"Hang on, there's a word on my back? You can see a word?"

"Some thirty years ago, while they were building an elementary school nearby, they uncovered some strange animal bones. Of course, everyone took some as souvenirs. Later on, archaeologists came along and asked everyone to hand over any bones they'd collected. They stayed at this inn. I saw them studying the bones—and this word was carved into them, more than once."

I no longer felt like having a bath. Instead, I dragged Mr. Liu to a quiet corner of the dining hall, sat him down, and asked him to tell me more. The kitchen was closed by then, so he had nothing better to do and was happy to tell me the whole long story.

It turned out that the archaeologists had come by less than three years ago. The local authorities had shut down the inn for them so they wouldn't be disturbed in their work. Mr. Liu, who'd already been working in the kitchen back then, was an inveterate busybody and would hover near the archaeologists, helping them with their work when he could. They'd seen him bustling in the kitchen, and he seemed enthusiastic, so they shut one eye and let him watch, as long as he didn't steal anything or make a mess.

Their haul consisted of a huge amount of turtle shell pieces and various animal bones. Every fragment had words and symbols carved on them, though much of it was too badly damaged to read and required a great deal of reconstruction.

Among all the damaged items was a giant turtle shell in almost perfect condition. The archaeologists washed it with a light acid solution, and Mr. Liu saw the markings on it come clear. The symbol that appeared most often was shaped like an eyeball.

He asked one of the archaeologists what the distinctive eyeball shape represented. The worker laughed. "It's not an eyeball; it's an ancient form of writing. It's—"

The archaeologist was interrupted by the expedition

leader, an academic named Professor Qiu, who cautioned that these were national secrets and should not be discussed with anyone. Mr. Liu didn't ask anything else, though his curiosity grew the more he thought about it. These objects were thousands of years old, so why would they still need to be kept secret? Was Professor Qiu just being a bully? In any case, he knew when he wasn't welcome, and he stayed away after that.

Ever since the giant turtle shell showed up, though, strange things started happening. There were a couple of small fires at the inn that left everyone unsettled. A few days after the incident with Professor Qiu, the archaeologists decided they'd gotten everything they needed and should get out of this fire-prone place. They packed everything up in wooden crates, which filled an entire truck. The crates were supposed to be airfreighted to Beijing, but the plane crashed on the way, and everything—including the giant turtle shell—was burned to ashes. Of the fifteen archaeologists who'd joined the expedition, only Professor Qiu survived. He had left his notebook at the inn, and in rushing back to get it, he'd managed to miss the plane. Professor Qiu was still in Gulan when he heard the news of the plane crash. He fell to the ground and couldn't be revived. Mr. Liu and the other inn workers took him to the hospital, where they brought him around. From then on, whenever Professor Qiu's work brought him near Gulan, he'd stop by to visit Mr. Liu, though no matter how many times Liu asked, the professor refused to tell him what it said on the turtle shell. All he would let slip was that the symbols represented great evil, and it was best not to know anything about them. He sighed several times after that, then muttered something about wishing he'd never set eyes on those wretched words.

"And didn't I look at that red mark on your back," Mr. Liu concluded, "and right away think of those horrible words? Truly, they're exactly the same. This isn't a sickness. What on earth have you been up to?"

"Mr. Liu, are you absolutely sure you don't know what it means?"

"My boy, all I know is that it's some ancient writing. I swear, I haven't the faintest idea what it actually stands for. But there's someone who does know. You're in luck—this Professor Qiu I was telling you about, he comes back to Gulan for a few days every year, and he's in town right now. He just checked in to the room just overhead!"

I grasped Mr. Liu's hand. "Then for the love of Buddha, you have to help me. Bring me to see Professor Qiu." Mr. Liu thumped his chest. "You can count on me. But this Qiu fellow is closemouthed. Whether he tells you anything, well, that depends on how persuasive you are. Maybe the mark on your back is special enough that he'll confide in you."

I asked Mr. Liu to wait for me while I ran a quick errand. First I rushed back to the dorm to tell Kai and Gold Tooth what I'd learned. We decided that Kai would stay put guarding the fragrant jade and Gold Tooth would come with me. After so many years of being a merchant, he was much better at getting information out of people than I was.

We quickly changed into more respectable clothes, then went back to Mr. Liu. I thought of something. "We shouldn't go up empty-handed, but it's too late to buy snacks."

"Professor Qiu won't mind if it's me who brings you up," said Mr. Liu. "But, ah, aren't you two in the antiques trade?

Best not mention that to him. He's bad-tempered, and he hates people in your line of work."

Gold Tooth and I agreed not to mention it. We'd make up some tale about being in Gulan on business and finding the strange symbol on my back. Once we got our story straight, Mr. Liu led us to the second floor and knocked on Professor Qiu's door. After we explained why we were there, Professor Qiu ushered us in.

He was around sixty, a scrawny, stick-dry man. His skin was dark, his back slightly hunched, no doubt the result of long years excavating archaeological sites. His face was covered in wrinkles, and he'd lost all his hair except a wispy outer ring. Despite his age, his eyes blazed with vigor. He didn't wear glasses, and apart from his funny hairstyle, he looked exactly like a village farmer who'd spent his life toiling in the fields.

Although he and Professor Chen had the same job title, they were completely different. Professor Chen was the very model of a scholar, the sort who sat in an office and acted all civilized. This guy was the practical sort, it seemed.

When Professor Qiu heard my story and saw the mark, he kept exclaiming how odd it was. I asked what on earth was on my back and if my life was in danger.

"Yes, this is indeed a symbol of the artifacts we uncovered a couple of years back," he replied. "The most complete turtle shell had one thousand one hundred and twelve words inscribed on it, resembling the classical Chinese script, but not the same. And this symbol, which looks like an eyeball, appeared seven times."

"Can you tell us what it means?" I asked. Professor Qiu

shook his head. "The mark on your back only looks like the ancient symbol—it can't possibly be connected. Two years ago, when the plane my colleagues were on crashed, everything we dug up was destroyed. There are plenty of coincidences in the natural world. Some species of beans, for instance, look exactly like human heads. You wouldn't think those beans had anything to do with actual human heads, now would you?"

Gold Tooth and I cajoled and pleaded, tossing out every bit of flattery we could think of, asking over and over what it said on that giant turtle shell. If he could just tell us the details, we'd be the judge of whether or not they were connected.

But Professor Qiu stubbornly refused to reveal any more. Finally, he snapped, "The two of you can stop pretending. You stink of dirt. I've been in this business long enough to know exactly what you've been up to. Only three people smell so strongly of soil: farmers, grave robbers, and antique thieves. And frankly, you don't look like farmers to me. So I'm not particularly disposed to help you. I don't know where you saw this symbol, but somehow making it look like a mark on your body and thinking you could fool me that way—I'd advise you not to think you'll get away with that. I only have two more things to say to you. First, you two shouldn't cause any more trouble—these ancient words are a national secret, and no ordinary person has the right to know about them. Second, and let this count as a friendly warning, you are absolutely not to think about these words anymore. They're a celestial secret too, which no mortal should know about. Anyone who gets too close to these words will find disaster befalling them."

CHAPTER NINETEEN

With those words, Professor Qiu stood and started pushing us toward the door. I thought how weird this old coot was, all smiles when he welcomed us in, then suddenly turning on us. Somehow he'd realized who we really were and changed his tune. But this was important—maybe a matter of life or death. Not just mine and Kai's, but Professor Chen and Julie might be in danger too.

"Professor Qiu, please," I said. "Won't you let me say one more thing? I don't know how you sniffed out the scent of dirt on us, but I swear, my gold-toothed friend and I aren't who you think we are. We're not grave robbers. For a while, I was recruited to lead a team of archaeologists into the Taklimakan

Desert. I worked for Chen Jiuren of Beijing, also known as Professor Chen. Perhaps you know him?"

The professor paused at Chen Jiuren's name. "Old Chen? You're telling me that you were on an expedition with him?"

I hastily nodded. "That's right. I imagine you must be the twin pillars of the archaeological world. In these circles, whenever your names are mentioned, everyone looks up with respect."

Professor Qiu's face softened, and he waved me into silence. "No need to flatter me. I know very well who I am. All right, if you know Old Chen, you can stay. Send the other two away."

Gold Tooth and Mr. Liu obediently left, and Professor Qiu shut the door tight behind them. He asked me a few questions about Professor Chen, and I quickly related the story of our expedition to Xinjiang, where we found the ruins of Jingjue City. Professor Qiu sighed. "I've known Old Chen for a long time. I'd heard he had a bit of trouble in the desert. He should count himself lucky he didn't end up buried in the sand. I wanted to visit him in Beijing, but then I heard he'd gone to America for medical treatment. Who knows if I'll ever see him again. He did me a great kindness once. Seeing as you know him well, I'll share what I can with you."

These were the words I'd been waiting for. "I suspect the mark on my back is the result of our having been to Jingjue City," I blurted out. "The ghost-hole tribe there worshiped the eye, and I think we may have gotten cursed. Then I heard that this was no eyeball, but rather a word, and I wanted to ask you what it meant, if only so I can be psychologically prepared for what's going to happen to me. I've escaped death countless times, so it's not my personal safety I'm concerned about, but to see poor Professor Chen in such a state—I won't lie to you, it's the old man I'm worried for."

Professor Qiu sat down in a chair. "It's not that I don't want to tell you the truth. I simply can't. Knowing these things won't do you any good at all. But I can say with certainty that this mark on your back isn't a curse, and it won't affect your health. You don't need to be anxious on that score."

I was growing increasingly frustrated. This was as good as not saying anything at all! At least it was nice to know that I wasn't cursed, but the more Professor Qiu refused to tell me anything specific, the more I wanted to know. Did the ancient writing still have meaning for us today? Surely it must, for it to appear on my body.

I kept prodding Professor Qiu, until he was forced to divulge a little more.

The professor had spent most of his career researching the ancient languages found around the Yellow River. He was an acknowledged master in this field, adept at decoding and translating these languages. When written words first appeared, it ended the period of barbarism, when humanity was able to keep records only by tying knots on a string. Language was able to hold a huge amount of information—in fact, unlike modern Chinese with its four tones, the ancient form of the language had eight, thus conveying unimaginably more. The other four tones became restricted to the elite, effectively a secret language for recording weighty matters the commoners knew nothing about.

Many of the records carved into the turtle shells were in this ancient language. People say the will of heaven needs no words, but that's an incorrect assumption. The will of heaven is just another language, though if you didn't understand it, you could be staring right at it and not know. Professor Qiu had made it his life's work to delve into these words no one else in the world could understand. He hadn't progressed very far—every step of the way had been torturous, and despite all the effort he'd put in, there hadn't been much in the way of results.

Then, over thirty years ago, his team excavated a Tang dynasty tomb that had been robbed many times. There were seven or eight entrances blasted into it, and the body had been badly damaged. The whole burial chamber looked ready to collapse, and most of the grave goods had been stolen. What was left was all but decomposed.

Various bits of evidence pointed to this being the tomb of Li Chunfeng, the famous imperial astronomer and yin-yang mathematician from the Tang dynasty. This period was a high point in Chinese civilization for technology, culture, finance, and many other fields, so the grave of a prominent scientist was expected to hold important materials for research. Unfortunately, it had all been destroyed. The archaeologists felt this loss keenly.

Still, they had to continue clearing out the place. When they reached the rotting coffin, they got a surprise: a secret compartment at the head of the coffin! This was unprecedented—even the most experienced expert had never seen such a thing. They opened it gingerly and found a leather pouch that contained something wrapped in oilcloth: a flawless white-jade box. Gold and silver bands wrapped around the box, and spirit beasts were carved into its surface. Its lock and clasp were made of pure gold.

Because of its unusual hiding place, this treasure had survived wave after wave of tomb robbers.

Anyone who knew antiques could tell at a glance that this was a great imperial treasure, possibly even a gift from the emperor himself to Li Chunfeng, who must have regarded it as supremely important, given its resting place. The artifact was brought back to base camp right away.

Inside the jade box were many important objects, including a piece of dragon bone (a nickname for turtle shell, because the dried bits of shell became bleached as bone) carved full of celestial writing. There was also a small slab of pure gold with animal heads at all four corners, words cramming its surface, some recognizable, some not.

Naturally, Professor Qiu and his team were called in to decipher the secrets of the dragon bone and gold slab. Upon accepting the assignment, Professor Qiu locked himself in his lab and began to work away like a maniac.

He'd seen dragon bones like this so many times before, but he was never able to work out what they meant or stood for. What were these records of?

The so-called celestial language was a gap in the knowledge of Chinese scholars. As soon as they worked out how to read it, many thorny difficulties would be solved right away. The problem was that their total ignorance of the language made this gulf insurmountable.

Some scholars attributed the language to a previous civilization, until carbon-14 dating showed that some clearly legible texts were the same age as the "celestial" ones, so the latter couldn't possibly predate Chinese civilization. Professor Qiu spent more than a month trying out one theory after another, until he finally cracked the secret. After examining the small gold slab with animal heads, he discovered that the language inscribed onto the dragon bones by the ancients was actually a high-security code.

Back in the Tang dynasty, Li Chunfeng had broken this code and received the gold slab from the emperor as a reward for his efforts. As for what was inscribed on the gold slab, it was a glossary—all the signs and symbols of the celestial language were explained.

This language was very simple, consisting of the four secret tones. By studying this gold slab, Professor Qiu was finally able to understand celestial language, which caused quite a stir in the world of archaeology. All of a sudden, large numbers of ancient texts could be read, revealing vast quantities of new information. Many matters previously considered to be settled fact now had to be revised.

After considering the situation carefully, the authorities issued a ruling that this decoded information should be treated with extreme caution and definitely not announced until it had been verified. Professor Qiu now said to me, "That mark on your back can't be called celestial writing—it's not part of the secret language. I've only seen it on the turtle shell found in Gulan. It represents a particular thing that people at the time had no word for, so they made one up. Calling it a pictograph is probably more accurate. I couldn't tell you what it means, though. It showed up amid a celestial writing text that looks like the record of some tragic event. I gave it only a cursory glance before it was shipped away—I didn't expect the plane to crash. Now nobody will ever know those secrets."

"Why didn't you photograph such an important object?" I asked. "You say this mark isn't a curse, but how can you be sure? I won't stop worrying until I know the details. Can't you tell me what was written on the turtle shell? Was it anything to do with the ghost-hole in Xinjiang? I swear, I won't tell a soul."

Professor Qiu abruptly jumped to his feet. "I can't tell you!" he yelled. "If I did, the whole world would fall apart!"

CHAPTER TWENTY

My encounter with Professor Qiu left me frustrated. I couldn't believe he refused to tell me what the symbols meant, or to elaborate on his cryptic parting words.

Back in Beijing, we had several scorching days in a row, the type that leave you drenched in sweat even when you're sitting still. Finally, the heavens sent a storm that left the roads steaming and the temperature a few degrees lower.

When the rain stopped, Pan Market filled with people.

As Gold Tooth negotiated with an old customer, Kai tried hard to push the embroidered shoe on a couple of blue-eyed tourists. "It's very ancient. Worn by a famous courtesan."

The couple barely spoke any Chinese but seemed interested in the shoe. Kai took advantage of their enthusiasm and named a steep price. It was enough to scare the couple off. Obviously, they didn't realize that in China, a customer is expected to haggle over the price. Kai had to run after them and offer a discount.

I sat in one corner, enjoying the bustle of the scene. After we'd returned from Shaanxi, Kai and I had gone to the hospital for checkups, but we were told there was nothing wrong with us. The marks on our backs were odd, but they didn't seem to be symptoms of an illness.

To be honest, we barely remembered they were still there. Business was going really well—the fragrant jade was fetching high prices. Still, every time I remembered Professor Qiu's words, a mountain seemed to crash down on me.

Although the dragon bones that came out of the soil at Gulan had been destroyed, Professor Qiu had surely made copies. What could I do to get ahold of them? I desperately wanted to be sure this mark on my back had nothing to do with the eye of Jingjue. Yet during our conversation, it took only one mention of the ghost-hole for him to have a complete breakdown.

The more the professor tried to duck my questions, the more certain I was that we weren't done with Jingjue. And if that was the case, I'd have to find a way to get some answers. I certainly wasn't going to spend the rest of my life with a giant eye on my back.

I was supposed to keep watch on our stall to make sure thieves didn't take off with anything, but in the summer heat, my eyes drifted shut as wild thoughts scrambled around my head.

I had a series of weird dreams. To start with, I had a mute girlfriend, who told me through sign language that she wanted to see a movie. We walked straight into a theater without buying a ticket, but the film didn't make any sense. There was an explosion onscreen, and a mountain fell apart. Without warning, we plummeted into a mist-filled cave. Alarmed, I told my girlfriend this was the bottomless ghost-hole deep in the desert, and we had to run. Her face was blank as she pushed me hard. I tumbled into nothingness, and far below me, a giant eye stared up at my falling body. . . .

Suddenly, I felt a twinge as someone pinched my nose. I jerked awake to see a familiar figure, her fingers still on my face. Half in the dream, I recoiled to find her eyes close to mine, and almost fell out of my chair.

Kai chuckled. "Sweet dreams, Tianyi?" he said as he and Gold Tooth burst out laughing. "Look who's back from America."

"Miss Yang came straight here," said Gold Tooth. "Says it's urgent."

Julie waved a handkerchief at me. "You were drooling in your sleep."

I dabbed my chin on my sleeve instead, stretched, and rubbed my eyes. "Your eyes . . . ," I said. "Good, you're back—we need to talk."

"It's too crowded here," said Julie. "Let's go somewhere quiet."

Leaving Kai and Gold Tooth to look after the stall, we went to a nearby park. Julie picked a stone bench by the lake and sat down. "Normally, only couples sit here," I said. "Hope you don't mind if people think we're on a date."

"What?" said Julie. "You mean people are only allowed to sit by the lake if they're in love?"

I had to remind myself that although she looked Chinese, she'd grown up in America and didn't always get our jokes. "No, of course not. This bench belongs to everyone. Anyway, we don't need to care what others think." I plonked down next to her, then asked, "How's Professor Chen?"

She sighed. "Still in America. He had too much of a shock to the system, and they're not sure if they can do anything about his condition."

"I'm sorry to hear that. What about you? What did you want to tell me?"

"Well, I'm worried about something. Strange red marks have appeared on my back, as well as on Professor Chen's."

"Kai and I have those marks too. How about Asat Amat?" I asked her. Five of us had returned from Xinjiang alive. Apart from Julie, Professor Chen, Kai, and me, there'd also been our desert guide, Asat Amat.

"I don't think Uncle Asat Amat would have one," Julie said. "He didn't set eyes on the ghost-hole. I'm pretty sure this mark has something to do with the tribe that lived there."

There were still many secrets about these mysterious people that we hadn't managed to uncover, but they were now all buried beneath the golden sands, along with the hole that led to who-knows-where. Nothing they'd left behind would ever see the light of day again.

I told Julie about meeting Professor Qiu, hoping he'd have an idea whether this meant we'd been cursed.

She listened carefully. "Professor Qiu—was his full name Qiu Yaozu? He's got an impressive reputation as a Western Regions expert and has decoded quite a few messages hidden in ancient scrolls and paintings. I've read his books. Back when they dug up Pharaoh Djedhotepre Dedumose's tomb, one of the artifacts they found was a scepter carved with all kinds of symbols. Many academics tried to decipher them without success, but then a French professor who knew Professor Qiu asked him for help, and he managed to crack the code—they determined that the scepter was the fabled Staff of the Underworld from ancient Egypt. The discovery stunned the whole world and made Professor Qiu famous. If he says this thing isn't an eye but it stands for something else, then I'm sure he's right."

I bit my tongue. Who would have thought this eccentric man who dressed like a farmer had such a reputation? "That's all well and good," I said, "but we need to find out if the mark singles us out for harm. And we have to find out if it's connected to the Jingjue Kingdom."

"I found some clues while I was home in the States," Julie said. "Remember the book of predictions we found in the Zaklaman Mountains that said one of us was descended from the seer? It's true—I'm the seer. My grandfather died last year. It was very sudden, and he didn't have a chance to say goodbye. I had the opportunity to go through his things recently, and I found a notebook. It was terrifying, what he'd written down. It proved that the seer was correct."

This was what I'd been most afraid of. The nightmarish ghost-hole was clinging to us like a Band-Aid. But why were we still cursed? Hadn't it disappeared into the desert, along with the entire Zaklaman Mountain range?

"It's not a curse," Julie went on. "It's worse than that. Let me tell you the whole story from the beginning."

CHAPTER TWENTY-ONE

THE ZAKLAMAN MOUNTAINS DEEP WITHIN THE TAKLIMAKAN
Desert hid many secrets beneath their obsidian depths—in
fact, in the ancient Uighur language, "Zaklaman" means "mystery." Long ago, a man known as "the holy one" was born in a
nameless village, which housed a tribe from the faraway Eu-
ropean continent. They'd lived here peacefully for many years,
until one of them stumbled upon the unfathomably deep ghost-
hole in the mountains. The village mystic told them that only a
golden jade eye could pierce its depths, so they fashioned such
an artifact. From that moment, misfortune descended upon
the tribe.

The gods abandoned the village, and one disaster after another befell them. The holy one, their leader, knew this was

surely connected to the ghost-hole, and that once the door to hell is opened, shutting it becomes near impossible. In order to escape further catastrophe, they had no choice but to abandon the land that had housed them for so many years, traveling toward the east and eventually being absorbed into the civilization of the Central Plains.

What exactly were these "disasters"? From a modern perspective, we'd call it a form of radiation—anyone who'd come into contact with the ghost-hole would, over time, develop indelible red marks in the shape of an eye. All of those so afflicted found themselves losing iron after the age of forty. Iron is what gives human blood its red color. Without it, blood thickens and can't hold oxygen, making breathing difficult. By the time of death, the blood of these victims had turned pale yellow.

This process took a painful ten years, and while their descendants weren't born with red marks, they inherited the same iron deficiency and died the same agonizing deaths. After the migration to the Central Plains, they discovered that the farther they were from the ghost-hole, the later the illness manifested itself, though they still got it in the end, generation after generation. No words can describe the torture of having your blood turn yellow and harden in your veins.

After many years of trying to find a cure, they finally got an answer during the Song dynasty, when a bronze urn from the middle Shang period washed up in the mud of the Yellow River delta. It was a deep vessel with four legs and delicate engravings. Artifacts like these had once been important in prayer rituals, and their carvings represented the emperor's devotion to his ancestors as well as his messages for the gods. They could also be commissioned as records of significant events.

The urn found by the Zaklaman descendants was one of the latter, depicting the discovery of a jade eye shot through with gold that had been found and presented to the Shang monarch Wu Ding, along with a scarlet robe. Emperor Wu Ding reckoned this must have been left behind by the Yellow Emperor after he became a deity and ascended to the heavens.

Quite a few of the Zaklaman descendants were mystics, and they cast the runes to learn that this gold-jade object was the eye of the divine. Offering it as a sacrifice to the ghost-hole was the only way to remedy the disaster that had befallen their tribe. But where was the eye? They knew it had slipped out of Wu Ding's hands and changed owners many times during the subsequent war, and it was quite probably buried in some aristocrat's grave as part of their burial goods. But there was no way to know for sure—the mystics' powers were of limited range, and they weren't able to pinpoint an exact location.

By that point, only about a thousand people were left of the five thousand who'd initially moved to the interior. They'd long been absorbed by Han culture, and even their names had changed. In a bid to escape the curse, the remaining tribe members fanned out across the country, seeking the eye of the divine in every ancient tomb they came across, becoming one of the four great clans of grave robbers who were active at the time.

Since the olden days, tomb raiders have used a variety of tactics, of which gold hunting was only one. The Zaklaman descendants mostly went the route of mountain moving, usually disguised as Taoist priests. As you can tell from the name, mountain moving is very different—essentially, it uses brute force to gain access, unlike the subtle techniques of gold hunting.

In the years that followed, who knows how many ancient tombs they mountain-moved their way through, following a trail of clues that broke and resumed over and over again. As the centuries trickled by, the eye of the divine's location continued to be obscure while the legions of mountain movers thinned, until by the twentieth century there was only a single young man with these abilities, the most famous grave robber in the Zhejiang region, known only by his nickname: the Partridge. He was an expert sharpshooter, and unparalleled at getting through the traps and snares of old graves.

Following the training of his ancestors, the Partridge sought out whatever slim threads of information he could, and he finally narrowed the location down to a treasure cave from the Western Xia Kingdom. The story was that this trove had been abandoned not far from the Western Xia city of Black Water and had been intended as a tomb for some important official, but the Mongols invaded before he could be interred. Yet because of this sudden event, the burial site was unlikely to be marked. So how was he to find it?

There were hardly any of his tribe left, and if the Partridge didn't find the eye soon, the rest of his bloodline would surely die out. As a mountain mover, he didn't know anything about feng shui, so he turned to someone who did: the gold hunters. This was during the time of civil war, and there were probably fewer than ten gold hunters left in the entire country. Indeed, most of the tomb raiding happening at this time wasn't conducted by experts, but rather rogue soldiers and desperate civilians.

The Partridge did everything he could to track down the remaining gold hunters. Finally, he found one—a reverse dipper of great renown, who'd since turned his back on the material world and was now a Buddhist monk going by the name of Master World's End.

The master advised the Partridge, telling him, "The human world is full of strife, and only Buddha can shelter you from that, bringing you peace with a single smile. Why must you be so sunk in gloom? Back in the day, the humble monk before you was a reverse dipper, but even though I gave everything I found to my people, my heart was never still, and I couldn't stop thinking how much unrest I was causing by bringing these precious things to the surface so people could fight over them. Our profession brings great harm, whether you use it for your own profit or that of others."

The Partridge had no choice but to tell him the full story. When Master World's End knew this was a matter of life and death, his compassionate nature nudged him to tell the Partridge what he wanted to know. According to the rules of gold hunting, though, the Partridge first had to carry out a mission.

"When I joined this monastery," said World's End, "I noticed an old grave nearby that had never been reverse dipped, about ten li to the southwest of here, amid deserted hills. There's only half a tombstone to mark the spot, with no writing. It's from the Southern Song dynasty. If you go in there tonight and fetch me a set of burial clothes, I'll teach you everything I know."

The monk gave the Partridge a set of gold-hunting tools and instructed him in the rules of their tribe. Gold hunters were the first ones to formalize the profession, and most of the oaths come from their original vows. Even the term "reverse dipper" comes from the fact that many of China's early graves were earth mounds that happened to be shaped like dippers for scooping rice. What the gold hunters did was said to be as easy as flipping a dipper over and helping themselves to its contents.

As he listened to the rules, a great many mysteries became clearer to the Partridge. He nodded at the instructions: light a candle in a corner of the tomb, and be ready to flee if it goes out; don't take too many items or you might anger the dead; only enter a grave once, and seal it after you leave.

That night, the Partridge went alone to the broken Song stone tablet. Clouds drifted across the dusky sky, the moon peeping between them. Dry leaves rustled in the wind, like the sobbing of ghosts.

Instead of using his usual mountain-moving techniques, the Partridge followed the master's instructions and opened a tunnel directly to the heart of the tomb. He had everything ready: black donkey hooves, candles, corpse incense, glutinous rice grains, pangolin claws—and also, to guard against more worldly dangers, a loaded Mauser pistol. He wrapped a damp cloth around his nose and mouth.

The monk had described this place as shaped like a broken sword, a design that should have prevented the dead from coming back to life. The Partridge wasn't worried—he'd encountered all sorts of dumplings in the course of his work, and the undead no longer frightened him. He thought, *So the old monk wants to test my skills and bravery? I definitely can't afford to look bad.* And with that, he took a deep breath, held his lantern high, and burrowed into the darkness.

He moved expertly through the space and was soon in the main burial chamber. This was a cramped room with a low ceiling, grave goods piled all over the floor. Without even looking at them, the Partridge picked his way through to the southeast corner, where he lit a candle. Turning, he saw that there was no platform, just a coffin made entirely of bronze. He'd never seen one like it. The metal was probably intended to hold the corpse in place—had it shown signs of being undead even before it was buried?

Mustering his courage, the Partridge used a pangolin claw to ease the lid open. Inside was a noblewoman of about thirty, who seemed to be sound asleep. Her cheeks bulged slightly, indicating she probably had a pearl in her mouth to prevent her body from rotting, and her hair was full of gold and silver ornaments. A light satin sheet lay over her, but he could see that she was dressed in many layers of fine robes. If he could just remove her outermost garments and bring them back, that would fulfill his end of the bargain. Stepping into the coffin, he got out his rope and wound it twice around himself, knotting it once at his chest and again around her neck.

He held his breath and leaned over her to burn a little corpse incense by her cheek. This fragrance would cause her body to unstiffen, making it easy to remove her robe. He was standing over her so that when she rose, her neck would be level with his chest. That was why the rope had to be arranged just so—many amateurs, only half understanding the method, would tie a noose around their own necks too and end up strangling themselves.

After a few moments, she softened and the rope lifted her. The Partridge was just pulling off her gown when he felt a gust of wind and turned to see the candle flame flickering like crazy, as if it might go out at any moment. "This is bad," he muttered.

Before he could untie the rope, the woman's mouth dropped open, and a purplish-black pearl rolled out of it. Right away, her face sprouted a layer of fine white down. She was becoming a white demon.

According to the rules, he wasn't allowed to take anything if the candle got extinguished. He'd started in this line of work at the age of fifteen and had been doing it for twelve years now. He could easily have departed at this point without any danger to himself at all, but it wasn't his style to retreat at the first sign of trouble. He had to get hold of that robe—without letting the corpse become a demon, or the candle going out.

Glancing down at the pearl, he recognized it as a mixture of scarlet sand and purple jade, a formula used to prevent corpses changing form. In noble families, because it was taboo to burn bodies, the only solution when someone showed signs of being undead was to secretly slip one of these into their mouths before burial.

Eyeing the guttering candle, the Partridge gave the rope a sharp tug. Softened by the corpse incense, the woman's neck jerked back and her mouth fell open. He quickly scooped up the pearl and popped it back in, then pulled the rope downward so her head tilted and her jaw shut.

In a single movement, he pulled the pistol from his belt and fired it behind him. The wooden rafters had circular tiles along them, one of which was struck by the bullet and fell, lodging in the ground by the candle and shielding it from the wind. The flame wavered a second longer, then stabilized.

He had to hurry to get the job done before dawn: "No gold hunting after the cock crows" was another of the rules. The reasoning was that no matter how pure your motives, reverse dipping is a dark art that should be carried out under cover of night. If the sun caught sight of what you were up to, well, there'd be no helping you. Trying to speed up, he sat on the corpse's leg to pin her in place as he started loosening her garments.

Then, suddenly, there was a tickle at his neck, and he felt something furry rub against his shoulder. As bold as he was, the Partridge felt his hairs standing on end. Keeping his body still, he slowly turned to see what was there.

CHAPTER TWENTY-TWO

A LARGE TABBY CAT WAS PERCHED ON THE PARTRIDGE'S shoulder. It must have sneaked into the chamber without a sound and was staring right at him with its large eyes.

He cursed under his breath. Every branch of reverse dipping is afraid of encountering animals, and cats are the worst of all. Cats are said to carry some sort of electric charge that can bring a corpse back to life if it comes into contact with one.

This wild cat didn't seem afraid of people. It lowered its gaze, seemingly drawn to the glittery grave goods, which must have looked like an array of cat toys. The Partridge's heart was in his throat. If the cat jumped into the coffin and came into contact with the woman, even with the pearl back in her mouth, she'd surely turn demonic again. Yet he didn't dare make any big movements, in case that put the candle out.

Whatever he did, it had to be fast—the sun would rise soon, and if he couldn't get the grave clothes back to World's End before dawn, he'd never learn the secrets of gold hunting.

He could have simply broken the rules to succeed, of course, but honor and trust are important to this profession, and a renowned expert like the Partridge naturally placed them above his own life. Even though reverse dipping is a dark art, its practitioners would still rather die than betray its principles, which are the only things differentiating them from common thieves.

It all happened very quickly. Barely had these thoughts passed through the Partridge's head when the cat, unable to stand the temptation any longer, arched its back and prepared to leap from his shoulder, toward the shiny baubles that captivated it.

The Partridge instinctively made a grab for the creature but stopped himself just in time. If he startled it, that might drive it toward the corpse. Instead, he had a thought. One of his many talents was that he could imitate almost any animal sound, and right now, after attracting the cat's attention with a whistle, he meowed a few times.

The cat froze, and its ears pricked up. Was there another of its own kind nearby? It looked around, puzzled not to find the source of those meows, which had sounded so very close.

Disaster averted, the Partridge tried to think of a way to lure the animal away. He needed just a bit more time to get the grave clothes off, after which the cat could go roll about in the coffin for all he cared. But how could he get those few minutes he needed?

Trying to further distract the cat, he did a couple of bird-calls. The animal looked swiftly around, then back at the Partridge. It pawed at the cloth covering his face, no doubt thinking a sparrow was hiding beneath it.

"Stupid beast," the Partridge said with a grin. "Imagine falling for that!"

While the cat's attention was on the black cloth, the Partridge stealthily reached out for the nearest piece of treasure: a bracelet woven from fine threads of pure gold. Moving very carefully so as not to alarm the cat, he hung the bracelet from his thumb, then, with a quick flick of his wrist, sent it spinning toward the tunnel he'd come in by.

The golden object arced through the air, clanking down by the entrance. It was so quiet in the chamber you could have heard a pin drop, and the cat definitely heard the clatter. Perhaps thinking the sparrow had flown away while it wasn't looking, the cat meowed furiously and made a dash toward the new noise.

Seizing the opportunity, the Partridge whipped out his pistol, intending to shoot the creature dead to prevent it from causing any more of a disturbance. Then a sound from behind him caught his attention, and he turned to see that another seven or eight cats of different sizes had sneaked in along with the big one, one of them only an inch from the fallen ceiling tile. The slightest nudge and that tile would knock the candle over, putting it out.

The Partridge broke out in a cold sweat. He'd survived all sorts of catastrophes and didn't relish the thought of it all ending here, in this tiny chamber, stymied by this weird situation. Had he accidentally attracted all these cats with his sparrow calls? Cats have sharp hearing, and would have come in search of a meal if they'd been within earshot. What was he to do now? It was almost dawn.

He stared at the line of cats, uncertain whether he should laugh or cry. What was going on? He'd averted one disaster, only to have a worse one pop up. Normally, getting a robe off a corpse would be no big deal, yet this was turning into one of the most difficult jobs of his career.

This reminded him of that old saying "Win or lose, it's all the same." His animal calls had saved him from one feral cat, only to attract a herd of others. Should he just shoot them all? The Partridge stiffened his resolve. Nothing in the world could stop him. Gritting his teeth, he worked hard to remain calm, trying to finish the task at hand before those wretched cats could spoil everything.

Moving lightning fast, he held the woman firmly in place and finished unfastening her outer robe. Lifting her left arm with his leg, he slipped it out of its sleeve. The movement attracted a couple of the cats, and they jumped onto the bronze edge of the coffin. Why were they so unafraid of people? It was probably that reverse dippers are filled with dark energy, dress in black, and take pills to slow down their pulse, so animals might see them as no different than corpses, and therefore no danger.

The cats, one black and one tortoiseshell, bumped into each other as they drew toward the glittering spoils. Immediately they started fighting, biting and scratching away, and in the tussle, they inevitably tumbled into the coffin.

Now they were right next to the corpse. The white hair had receded after he got the pearl back in her mouth, and she looked like she had when he'd come in. But if the cats were to touch her, all bets were off. The Partridge had seen white demons before. They were fearsome, not easily defeated. The roosters would start crowing for dawn in the time it took half an incense stick to burn. On one hand, the demon would stop moving at dawn. On the other, if the Partridge didn't get the robe off by then, he'd have to leave it behind.

This was where his fine physical skills came in handy. A second before the cats touched the woman, the Partridge straightened his torso, and with a firm thrust of his legs, he leaped straight out of the bronze coffin, the corpse still attached to him. They landed lightly on the floor of the burial chamber.

Another three or four cats had jumped into the coffin too and were now prowling about inside, treating it as a giant kitty playpen. A close shave. No time to waste—he shoved the corpse away, raising her arm with his leg again. Before he could get the other sleeve off, he noticed by the flickering candlelight that her mouth was wide open. That must have happened during the jump—he'd shaken her jaw loose. And now the white fur was returning, sprouting from her like mold on food left out too long, growing thicker by the moment. A black fog drifted from her open mouth, sending a shiver through him. This was dark energy, thick and cold, and if he hadn't taken those heart-stilling pills, the fog might well have metabolized through his body and killed him at once.

The Partridge didn't dare get careless in the face of this corpse breath. Keeping his head down to avoid breathing it in, he saw the purple pearl had rolled across the floor and lodged against the fallen tile. There was no choice—he couldn't risk her fully transforming into a white demon—so he let go of the robe. He had to stop the change before it became irreversible.

Lunging across the floor, the corpse still in his grasp, he dragged her to the southeast corner of the chamber. This was where the light from both the lantern he'd hung from the coffin and the candle faded into nothing. Now and then, a stray flicker from the candle showed him where the pearl had rolled to, but otherwise it was swallowed by the dark.

The Partridge got close enough to reach for it, when an enormous cat pounced from the shadows. It was the first one that had come in, the one that had started this whole mess. It must really have been starving, because even the pearl was starting to look appetizing. Opening its mouth wide, it prepared to bite into it.

The Partridge could have throttled the creature. There wasn't enough time to snatch the pearl, so he did the only thing he could: he squeaked like a mouse. Sure enough, the cat fell for the trick once again, freezing in place and staring wide-eyed at the man, as if baffled at this giant mouse.

Taking advantage of this confusion, the Partridge grabbed the pearl and stuffed it into the corpse's mouth, nudging the cat aside with his boot. It yelped and scuttled away. The Partridge thought vengefully about how much trouble the cat had managed to cause, but he let it go and focused on his work.

He had an animal's instinct for time and sensed the cocks would crow any minute now. There was no time left. Pulling the corpse up by the rope, he finally managed to get the robe completely unfastened. She was wearing at least nine layers of clothing, so this topmost one was jammed on tight, but if he used the right technique, he would probably be able to get it off without too much trouble. Spinning her around, he took hold of the sleeves. This way, he wouldn't need to mess around with her arms—he could just let go of the body and she'd drop out of the garment.

Before he could do this, though, he felt a sudden movement. It was the other cats, who'd heard his mouse cries, and being just as hungry as their friend, they had come over to investigate, scurrying around the Partridge to find the mice.

There were more than a dozen cats now. Even if he had three pairs of arms, he'd never be able to deal with them all. He felt himself go cold. *All right, I give up. I guess fate isn't going to let me learn gold hunting.* But even as this despairing thought was running through his head, another idea came to him. "Meow," he called. "Meow, meow!"

Wild cats are cautious by nature. Hearing this strange creature who'd been squeaking a minute ago now suddenly sounding just like them, they couldn't understand what was going on. So the cats stayed put till they could be sure, their eyes fixed on him.

In the inky dark, the cats' eyes glowed eerily like little lamps. The Partridge left them to it, pulled the corpse to him, and got to work again. At the same moment, the cats seemed to make up their minds all at once that whatever he was, whether a mouse or a dead person, he might be edible, and they'd take a bite to make sure, never mind what sound it made. Moving in unison, they suddenly swarmed toward him.

This long, awful night would reach its conclusion in the next few seconds—success or failure hung in the balance. In this tiny fraction of time, the Partridge had to do three things: not let the cats touch the corpse, not let the candle go out, and get the robe off the corpse before the cock crowed.

He took a step back, finding the tile and bracing his foot against it. Reaching out with his other shoe, he flicked the nearest cat smartly on the nose. It yowled in shock and darted aside in a hurry.

Now the Partridge dropped to the floor, flinging himself over the corpse, so the two cats that had been lunging at them flew harmlessly through the air. He grabbed the candle and held it to the corpse rope with his right hand, singeing through it, while his left hand clutched her lapel. Her back was to him, so he just had to kick gently for her to slide away, leaving her robe behind. The candle flickered out, and in the distance, he heard the cocks crowing, their cries drifting into the tomb on the morning breeze.

You don't often see cats eating a human body, but at that moment, more than ten feral cats, wild with hunger, descended at once on the corpse left behind from the Southern Song dynasty.

CHAPTER TWENTY-THREE

The Partridge pulled the black cloth from around his mouth. The hungry cats gnawed and clawed at the corpse so ferociously that he shuddered. They were more like evil spirits than animals. The cocks had crowed three times now, so the corpse would no longer be able to transform. The cats would be able to gorge themselves to their hearts' content. Of course, the purple pearl in the corpse's mouth, which had kept her flesh from decaying, was probably filling her body with dark forces—but he wouldn't be around to see what effect that would have on the cats.

The Partridge carefully folded the robe, picked up the lantern, and made his way back through the tunnel into the open air. Despite the roosters' noise, the sky remained dark.

He quickly filled in the hole and replaced the broken stone tablet. When he looked back, it appeared as if the grave had never been disturbed.

Back at the monastery, he bowed to World's End and offered the robe to him with both hands respectfully outstretched, describing the events of the night in detail and finishing with, "The cocks crowed and the flame went out almost at the same instant I laid my hands on the grave garment. It's impossible to say which came first. I can't swear I followed the rules. I believe that means I have no right to your tutelage. If I remain alive, I'll surely visit again and open my ears to your wisdom. Now I must depart."

The monk had been around long enough and understood perfectly well what the Partridge was doing—he was using a fine reverse-dipping technique and retreating in order to advance.

Gazing at the Partridge kneeling at his feet, World's End thought of his younger self and how similar he'd been to this fellow.

Having heard the whole history of the Partridge's mountain-moving tribe and their predicament, he made up his mind to help. In the first place, as a Buddhist, he could hardly stand by and do nothing now that he knew the secret of the Zaklaman descendants. Second, he was growing quite fond of this young man, who'd confessed frankly that he wasn't sure if he'd obeyed the rules, a rare act in a society where morality was going downhill. World's End had a lot of secret knowledge and skills to pass on. Why not to the Partridge?

The monk raised the Partridge to his feet and said, "Even if you only got the grave garment as the cocks crowed and the candle went out, that doesn't mean you didn't follow my instructions. I said you had to stop after these events had taken place, but I mentioned nothing of during."

The Partridge's heart was filled with joy, and he bowed again in thanks. "Please accept my worshipful devotion, oh great master. It is three lifetimes of good fortune to be received by you and share in your wisdom."

World's End hastily stopped him. "None of that here. We gold hunters have never believed in these hierarchies, unlike the mountain movers. We're all equal. I'll pass my knowledge on to you, and you'll pass it to someone else. Any reverse dipper using the techniques of gold hunting, and following the principles of our clan, is automatically one of us. It seems to be destined that I will tell you my secrets, but we will not speak of master or disciple. We are simply of the same clan now."

Even after that speech, the Partridge insisted on bowing deeply, then stood with his hands respectfully clasped, preparing to receive instruction. World's End was delighted to have acquired this robe, which he planned to ceremonially burn while chanting prayers, in order to allow the dead woman to gain happiness in the afterlife.

The only harsh words he had to say were about the Partridge's treatment of the cats. Even if they had inconvenienced him, he ought to have made sure they could get out before sealing the tomb behind him, possibly trapping them in. He shared many Buddhist philosophies with his new pupil, urging him to act with kindness, and to always show mercy to his opponents, rather than fighting to the finish. This way, he would build up good karma.

While the Partridge respected the monk a great deal, he

found this a bit preachy. They were just some cats, after all—what was the big deal? But he bit his tongue and tried to be patient, nodding along to the sermon instead.

World's End went on in this vein for quite some time before he finally exhausted the subject and moved on to the meat of gold hunting. He explained the various traditions and practices one by one. The rules he'd listed before had been extremely abbreviated, and now he went into them in detail, until the Partridge understood them inside and out.

Reverse dippers aren't really people, more half human and half ghost entering ancient tombs to seek treasure while regular folk are sound asleep. They might take one day or ten to find their way into a grave, but once they're inside, the ironclad rule is that the coffin cannot be touched after a cock crows. Once the world of daylight asserts itself, the kingdom of night must retreat. As the rhyme goes, "Gold hunters hide from sunny skies, stop work once the rooster cries." There's no way around it.

After entering a tomb, gold hunters always light a candle in the southeast corner of the chamber before raising the coffin lid. This is, first, to prevent poisonous fumes from building up and, second, because an agreement was reached millennia ago between the living and the dead: If a candle goes out, that means the treasures in the grave are not to be touched. If you insist on helping yourself anyway, then you'd better be prepared to face the consequences. If your fate is strong, you might well be able to pull this off, but it's still a route fraught with danger. Nine out of ten people who try this lose their lives. Seeing as the world is full of ancient tombs bursting with precious items, it seems silly to risk your life over some baubles the deceased aren't ready to let go of yet. Most gold hunters choose to follow this rule and leave well enough alone if a candle flame goes out on them. Besides, an extinguished flame is often a sign that a corpse is about to transform into something undead, and it can also mean that a curse has just been activated. The lighting of a candle is one of the main things that distinguishes gold hunting from other branches of reverse dipping, and there are very good reasons for this practice.

The Partridge absorbed all this. From here on, he would say goodbye to mountain moving. He was a gold hunter now.

World's End pulled two gold charms from his pocket and said, "Knowledge alone makes you only half a gold hunter; you also need to have at least one of these in order to fully enter the clan. This pair is more than a thousand years old. They belonged to me and one of my colleagues. We pulled off quite a few big jobs together, but he was killed twenty years ago by a nail trap during a reverse dip in Luoyang. Ah, those were heady times . . . but best not to bring it up now. These charms are yours to keep, and as long as you abide by the rules, you have every right to call yourself a gold hunter for the rest of your days."

The Partridge reached out with both hands to receive this gift. He hung the charms with pride around his neck, where they could rest against his skin. Again he bowed to World's End.

The monk asked more questions. He wanted to know about the ancient village, the ghost-hole, the eye of the divine, and finally, the treasure cave in the Western Xia Kingdom.

After hearing the explanation, World's End nodded slowly. "As for this eye of the divine, I've heard a little about it. It's also known as 'phoenix gall.' They say the Yellow Emperor left it behind when he ascended to the heavens, though others believe it comes from a thousand leagues beneath the ground, that it is a gift from the Earth Mother, or that phoenix breath hardens into this stone. In any case, it's in the shape of a giant human eye and might be one of the true marvels of this world. Initially buried with Emperor Wu at Maoling, it was later liberated by the Scarlet-Browed Army, who declared that the Maoling grave goods belonged to the people. Who would have thought they'd end up in the hands of the Western Xia?"

The Partridge replied, "Your humble servant has seen many of my tribe wither and die in unspeakable agony, thanks to the curse of the ghost-hole. For generations, we've been told that this was the result of a long-ago mishap, when a prophecy told of an eye-shaped jade that could look into the ghost-hole. In their ignorance, they created a false eye of the divine, and when they attempted to use it to pierce the depths, they brought upon themselves a curse that could only be broken by finding the true eye. From then on, every single one of us has been engaged in a search for this mysterious artifact. We've poured our souls into the hunt, to no avail. Finally, I tracked down the information that it had entered the possession of the Western Xia, and the Mongols had sought it there, but because the kingdom's treasures were in a secret hiding place, they weren't able to find it either. The legend tells us of a Western Xia city known as Black Water. A temple near this city, once part of its border wall, is known as Black Water River Meets the Sky. A great minister of the Western Xia, Hu Jing, was passing by Black Water one night when he saw in the sky, ten li from the city, three stars blazing and purple mist drifting between the clouds, and he decreed that the fortification beneath this omen should be turned into a temple, where he hoped to be buried after his death. Unfortunately, he didn't get his wish when he was assassinated, and so the mausoleum readied for him stood empty. When the Black Water River changed its course, the city that shared its name was swallowed by the desert, and humankind abandoned it. As the rampaging Mongol hordes entered the kingdom, the last Western Xia emperor decreed that all the remaining wealth, the rare treasures and precious artifacts, should be concealed in this vacant tomb. The eye of the divine would have been among them. Everything aboveground in that region has long been eradicated, and only mystical methods can now tell us where this temple once stood."

World's End nodded. "Black Water City lay beyond the Helan Hills, against Green Mountain at one end and the Jade Belt at the other. This is a region rich in feng shui. The Western Xia absorbed the energies of previous dynasties to grow on a vast scale. They were a people heavily influenced by Buddhism but also steeped in folk traditions, so their graves are of an unusual design, hard for those who came after to penetrate. The lost language of the Western Xia might resemble the writing of the Central Plains, but it is far more complicated."

The Partridge gave a quick nod. "Then a few years ago," he elaborated, "explorers from the west worked together with local thieves to rob Black Water City of its ancient treasures. They unearthed seven Buddhist towers and took their contents, including many sacred texts in the Western Xia language. These might have included a record of the eye of the divine's hiding place, but these manuscripts have been taken out of the country now, and we have no way of reading them. If only we could find a reference to the Black Water River Meets the Sky Temple somewhere, that could tell us everything we need to know—and save a lot of trouble."

"The Western Xia language is mostly indecipherable to us," cautioned World's End, "so even if there were such a record, we wouldn't necessarily understand it. But we know of the three blazing stars and the purple mist, which must refer to some sort of dragon palace—there would surely be a spiritual residue we could uncover with gold divining, even if there are no worldly traces left."

Gold divining is a branch of feng shui, the most difficult one, because it requires knowledge of both the heavenly arts and geography, using the language of sun and stars to understand the delineations of the Earth. Starting from the basic principles of feng shui and building up, even the most expert student would take five or six years to learn this craft.

World's End knew that the Partridge was filled with impatience, and so he proposed that they should visit Black Water City outside the Helan Hills together to see if they could get hold of the eye of the divine. Once they'd done that, there'd be plenty of time to learn gold divining.

Hearing that Master World's End was prepared to intervene personally to help him, the Partridge swelled with gratitude. They quickly made their preparations and set out. Being a monk, World's End simply changed into his traveling habit. The Partridge, like most mountain movers, went about in the disguise of a Taoist priest—but since it would have attracted too much attention to have a Buddhist and Taoist on a journey together, on this occasion he put on civilian garb, taking on the role of the master's secular servant.

It's an arduous trek from Zhejiang to the Helan Hills. Luckily, Master World's End had a reverse dipper's hardiness, and advanced in years as he was, he remained nimble and strong. They got a carriage to the Yellow River, where they would catch a ferry that took them as far as Wuxiang Hold, a short distance from Helan.

Waiting for their boat, they looked out at the twists and turns of the river, like a long jade belt winding spectacularly across the landscape. Idly chatting, they got onto events from the past, and World's End began telling a story from that region.

This was before he'd taken orders, back when he was still a significant figure in the reverse-dipping world. His nickname then was "the Flying Lion" because of his speed and prowess. On one occasion, he was passing through the Green Bronze Valley to the hundred and eight towers in the north. Locals said the river spirits were particularly strong here, and they had to fling some of their possessions from the boat in order to pass.

The Flying Lion had happened to be on a boat transporting scorched earth, making its first voyage along this route. The owner was a miserly salt merchant who ignored the captain's advice to make an offering. He wouldn't give up so much as a sack of his cargo, instead scattering a grudging handful of salt into the water.

They'd spent the night just outside Green Bronze Valley. At the inn, an old man with a green hatpin appeared. At the time, everyone wore red pins in their hats, so a green one was very eye-catching. He had a ladle with him and had come to beg for a scoopful. Scorched earth was a highly valuable commodity, so of course the merchant refused to give him any, chasing him off instead.

Compassionate even as a young reverse dipper, the Flying Lion took pity on the old man and used his own money to buy him some scorched earth. This substance could be used instead of lime in coffins as a dehydrating material with a distinctive fragrance—not that the Flying Lion knew what the man wanted to do with it, but he handed it over, and the green hatpin man departed with thanks.

They continued their journey the next day, but when they reached Green Bronze Valley, an enormous turtle easily the size of two or three houses put together, appeared in the river. It rushed toward the boat and overturned it, so the entire cargo sank. Not a single person was harmed. They were all caught in a wave and gently washed ashore. Later on, everyone said it was because World's End had offered the old man a scoopful of earth that the River God had spared their lives.

The Partridge listened to this story with his mouth agape, marveling at his mentor's escape from the raging Yellow River itself. So it turned out that compassion brought its own rewards. Then he thought of something else, and said, "I've heard that there are a lot of rituals to be followed when taking boats across rivers or oceans. For instance, you can't talk about sinking or capsizing, because if you mention these things, they will surely happen. There are others—probably as many rules as for gold hunting."

World's End was about to reply when the people around

them rushed toward the water. The ferry had arrived, so they stopped their conversation, the younger man helping the older on board.

The sky was clear and the sun scorching. They moved quickly over the calm river, not a speck of wind or waves to be seen. There were many passengers, and as neither man was fond of crowds, they tried to find a quiet spot. Leaning against the railing, they watched the passing scenery. Master World's End pointed out feng shui elements to his new pupil as they came up.

Then, in the middle of a sentence, the Partridge suddenly lowered his voice. "There are ghosts on this boat," he whispered.

CHAPTER TWENTY-FOUR

THE PARTRIDGE WAS REFERRING TO THE HANDFUL OF WHITE men on the boat. He'd been sneaking glances at them for a while, finding them suspicious. They all clearly had concealed guns, and their luggage was full of shovels, spikes, and long ropes. They huddled together, muttering.

The strange thing was that these foreigners weren't like any he'd ever encountered before. He'd met quite a few Westerners, and spoke some of their languages, but these men didn't seem like cautious Englishmen, or stern Germans, or laid-back Americans. They had pale skin and flaxen hair and exuded a gangster-like aura. Where on earth could they be from? Frowning, he examined them more closely, and then he had it: they were Russians.

Could they be on their way to dig up Black Water City's antiquities? After the Russian Revolution, many people had left the country to live in exile, and quite a few had ended up in China, making a living through black-market dealings.

World's End, being fairly cosmopolitan himself, naturally understood what the Partridge was driving at. He murmured back, "We're on a secret mission, and we don't want to attract attention. Best not to get involved."

The Partridge replied, "I'm just going over to have a look. If those foreigners plan to steal from Black Water City, that's close to our target—they might get in our way. We'll lure them somewhere quiet and finish them off—that's the safest thing."

Before World's End could talk him out of it, the Partridge squeezed through the crowd until he was close enough to eavesdrop. It turned out that of the six people in this group, only five were Russian; the final one was American. The Russians were the descendants of tsarists, currently engaged in the arms trade. They'd heard that Black Water was full of buried treasures and thought they might try their luck to see if they could make a quick buck there. The American was a young priest who'd spent the last few years doing missionary work in China. During his travels, he'd stumbled upon the ruins of Black Water City. While spreading the word of God elsewhere, he'd gotten talking to these Russian adventurers on the road, and when he happened to mention his discovery, they'd jumped on him and said they had to do some business there, and could he please lead the way back to the city? They'd love to have a look.

Not many people would try to pull a scam on a member of the clergy, and the priest was taken completely unawares.

Besides, the Russians barely spoke any English, and the American knew no Russian, so they were able to communicate only in Chinese, which they'd all spent long enough in the country to have learned.

Pricking up his ears, the Partridge noted that every third sentence they spoke had to do with Black Water City. The priest had no idea they were going there on a looting expedition, so he was artlessly describing everything he'd seen, down to the smallest detail. The holy towers were half-buried, he prattled, and full of Buddha statues, every one of them plated in gold and silver, exquisitely crafted. Other figures were carved out of ivory or ancient jade, each more beautifully mystical than the last. It was as if the heavens themselves had created these marvels.

The Russians practically drooled, glugging down vodka from their flasks and wishing they had wings so they could get to Black Water quicker. As soon as they'd dug up these precious items, they'd surely unload them as fast as they could for big money.

The Partridge chuckled grimly to himself. He'd visited these towers himself and was very familiar with the ruins being described. What these foreigners didn't know was that at the beginning of the nineteenth century, there'd already been an archaeological frenzy from Europeans heading to China, and Black Water had practically been picked clean. The ruins now held nothing but worthless clay figurines and tiles, most of them smashed. The American priest had no appreciation for antiquities and had apparently taken these crudely colored statues to be ivory and the like. To think the Russians actually believed him.

But then the Partridge thought, *Wait, that can't be it.* No one would mistake broken clay for silver or gold plating. The American had perfectly good eyesight, it would seem. So what was going on? Had this hapless priest stumbled upon Black Water River Meets the Sky itself, and not just the lesser pavilions? What he was describing sounded more like this mystical buried site than the towers that had already been excavated.

This was when the Partridge realized something might be wrong. Before he could hear any more, the boat shook violently, then swerved across the river so it lay horizontal. The hundred or so passengers lost their footing, tumbling this way and that, screaming in pain and confusion.

Worried about World's End, the Partridge left the Russians and barged back through the crowd. His master was still upright, looking uneasy. "This isn't good," he said. "There's something in the water."

Indeed, the once-placid surface was now stirring like a boiling pot, spinning the ferry around in the middle of the river. The passengers, just getting to their feet, fell over again. Like a stage magician, the captain produced a pig's head and dropped it overboard, followed by a platter of roast chicken. He then lit some incense and knelt on the deck, kowtowing to the river.

This ritual didn't do the slightest bit of good. The boat continued churning, and nothing they did could induce it to move ahead. The captain suddenly knelt before the passengers, bowing again and again as he said, "Ladies and gentlemen, brothers and sisters, could an individual on this vessel have spoken some inauspicious words? The Dragon King appears to have taken you seriously, and if you don't placate him, none of us will survive this. Which one of you was it? Don't drag us all down with you." His head thudded against the deck as he kowtowed.

Walls of water were closing in on them, and everyone was pale with fright. If someone really had said the unsayable, there was no way out of this.

Just as everyone was about to panic, a merchant hollered, "It was her, it was her! I heard her."

They turned to see him dragging a young woman with a small child forward. "Her kid was raising a ruckus!" he shouted. "She got fed up, so she said she'd throw him into the river."

The people around them were nodding to indicate they'd heard her too. The child had been sitting on the deck, howling away, and the woman had tried to comfort him, before finally snapping, "Stop that, or I'll feed you to the fishes."

Her dire warning didn't do any good at all—the child kept making a racket, but at that moment, the boat had stopped moving forward and started spinning in place instead. The woman hadn't seen much of the world and didn't know how powerful words could be. When the accusing eyes bore down on her, she hugged her child, terrified, and slumped to the deck, now weeping too.

The captain crouched beside her. "Miss, how could you say something like that on board my boat? It's too late now. The Dragon King heard you, and he's waiting for you to drop your child into the water. If you don't, we're all finished." With that, he snatched the child into his arms.

Naturally, the woman wasn't able to just give up her own flesh and blood like that. She screeched and tried to grab her child back, but the captain was a burly man and fended her off easily. She turned beseechingly to the crowd around her, but they glared at her stone-faced, not lifting a finger. They all clearly thought that the child had to die, or else they all would, and there was nothing more to be said. Of course they felt sorry for the child, but the mother had to take the blame. Who asked her to spout such nonsense on a boat? Everyone knew you had to watch your words around the water gods. She'd brought this on herself.

World's End looked on with a pang, and he was about to nudge the Partridge to say the two of them should step forward, when someone burst out of the crowd and grabbed the captain's arm: the American priest.

Waving his copy of the Bible, he declared, "Captain, in the name of Christ, stop!"

If anyone else had tried to intervene, the captain would have knocked him out at once, but he didn't dare offend a white man. Still, the boat was spinning perilously, and they could overturn at any moment. Glaring at the man, the captain snarled, "You stay out of this. If this kid doesn't go into the river, the Dragon King will swallow all of us, and my boat too. When that happens, your little black book isn't going to save our lives."

The American was about to say something else, when one of the Russians, a stout, red-nosed man, pulled him aside. "Father Thomas, this isn't any of your business. These are mystical Eastern rituals that might not make sense to us, but we have to let them do what they have to do. If not, we really might all drown."

Father Thomas raged, "Mr. Andrei, I can't believe you'd say

such a thing. Only a demon would think it was right to throw this child into the river."

While the two foreigners quarreled, the captain took advantage of their distraction to trip the woman up, and while she lay on the ground, he flung the child over the railing. The woman screeched and fainted dead away.

Before World's End could shout at the Partridge to do something, the Partridge had already leaped forward. Although he generally kept to himself, he couldn't bear to see this innocent child get killed. His flying-tiger claws were already out and hurtling through the air. These were made of superior steel, a set of razor-sharp blades articulated like a paw, hanging from a string so they could grab things from a distance. Now they swung overboard and snagged the boy's clothes, and with a sharp flick, the Partridge had hauled him back on board.

The other passengers stared, slack-jawed. No sooner had this happened than all five Russians had their revolvers cocked and pointed right at the Partridge's head.

The river was roiling ever more fiercely, and everyone was dizzy from the motion. They might go over any second now. The Russians had been in China long enough to understand that the captain's words were no mere superstition, and if the river gods didn't get the sacrifice they'd been promised, there was no way out of this situation. They had breathed a sigh of relief when the child went over, only to see him get pulled back, and they responded in the only way they knew: by drawing their guns to deal with this new threat.

Before any of them could pull the trigger, there was a

mighty boom. Everyone ducked, then looked around wildly. Who had fired?

It was the Partridge again, imitating a gunshot as accurately as his animal cries that had so confused the cats. He picked up the child and tossed him to World's End, then pulled out his Mauser pistol and started firing from the hip. The five Russians crashed to the deck, lying in a growing pool of blood.

The passengers stared, their faces the color of clay. Five people had died, just like that, from guns drawn in the blink of an eye. This strange man stank of death, and he'd murdered them all as if he were a demon rather than a human being. The Partridge didn't care what anyone thought of him, and he quickly scooped up the corpses and tossed them overboard.

As the saying goes, even gods and ghosts are scared of evil men. The moment the Russians plunged into the river, the boat stopped spinning and could move forward again. The water slowly calmed and was soon smooth as before. The Partridge asked the captain to pull ashore.

Scared out of his wits, the man did as he was asked. He yelled at his crew to tack to the side and set down the gangplank when they got close enough to land.

Master World's End handed the boy back to his mother, admonishing her to mind her language in the future or she might not be as lucky the next time. The Partridge had killed five people in cold blood, which wasn't something they could smooth over. The best thing now would be for them to go undercover for the rest of their journey. As they disembarked, they brought the American priest with them. If they did encounter the army or police after this, it would be good to have a foreigner with them. Besides, he'd been the only one traveling with the Russians, and with the dead men's bodies at the bottom of the Yellow River, no one would be able to identify the deceased if the priest wasn't around to bear witness.

The Partridge and World's End stood on either side of the American, who walked along in a daze. Luckily, they weren't far from the Helan Hills and would arrive in three or four days. The area was fairly deserted, and they were unlikely to run into anyone on the way.

Father Thomas, imagining he'd been kidnapped by a pair of ruthless killers, begged them to think of the Lord's mercy, urging them to mend their ways, especially this old monk, who looked the picture of kindness. How could he take part in this abduction at his advanced age? Wouldn't it be better if he converted to Christianity, a religion that promised eternal life?

Three days later, the American priest came to the conclusion that they weren't actually kidnapping him—they seemed to be on their way somewhere, making a beeline for the northwest. Unable to fathom what was going on, he finally asked what they intended to do with him.

"You were tricked by those Russians," the Partridge said bluntly. "Didn't you see all those tools they had with them? They were planning to loot the treasures of Black Water City. When they heard you'd been there, they asked you to show them the way and would definitely have killed you once they arrived, to make sure you kept your silence. I saved your life. You can relax—I don't believe in slaughtering innocent people. When we've taken care of our business in Black Water City, we'll let you go. Right now, we're just trying to make sure there isn't any trouble before that."

The priest seemed calmer. "You drew your pistol at the

speed of lightning," he said. "It was quite a sight. I'd been thinking there was something fishy about those Russians too. They said they were planning to go into mining, but I guess it makes sense that it was looting they had in mind. And now, God will punish them."

The Partridge asked Father Thomas if he could describe the Buddhist towers one more time.

"What? Don't tell me you're planning to dig up the treasures yourself?"

The Partridge decided he liked this American enough to tell him the truth. "Not at all. There's something important I need from there. It's the difference between life and death for my tribe. It's a big secret, so I can't tell you any more."

"Okay," the American said, nodding. "I'll believe you. Here's what I know. Many years ago, I visited the ruins of Black Water City. I was hiking across the desert nearby when I stepped into a patch of quicksand. I thought my time had come to meet my maker, but instead, I was sucked down into an underground chamber, some sort of prayer hall. It was full of gleaming statues of the Buddha. I was hurrying to spread the word of the Lord, so I didn't stop for a closer look. If I went back there now, I'm not sure I could tell you the exact spot. But it's close to Black Water City, maybe six or seven kilometers away."

This jibed with what the Partridge knew. So it seemed this temple was close to the surface, and as long as they got the location right, it would be easy to dig a tunnel down into it.

The legend of Black Water River Meets the Sky was that it contained a giant reclining Buddha, beneath which was a mausoleum that had never received its intended body, but instead became a secret repository for the Western Xia Kingdom's treasures. The Partridge was heading for this spot.

Black Water City would be easy to find—there were many broken buildings remaining aboveground, and holy towers signaling its location from a distance, still rising majestically into the air. It was almost dusk when they got to the ruins, the gray outlines of the distant mountains still visible in the distance.

This ruined city was completely silent in the dusk, as if every living thing there had been snuffed out a moment ago, leaving a desolate atmosphere. Impossible to imagine this had once been such an important metropolis for the Western Xia dynasty.

Here they were: a Buddhist monk, a Christian missionary, and a fake Taoist priest. A bizarre trio, on their way to find the hidden wealth of a lost dynasty.

Near Black Water City, they watched silently as the moon spilled its cold light over the earth. They were in the high plains of the northwest, and the air was thin. A million stars glittered overhead—more of them, glowing much more brightly, than back at sea level.

World's End looked up, got out his feng shui board, and began calculating their gold-divining coordinates. Above them were the constellations of the Giant Door, the Hungry Wolf, the Guiding Star. And on the ground was the meridian of the dragonfly, which at that moment told him exactly where they needed to be.

Fixing his eyes on the spot, the old monk led the Partridge and Father Thomas through the moonlight. Pointing at the place, he said, "This is it, the great hall of the Black Water River Meets the Sky Temple. But I have to warn you, there seems to be something else buried here: a one-eyed dragon."

CHAPTER TWENTY-FIVE

NOT UNDERSTANDING THE LANGUAGE OF FENG SHUI, THE Partridge seemed bewildered, then asked, "What's a one-eyed dragon?"

Staring into the moonlight, World's End explained, "Beneath the ground here lies a sort of tunnel we call a dragon—but a much smaller one than usual, and there's only one opening through which air can pass. This is known as a one-eyed dragon, or sometimes as a dragonfly meridian. The purple mist and three stars, if clear and shapely, belong to the loyal warrior. But if mighty and fierce, they belong to the conquering army. If the purple mist is like a tree, its roots will tangle your feet; if like a hill, swollen on the surface, it's about to explode. In any case, these are ill omens. Because the Black

Water River altered its course, the structure of this cave has long been compromised. This precious eye of the dragon is now a cancerous tumor. If someone were buried here, their descendants would be in trouble." He pointed up at the thin sliver of the new moon. "We didn't consult the almanac before we came, and yet look, even the moon is barely present. Buddha himself is shutting his eye."

The Partridge had unsurpassed courage and had been seeking the eye of the divine for many years; it was a search that had consumed his tribe for millennia. How could he bear to wait a day, with the temple beneath his feet? He said to the monk, "The legend says the treasure is in an empty tomb. If no one is buried there, then we don't need to worry about the rules—it's not actually a grave without a body. So I'm going to get my shovel out and dig a hole, grab what I need, and leave. We'll just be careful, and nothing will go wrong."

World's End thought about it and had to agree—perhaps he had been overcautious. This was a treasure vault, not a burial site, so the normal rules didn't apply. They didn't even need to worry about lighting a candle or the three forbidden heists. He nodded his assent.

The Partridge got a metal club from his bag. Its hollow center had a mechanism in it, and its surface had been rubbed shiny and smooth by frequent use. Who knew how many hands it had passed through? Next, he pulled out nine steel blades, which fitted like flower petals into grooves down the length of the club, specially designed to clamp firmly around them as soon as they were inserted. Finally, he clicked a revolving handle to the end of the implement, and now it was a whirlwind digger, one of the best tools for entering a tomb. It could expand or shrink at will, adjusting to the size of the tunnel it was digging.

While the Partridge got to work with the digger, he asked Father Thomas to help clear away the mounds of dirt it was leaving behind. The American priest obeyed, grumbling, "Didn't you say you'd let me go once we got to this place? Now it seems you have all kinds of little activities lined up for me. You have to understand that Western priests such as myself are servants of the Lord; we don't normally engage in manual labor."

Neither the Partridge nor World's End could understand what this foreigner was mumbling about, so they ignored him, focusing instead on the tunnel opening up before them. In the time it took to smoke a pipe, the digger had reached the roof of the buried temple, revealing a patch of green crystal tiles like gleaming fish scales. Along the gutters were carved figures of the arhats, much grander than any normal building. You could tell at once that this must have been a magnificent structure.

The Partridge lifted a dozen tiles out of the sand pit he'd created and flung them to one side. Lowering his lantern on a string, he saw rows of wooden rafters, and beneath them an awe-inspiring great-man chamber. The "great man" was what Buddhist disciples respectfully called the Shakyamuni Buddha, because like a great warrior, he feared nothing. With his infinite power, he'd defeated the four demons of darkness, rage, death, and power. The lantern didn't quite reach the far corners of the hall, but the Partridge could just about make out a "three-bodied Buddha" in his incarnations of mortality, karma, and transformation, with bodhisattvas on either side.

Buddhism had been on the ascent during the Western Xia

dynasty, so it was natural that this temple would be on a grand scale. The Partridge nodded at World's End to say it was fine to go in. He normally worked alone, and had planned to enter first, but World's End had argued that this treasure trove was almost certainly booby-trapped, and gold hunters were skilled at seeking out such dangers, so it made sense for the two of them to go in at the same time. This would be a further step in their cooperation.

And so the two men each took a heart-stilling tablet, washing it down with a flask of sky dew. These were precautions to keep themselves from losing consciousness in the stagnant air of underground places. Then, with their charms around their necks, black cloths across their faces, water-fire shoes on their feet, and tools firmly in place, they prepared to enter.

The Partridge remembered that Father Thomas was still there, and while he didn't seem like a bad person, it didn't seem safe to leave a foreigner alone while he and the monk were inside. If the American did turn out to have ill intentions, it might spell trouble. Better to bring him along and hope he was good at following instructions. If not, well, he could be fodder for the traps.

With this in mind, the Partridge beckoned the priest over and tried to feed him a heart-stilling pill, but Father Thomas refused to open his mouth, convinced this was some sort of Chinese poison. Rather than trying to explain, the Partridge prodded him sharply in the ribs, and when the priest gasped, he popped the pill right down the man's throat. The American could only look up at the sky and proclaim, "Merciful father, forgive these men. They know not what they do."

The Partridge nudged the American to the hole in the roof

and got his flying-tiger claws, preparing to let him down first. Father Thomas was shocked—wasn't it enough that these barbaric Easterners had poisoned him? What was happening now? Was he going to be buried alive?

World's End said soothingly, "Mr. Foreign Priest, please don't worry. You and I have both taken orders, and my Buddha is all-encompassing and compassionate, so a monk like me will be kind too. I would never step on an ant, and I shield my candle flames so they won't kill moths. Of course I wouldn't hurt you either. It's just that what we're doing has to remain secret, so we're inviting you to journey with us, and as soon as the trip is over, you'll be free to go."

Reassured, Father Thomas calmed down. No matter what, this Chinese monk was also a spiritual worker, and such a man would surely never participate in a murder. He allowed the Partridge to lower him through the roof on the flying-tiger claws.

World's End and the Partridge followed behind him, and when they were all in the great-man hall, they shined the lantern around for a closer look. Sure enough, this was a truly astounding chamber. Every inch of the Buddha glittered with precious gemstones, and even the lotus throne was made of precious metals. The temple was a sturdy construction held up by thirty-six vast pillars.

Seeing the Buddha, World's End immediately knelt and began kowtowing, chanting his scriptures. Having been a fake priest, now back in civilian clothing, the Partridge saw no problem with kneeling down too, asking the Buddha for help with ridding his tribe of their misery. He was completely sincere in his prayers.

When they were done with their devotions, the two men continued looking around. The outer chamber was completely collapsed—there was definitely no way in. The side rooms were full of arhat statues, all exquisitely made and carved with consummate skill. Any one of them would have been priceless, which went to show how influential Buddhism had been during the Western Xia years.

Yet there was something about these figurines that seemed somehow different from the ones they'd seen elsewhere. They couldn't have said what exactly; there was just something odd about them.

Then World's End realized what it was. He said to the Partridge, "The Western Xia dynasty was led by the Tangut people, who arose from the Tibetan lands and helped the Tang emperor open up his kingdom. For their service, they were bestowed the surname Li. As a minority, they were much more influenced by Indian Buddhism than the Buddhism practiced in the interior, so these statues are dressed in Tang robes, but their features are much closer to the people of Buddhism's source, unlike in the temples of the interior, which are more dominated by Han culture."

They'd worked out that the treasure trove was probably not far from the great-man hall, or perhaps in the chamber itself, because this tomb would have been constructed according to feng shui principles, and with such a narrow meridian, there weren't many places where it could be.

Father Thomas wandered around with them, finding this stranger and stranger. Why had they chosen to go digging in such a random spot, finding a giant temple right away? And now that they were in here, he thought this all looked familiar, particularly the beautiful statues. Surely this was the hole he'd fallen into all those years ago. That had been an accident, and he'd never have been able to find his way back here. So how could this old monk have done it, just by looking at the stars? This Eastern mysticism was so hard to understand, so full of secrets. The American priest looked at the two men with more respect now and bit his tongue when he felt like complaining.

The trio made three rounds of the chamber, examining virtually every brick and tile, but there was no sign of a hidden room.

Finally, the Partridge said to World's End, "If there's nothing here, then perhaps we should check in the back room."

The monk nodded. "Since we're here, there's no rush. We can take our time to examine the whole place. There's probably a reclining Buddha in the rear—let's see what we can find."

The passageway to the back of the temple was decorated in the Song dynasty style, with pictures of lotus blossoms. It gave them a sense of peace to look at images of these flowers, which rose from the mud to bloom gloriously, leaving behind the earth they'd risen from.

After spending so much time with World's End, the Partridge had heard quite a bit about Buddhist thought, and his inner rage had subsided a fair bit. At this moment, in this underground sacred place, he suddenly felt a great weariness descend over him, and all his plans of reverse dipping seemed unspeakably exhausting. He wanted only to find the eye of the divine, finish his life's work, and spend the rest of his days in seclusion, devoting himself to reflection.

This thought flashed through his mind swiftly, but he knew he couldn't afford the slightest sluggishness at this time. He needed to concentrate on the business at hand, which was to uncover the hiding place of this treasure.

They soon got through to the rear chamber, which, as World's End had expected, was a stately room occupied by a vast stone Buddha lying horizontally, decorated with seven types of jewels. He must have been fifty meters from head to toe, asleep on his lotus dais, his large earlobes dangling.

Ceramic urns stood at either end of the room, once filled with hardened dragon oil, a sort of solid fuel that could burn for a hundred years without going out. The long-burning crystal lamps used for ancestral worship are usually filled with this substance. Now, though, enough time had passed that the urns were empty and the flames extinguished.

Stone tablets were dotted around the room, inscribed with the impossibly complicated Western Xia language—probably something to do with Buddhist teachings. The Partridge roamed around the room a few times, before finally stopping and staring at the giant Buddha. "There's something wrong with his posture," he said to World's End. "It looks weird to me."

World's End had a closer look and realized he was right. "Ah yes, that's correct. Good observation, no doubt due to your mountain-moving skills. This Buddha's head has a mechanism in it—the entrance is probably somewhere inside there. But I can't tell how exactly it works, and I'm afraid if we start fiddling with it, it might prove dangerous."

The Partridge clasped his hands and bowed deeply to the sleeping Buddha, then leaped up onto the dais. The Buddha's lips were very slightly parted and looked like they might be able to open wider. Only an expert reverse dipper would have noticed such a detail. Could the tunnel be inside his mouth?

But those lips could also be concealing flying daggers or poisoned arrows, all manner of traps just waiting for someone to activate them. The Partridge studied the statue's face carefully and saw that the mechanism was fairly straightforward. There were no traps here, just a simple lever that would open a tunnel. Summoning Father Thomas to help, he got to work pressing down on a particular petal on one of the lotus blossoms.

With a loud grinding sound, the giant lips moved apart. Inside the mouth was a tunnel leading straight down, with a ladder fixed along its wall. Father Thomas exclaimed at the sight, and without even waiting to be asked, started clamoring to go first so he could see what was down there.

The Partridge knew this had been built as a tomb before being converted to a treasure store, which meant the Western Xia rulers would surely have put in some sort of safeguards to prevent theft. Sending the American down first would mean his certain death, and he seemed like a decent fellow, so the Partridge said he should go in the middle, with World's End bringing up the rear.

No grave robbers had disturbed this ancient tomb before. It was anyone's guess what unusual features lay within. All they knew was that the Han civilization had barely influenced this kingdom, so it would be unlike anything they'd seen in the rest of China, and they'd just have to proceed one step at a time. With a mountain-moving expert like the Partridge leading the way, they were definitely in safe hands.

To check on how the air was circulating below, the Partridge handed the lantern up to World's End, while fitting a phosphorous cylinder to the end of his steel umbrella—an implement used by all gold hunters, constructed entirely of metal and therefore impenetrable to attack. The phosphorous cylinder could test air quality while providing illumination—in modern scientific language, we'd say it consisted of a biological glow, like a firefly or luminous sea creature, and it was fueled by ground-up bones of the dead mixed with red wormwood, which produced a cold blue glow that could last up to an hour.

With the cylinder lighting their way, the Partridge allowed the steel umbrella to dangle below him on the flying-tiger claws as a shield. Inching down the ladder, he soon felt a tightness in his chest. There was no air circulation to the lower level, and if they hadn't taken precautions, they'd probably have lost consciousness by this point and plummeted to their deaths.

He glanced up to see how the monk and American priest were doing, and yelled that they could take a break before going on, but they said they were fine, it was still endurable. They were more than halfway down and might as well go the rest of the way.

Sure enough, they were at the bottom in about a cup of tea. (In gold-hunting slang, a cigarette is three to five minutes, a cup of tea ten to fifteen, and a bowl of rice twenty to thirty.)

At the bottom of the shaft were four icy-cold stone walls. The air was very dry. The Partridge spun the cylinder around, trying to see what else was down there. Without warning, a warrior in golden armor loomed out of the darkness, frowning and silent, clutching an enormous ax in both hands, which he was now bringing down toward the Partridge's head.

CHAPTER TWENTY-SIX

REACTING QUICKLY, THE PARTRIDGE JUMPED BACKWARD WITH a shout, pressing himself against the stone wall and opening his steel umbrella as a shield. In the same movement, he pulled the Mauser from his belt and rested it on the rim of the umbrella, ready to fire at the warrior.

Why had he shouted? It has to do with the practice of martial arts—when making a vigorous movement, involuntary sounds come from your mouth, just as naturally as breathing, to avoid internal injuries. He definitely wasn't screaming out of fear.

There was an unexpected consequence, though—Father Thomas, still several feet from the ground, had been startled into losing his footing on the ladder, and he tumbled right down.

Hearing the whoosh of air above him, the Partridge knew something was about to land on him, and he quickly raised the umbrella so the American landed on its dome—fortunately from not too high up—and slid off onto the ground. Although the impact jarred Father Thomas's limbs and left him aching, he didn't suffer any great harm.

At the same time, the Partridge lifted his glowing blue light to take a closer look at this ax-wielding warrior. As it turned out, there was no need to be scared—he was just a painting on the wall, so realistically done, in such vivid colors, that he'd seemed exactly like the real thing, life-size and glowering in his majestic suit of gold armor. It was truly a great work of art—energy pulsed through every inch of his muscle, and even now that the Partridge knew what this was, he wouldn't have been surprised if it had leaped right out of the wall.

World's End had now reached the bottom too, and he stared at the painted warrior. Together, they decided that this gold-armored man had to be a great general named Weng Zhong, from the Qin Kingdom, whom it was said even ghosts were afraid of. By the start of the Tang dynasty, every highborn person's tomb came decorated with Weng Zhong's portrait, so that he could guard the doors and keep the place safe.

Most such images of him were slowly eaten away by exposure to the air, and besides, grave robbers tended to tunnel their way in or blast through a side wall, so they never actually confronted this legendary general. This was the first time either of them was meeting him, and they wanted to take a closer look.

The Partridge said, "Master, the Western Xia people were certainly influenced by the culture of the Central Plains—look, they even invited in this Qin general. And if he's standing guard here, that means we must be near the location of the tomb."

World's End held up the lantern and stared at the stone wall Weng Zhong was on. He nodded. "There are nails hammered into this; it's definitely the entrance." Before he'd finished speaking, Weng Zhong shimmered and vanished.

Father Thomas, already in a nervous state from the eerie surroundings and flickering lamplight, was so stunned he went pale and hastily made the sign of the cross.

World's End turned to him. "Don't be scared, Foreign Priest. As fresh air starts to flow through here, the ancient pigments crumble to dust. That's all. Nothing ghostly happening."

The American calmed down, though he still thought the place was spooky. Perhaps not even the all-seeing Lord knew what lay in the world beyond this door. Just his bad luck that these two Chinese men had dragged him here. What if this underground place belonged to Satan? Or there could be werewolves, vampires, or zombies lurking down here. Thomas might have been a priest, and strong in his faith, but he'd never stopped being afraid of the dark. He often blamed himself for this, feeling it showed a lack of faith. This encounter was a test sent by God, and he had to find a way to conquer his terror in order to pass. Yet how could he overcome it so quickly?

The Partridge didn't have time to deal with the foreign priest's complicated emotional state. He was examining the wall and saw that it was a sand barrier. This was a fiendish design that, after the deceased was buried and the door closed behind the mourners, would cause a huge quantity of sand to fill the passageway, wedging the entrance shut so it was impossible to open from the outside.

Luckily, World's End noticed that there was a tiny crack at the bottom of the door to accommodate the tracks it glided on, and not one grain of sand was falling from that opening. This suggested the mechanism had never been activated, probably because no one was actually buried here, and when hiding their treasures, the Western Xia court would have left the place unsealed, to make sure they could come back to retrieve them.

That saved a lot of time. They needed to break through the side wall, but could simply open this stone door. And so the three men put their shoulders to it and heaved.

The door wasn't latched, just heavy. Still, it was only a few hundred pounds, and the trio was able to get it open a crack without too much effort—just wide enough for one person to enter.

The Partridge walked through, still holding his umbrella. He shot a flare, which shone long enough for him to get a clear view of the entire tunnel. The two tanks on either side of the door weren't even filled with sand, but stood empty. The floor was level, neatly paved—and he knew that the more orderly it looked, the more likely it was to conceal a trap of some kind.

Behind him, World's End was urging him to be cautious. The door hadn't been sealed, which might have been because the men who hid the treasure were fleeing for their lives, but that might also be intended to lure him in and catch him off guard. As the saying goes, "If the door's open wide, what's inside might finish you off." Some doors were thick and sturdy, with sand piles or giant stone balls behind them, but that was a crude defense and could be overcome with brute force. The real tests came in the passageway and grave chamber, two places a would-be thief would definitely have to pass by.

The Partridge was naturally very careful—after all, he'd never been into a Western Xia tomb before and didn't know what to expect. Holding his breath, he walked about seventy yards down the corridor, at the end of which was another big door.

This was a more normal-looking one, tall and wide, with a round arch like a city gate. It took up the entire width of the passageway, beautifully carved from white jade, but not with pictures, just words—all in the Western Xia language. They didn't know what it meant, but again guessed it was Buddhist scriptures. A metal bar lay across the door, held in place by a giant lock, no key in sight. The treasure must be on the other side.

The strange thing was, on either side of the jade door were two deep round holes. Neither the Partridge nor World's End had seen anything like this, but they were clearly man-made, exactly the same size and symmetrically arranged. The whole mausoleum was solidly constructed, the stone walls as smooth as mirrors, three or four yards high. It had taken a long time to build, and every feature of it must surely be there by design.

World's End thought this must be some kind of mechanism and wanted to talk about what it might be. The Partridge interrupted, "That lock on the door—I'm good at picking locks. Only, what if damaging the lock sets off some sort of trap?"

The monk waved the thought away. "You won't get this open. Why put a metal bar over the door? That seems unnecessary. Anyone who could make their way in here isn't going to be deterred by a puny thing like that. But examine the lock—in the Song dynasty, they were attaching them to doors as protection, and if you tugged at it, poison gas or something like that would surely seep out."

The Partridge didn't dare touch the lock but looked at it very carefully, and sure enough, it was built right into the door, which meant the slightest touch could set something off. He broke into a cold sweat. He was normally so calm, but today for some reason he was losing his cool. Maybe because if World's End hadn't spotted the danger, he'd probably be dead by now.

Meanwhile, the monk had worked it out. "The white-jade door is a ruse. Never mind how pretty it is, it's a fake. You won't get in that way. This tomb isn't large, but it's impressively designed. The only way in is from below. No matter how ingenious the Western Xia people were, you can't get away from feng shui. If my calculations are right, these paving stones should move—probably the only entrance."

The Partridge did as he instructed and lifted slab after slab, and sure enough, a large tunnel was revealed, leading to the chamber behind that jade door. The Western Xia subterfuge was no match for the experienced eye of a reverse dipper like World's End.

Still leading the way with his steel umbrella, the Partridge walked slowly in with the other two behind him. An enormous black object, shaped like a beehive, was suspended from the ceiling of the tunnel. They couldn't tell what it was—by the light of the cylinder, it could have been stone or jade. Best to stay away—they sidled around it without touching it.

The darkness seemed to lighten once they got in. The room, twenty yards wide, was full of jewels of all sorts, gleaming and reflecting the glowing cylinder. The most eye-catching was a coral tree in the center of the room, draped with baubles and gems. Sure enough, these were extraordinary treasures. There were also countless scrolls and trunks both big and small. Everything valuable from the Western Xia palace had been moved into this space.

Father Thomas was bug-eyed, and he began pestering World's End to let him take one or two objects with him. Any of these things could be sold for enough to build several churches, places where street urchins could come for a meal and to learn about Christ.

World's End replied, "That's a laudable aim, but these are national treasures, and we can't touch them. My family has some money, and I'm happy to put some toward your church. Us spiritual workers might as well use our money for good; it's not like leaving our gold and silver behind will be any use."

For his part, the Partridge was blind to all these glittering artifacts—he only cared about getting his hands on the eye of the divine. The rest might as well be weeds that he'd trampled across in his search. Abruptly, he froze. Pointing behind World's End, he said, "We're in trouble. There's a dead person there."

World's End spun around, startled. He hurried over, and sure enough, a pile of bones lay in a corner of the chamber. This skeleton was quite a bit taller than a regular human being, its white bone hand clutching a bunch of keys. Behind it was a dark Buddha of a thousand hands, neither stone nor jade. When the Partridge held the glowing cylinder up to it, it absorbed all the light. The contrast between this darkness and the gleaming white bones was chilling.

World's End felt his heart sink. "This isn't good. It's the new moon tonight; the Buddha's eye is shut. All our charms will have lost their effectiveness. If there are evil spirits here, then this tomb will soon be our tomb too. But the strangest thing is, how could there be this statue with a thousand hands and eyes—a dark Buddha?"

CHAPTER TWENTY-SEVEN

THE BLEACHED BONES HAD ALREADY GIVEN THE PARTRIDGE AN uneasy feeling. The monk's solemn tone told him this was serious. He asked what the Buddha signified.

"The eye of the moon is shut tonight," said World's End, "and evil is afoot. At times like this, when yang is weak and yin is strong, that's when strange things take place. Who would dare go reverse dipping on such a night? I thought this was an empty grave, but now here's a skeleton, and even more ominous, a thousand-eyed Buddha. This statue is no ordinary object. There are surely dark forces at work here. Normally, we'd defend ourselves with black donkey hooves and rice, but they've lost their power for now. We should leave."

The Partridge was reluctant to go with his mission unfinished, but he could tell how dangerous this was. He nodded. As they rushed back toward the tunnel, Father Thomas, desperate to get out, pulled out the candle the Partridge had given him earlier to light the way.

World's End yelled, "No!" and pulled him back. At the same moment, a vast plume of black fog rose from the hole in the ground. If the American priest had been a tiny bit closer, it would have swept him up, and he'd surely have met his maker. The fog was poison. World's End was familiar with it; many graves had such a mechanism, and one of them must have bumped into it. Luckily, the monk had enough experience to realize what was happening, and he dragged the priest out of the way in time.

The fog must have been infused with centipede venom, because it lingered like a solid black mass, refusing to disperse. More and more of it was pumping out of the tunnel. The three men gulped down scarlet antipoison pills, though the gold-hunting medication was mostly used to combat toxic fumes from corpses. How they would fare against something this virulent was anybody's guess.

With the fumes slowly taking over the room, the trio slowly backed into the corner where the skeleton was. It didn't matter that this was a dead end—the Partridge's whirlwind digger would be able to get them out, but not before the poison got hold of them. They had to find a way to stop the fog from advancing.

Nothing in the Partridge's skills or World End's experience had prepared them for this. If it had been regular poison gas, they'd have held their breath and slowed their heartbeats till they managed to get out, but this thick miasma was clearly too powerful for that. Where was it coming from?

With their backs to the stone wall, they stared helplessly as their doom rushed at them. But the Partridge rallied. He wasn't afraid of anything. Pressed against the wall, he felt something cold against his back. When he turned his head, he saw a lamp fixed to the wall, probably the long-burning light designed to hang over the coffin.

There was no coffin, just the lamp on the wall. Something was wrong. The feng shui rules stated that such lamps should be three feet, three and one-third inches from the ground, but this was half an inch lower than that, and pointing downward. It must have been a hidden mechanism. If they pulled it back up into place, the wall would flip over, revealing the secret chamber behind it. These rooms were where the most important grave goods were kept, so that even if thieves did manage to break in, they wouldn't get the best stuff.

The fog was growing thicker now, and at the last possible moment, the Partridge grabbed the lamp and yanked it up sharply. It moved easily, and with a grinding noise, the wall behind them suddenly revolved, sending bits of dirt flying so they were speckled with it.

The inner room had a lower ceiling. The wall completed its turn and clicked into place, bringing the thousand-hand Buddha and skeleton with it. There were no piles of jewels here, just a locked box.

Before looking at what they'd uncovered, the Partridge quickly pried a couple of tiles from the floor, then scooped up the dirt beneath to fill in the spaces around the revolving wall. They couldn't risk any poison seeping in. He was heartened to find the soil loose and springy. He would be able to dig them out in a couple of hours, and there was enough air in here to keep them going till then.

After a lifetime of reverse dipping, World's End was used to narrow rooms like this. Seeing the Partridge get his tools out and start digging an escape tunnel, the monk sat cross-legged and, running his prayer beads through his fingers, sank into meditation.

As the Partridge worked away, Father Thomas couldn't help asking World's End, "Did you notice something in the black fog outside? It didn't look like poison."

World's End slowly opened his eyes. "What?" he said quietly. "You saw it too?"

Father Thomas nodded. "In the last second before the wall spun us around, I saw a human figure in the fog. It looked like the Buddha. Could it be . . ."

Hearing this, the Partridge stopped his digging and looked up. He'd seen the figure just before they'd entered this room.

World's End thought about it, then pointed at the dark Buddha statue. "According to legend, this is an evil spirit worshiped by ancient people. The cult that followed him was wiped out by the government in the late Tang dynasty, and yet here in a Western Xia tomb, there's a dark Buddha statue. It's probably made of putrid jade from ancient Persia. This is a rare stone, and despite the name, it's not a type of jade at all. They say any person or animal who touches it will find their organs turning to liquid, their flesh melting off until nothing's left but bones. And then their soul will be chained to the dark Buddha, trapped here forever."

The Partridge looked at the bones. "This skeleton might

once have been a loyal attendant who chose to stay behind to guard the treasure, only he touched the putrid jade and died. Maybe that black fog wasn't poison, but . . ." He didn't need to finish the sentence for them to know what he meant.

World's End urged the Partridge and Father Thomas not to go anywhere near the Buddha, and to dig that tunnel out as quickly as possible. If the dark Buddha was messing with them, this inner chamber wouldn't keep them safe. His eye was drawn again to the keys in the skeleton's hand. He grabbed them, then the locked box—perhaps the eye of the divine was in there, and perhaps these keys would open it. No way to know except by trying.

The monk lit a candle. He tried the keys, and sure enough, one of them fit. The Partridge was a few yards into his tunnel by now, and when he stuck his head back out to clear the dirt away, he saw the open box and stopped his work to look inside. All it contained, though, was a dragon fossil carved with strange writing.

He'd allowed his hopes to rise, and this was like having a bucket of cold water poured over him. He stood there, the disappointment stinging, and then there was a sudden tickle in his throat, and before he knew what was happening, he was spitting a mouthful of blood onto the dragon fossil.

World's End jumped back. He'd known the Partridge was too passionate and took things too seriously, so great emotion could indeed make him vomit blood. Afraid the Partridge would faint, the monk asked Father Thomas to hold on to him.

Turning, World's End caught sight of the dark Buddha, whose eyes had suddenly blinked open, dozens of them, shining in the gloom, glaring malevolently at the trio.

CHAPTER TWENTY-EIGHT

Father Thomas stared in horror at the Buddha's open eyes, all of them white with no pupils. "What . . . what are those? When did those eyes open? Are they eyes or giant maggots?"

And now those eyes were emitting a thick black fog, so dense it was almost solid. In the flickering candlelight, they watched as this mist coalesced into a blurry shape: a second dark Buddha. The priest got out his flask of holy water, which he splashed at the creature. Although it had been moving sluggishly, it reacted swiftly, a gap appearing in its center so the liquid passed harmlessly through without touching it, splashing on the ground. The hole happened to be in the center of the dark Buddha's face, making it look like a vast mouth had opened, roaring at the three men.

Realizing the fog monster was afraid of holy water, the Partridge yelled at the American to try again, but Father Thomas shouted back, "That's all I had!"

"The foreign priest has the right idea," World's End said. "Sacred artifacts frighten it. The new moon must have passed, so our charms will work again. Watch me." As he spoke, he snapped the string of his prayer beads and flung the beads at the black fog.

Unexpectedly, the monster didn't react. In fact, it didn't even seem to notice the beads, which simply went through it as it continued to advance. Crestfallen, World's End could only mutter, "That's so peculiar. My Buddhism has no effect. Could it be less powerful than Western holy water?"

The fog stopped, as if an invisible wall were in its way. It turned toward the candle, which they'd left at the far end of the room.

"What is it?" shouted Father Thomas.

The Partridge had seen the same thing. "The fog . . ."

Then all three men at once: "The candle!"

The candle had caused the temperature of the air around it to rise! Whatever it was made of, the black fog was like a moth seeking out flames, and the candle was attracting it. It was some kind of substance that lay dormant, coming to life only when sufficient heat was applied, then rampaging through the space until everything hotter than room temperature had been eliminated.

Sure enough, the fog now sought out the candle as its first target. Although formless, it seemed to have some mass, and in an instant it had squashed the flame out. The room was now pitch-dark.

The men knew they were in trouble. This fog would now look for the next-warmest objects, and that happened to be the human beings.

Once the trio had worked out what triggered the fog, it was easy to divert it: they lit every candle they had and lured it to the far corner, away from the revolving wall. There was no time to finish digging the tunnel out; their best bet was to clear a path back to the main chamber, leaving the miasma stuck here behind the jade door.

As they fled toward the revolving wall, World's End scooped up the dragon fossil. It had all kinds of strange symbols on it, some of which looked like the eye of the divine. Perhaps this would give some clue to its whereabouts. In any case, it must be a valuable object to be stored in this secret inner chamber.

The Partridge and Father Thomas were already at the wall, yelling at World's End to hurry. As soon as he joined them, they pulled the sconce lever and it started turning, only to creak to a halt halfway through. The mechanism was jammed.

CHAPTER TWENTY-NINE

As the wall stopped moving, the black fog in the main room, which had been drifting aimlessly, suddenly found its target and formed a giant face zooming toward the three men. Meanwhile, the cloud behind them, having extinguished the candles, was also hurtling toward them. They were hemmed in, two deadly masses closing in on them from either direction with a fearsome rumbling.

"Quick!" shouted World's End. "Light a candle to lead them away." The Partridge reached forlornly into his bag, but they'd used up their entire supply.

They were inches from their doom now. Luckily, the Partridge wasn't the sort of person to let himself get turned into a skeleton.

He suddenly remembered the coral tree draped with jewels in the center of the room. What if he could use his flying-tiger claws to haul them onto the tree's branches? The rope was sturdy enough to support the weight of ten people, so three should be no problem. The question was whether the tree would be equally strong.

No time to worry about that. He sent his claws shooting out so they hooked onto the top branch and swung around it a few times till they were secure.

Clutching the rope, he called to World's End and Father Thomas to hold on tight and keep their legs up in the air. Not waiting for an answer, he yelled, "Now!" A tug of the rope and they were soaring through the air, leaving the jammed revolving wall behind them.

As soon as their feet left the ground, both banks of fog surged forward and met at the spot where the three men had been just a moment ago. Father Thomas stared, petrified, his teeth chattering so badly he couldn't even form the words to a prayer. Holding his legs as high as he could, he thought frantically that if the rope didn't snap, it would surely be a miracle.

The coral tree swayed alarmingly. In midair, the trio suddenly felt a jerk. Father Thomas didn't dare open his eyes, but the other two turned back and saw that the skeleton had somehow attached itself to one of World's End's feet. The old monk let out a sharp breath at the sight.

At that moment, the tree branch groaned and snapped in two. The three men crashed to the ground. Luckily, they'd gotten clear of the fog, landing just beyond it. The Partridge grabbed his companions and urgently pulled them away. But now his left hand was numb—it had touched the fog.

As he watched, the flesh on his hand dissolved, leaving only white bones. The muscles of his arm were going too, the rot slowly creeping upward from his wrist, raw pain clutching every one of his nerves. If he didn't find a way to stop this, soon his whole body would go the same way. But with the fog so close to them, the main thing was to escape.

Enduring the awful pain, the Partridge grabbed Father Thomas and World's End.

Father Thomas shrieked and jumped up, patting himself all over. He hadn't been touched at all, but he was looking at the stark white bones that were the Partridge's left arm. World's End was unconscious—probably from hitting his head when they landed. The Partridge had to manhandle him toward the tunnel.

Beads of sweat were running down the Partridge's forehead from the agony, while the flesh was gone almost up to his elbow. The only remedy was the same as for a venomous snakebite, but there was no time to chop off his own arm. Their exertions had raised their body temperatures, and the fog was drawing closer and closer. With his right hand, the Partridge pulled out his pistol and sent five shots thudding into the dark Buddha's body.

The fog was now attracted to the heat of the muzzle, and it swarmed in that direction. Almost fainting from the pain, the Partridge muttered to Father Thomas, "Let's go."

They jumped down into the tunnel, carrying World's End between them. Again they were confronted with the suspended black rock, only now they knew what it was—the source of the first cloud of black fog. That must have been when Father Thomas lit his candle in this passageway.

They hurried past the putrid jade to the end of the passage. When they got out, the Partridge yelled at the American priest to seal the gap behind them so the fog couldn't follow. Ripping a strip of fabric from his shirt, he wound it tightly around his arm, then activated the whirlwind digger and put one of its blades straight through his injured limb. The infected forearm thudded to the ground, and even with the tourniquet, blood gushed from the wound like a fountain. Before he could stop the flow, a dark curtain came down over his eyes and he fell into a dead faint.

Father Thomas was now the only person left standing. With no time to waste, he had to get the two Chinese men back out into the open air. Just as he was about to grab hold of the Partridge, he saw something horrific: the amputated limb, now mostly liquid and bone, was lying in a puddle on the floor—and black specks were rising from this puddle, swirling through the air.

Sunk in despair, Father Thomas was about to give up hope, when he heard a cough behind him. Spinning around, he saw that the Partridge had come to. Hurrying over, he helped him up and pointed at the miniature black fog, too anxious to speak.

The Partridge was pale and trembling from loss of blood. It was a good thing he'd thought to tie a cloth around his arm, which had more or less staunched the flow now. Once upright, he felt most of his alertness come flooding back. A small cloud of black particles was hovering in front of the jade door, searching for warmth. He quickly got out his pistol again and fired it into the padlock.

The lock juddered as the bullet ricocheted off it, and an

ear-shattering rumbling came from the two holes on either side of the door. Sand began to pour out in a great flood.

The Partridge and Father Thomas dragged World's End frantically toward the exit, not looking back to see what was happening, though they could hear the sand continuing to spill behind them. It was probably designed to fill the entire passageway.

They got through the door and were standing in the shaft with the ladder before they had a chance to draw breath. The Partridge smeared some Yunnan white ointment onto his stump, though there was no way he'd ever get this arm back. It looked like his reverse-dipping career was over. He could have vomited blood again with frustration, so he quickly gulped down two more heart-stilling tablets to calm himself.

He was most concerned about the state of the old monk. The other two had only come to Black Water City because of him, and if the journey were to cost World's End his life, that'd be a bigger sin than he was prepared to take on. He and Father Thomas propped the old man into a sitting position and examined his injuries.

The American priest touched his back, and his hand came away bright red. "It's blood! The monk is wounded."

During their headlong flight, there hadn't been time to see what had knocked out the monk. Now it was clear: in the fall from the coral tree, the skeleton attached to World End's foot had broken apart on impact, and one of the bones had shattered and lodged deep in his back. There was a good chance it had pierced a major organ—in which case the old man might be beyond help.

The Partridge emptied the entire bottle of Yunnan white

ointment over the wound, but blood kept gushing and washed it away. Helpless, he wept as he got a northern pearl from his bag, crumbling it under the monk's nose, hoping to revive him for at least a few moments to hear his last words.

As the powder entered his nostrils, World's End coughed a couple of times and awoke. He looked groggily at the two sobbing men, then gazed down at himself and knew he didn't have long. Clutching the Partridge's right hand, he said, "I'm leaving this vessel that is my body, but don't be sad. Listen well; I need you to remember these words."

The Partridge nodded, and the monk went on. "I haven't been a gold hunter for many years now. My charms belong to you, though it's a shame I didn't have time to teach you all the secrets. If you have a chance, go look up my old colleague Golden Abacus. He goes around disguised as a merchant, and he operates on the banks of the Yellow River. He's peerless. The only one who could give him a run for his money when it came to yin-yang feng shui was Third Master Zhang, who is, alas, deceased. As for gold diviners, once I'm gone, there won't be any more in the world except Golden Abacus. If you bring my charms to him, he'll help you. Oh, and here's the dragon fossil I picked up from the inner sanctum. It's covered in references to the phoenix gall, and it might hold some vital clue. You might be able to find the eye of the divine just by studying it."

Again the Partridge nodded, though he knew that with his arm gone, he might not be able to get hold of this artifact, even if he found out exactly where it was. The old monk was fading fast. He seemed to have a few final thoughts but was choking too much to open his mouth. He bit his lips, trembling all over.

With the last of his strength, World's End managed to say, "You . . . must remember . . . don't kill . . . reverse dipping is bad karma . . . be merciful . . . I'm fading . . ." And with that, he quietly slipped away.

The Partridge knelt by him, kowtowing again and again. Father Thomas had to beg him to stand. This was no place to linger. The two men climbed back up into the temple, then ceremonially burned the monk's body in front of the jeweled Buddha. With tears in their eyes, they finally departed.

For many years after that, the Partridge did as World's End had urged him, seeking out the Golden Abacus in the valleys around the Yellow River. He traveled the whole territory without a single sighting of him. He also showed the dragon fossil to every scholar he met, and not one of them could tell him what it said.

The world was in chaos at the time, and an enormous war was brewing. With Father Thomas's help, the Partridge was able to emigrate to the faraway United States. Brokenhearted, he settled in the state of Tennessee, where he was determined to live out the rest of his life, secluded from the world.

After that, a series of wars tore China apart, and it would have been hard to find the eye of the divine. As for the Partridge's tribe, their numbers withered away. The Partridge was crushed to think that in a hundred years at most, the bloodline was likely to be broken, and his ancient people would be no more.

The Partridge didn't remain alone in his adopted home. He married, and he and his wife raised a daughter. In turn, she married and had a daughter of her own—Julie Yang.

The Partridge's son-in-law, Yang Xuanwei—Julie Yang's

father—learned about the Partridge's story. He was fascinated by archaeology and loved adventure, and wanted to save his child from the iron sickness. He put his plan into action. As a young man, he'd immersed himself in the culture of the Western Regions, though he'd mainly studied the Han and Tang dynasties, when this part of China was at its most prosperous. Yang Xuanwei didn't know much about the Jingjue Kingdom, but he was certain that its ghost-hole contained some important clues. He was a man who believed that everything could be understood through science.

When China reformed and opened its borders, a second wave of desert explorers arrived. Joining them, Yang Xuanwei assembled a team and launched an expedition. Unfortunately, after entering the desert, they were never seen again. And when Julie Yang, in turn, enlisted Professor Chen and his students to help find her father, we passed through the black valley of the Zaklaman Mountains, ending up in the ancient Jingjue City, where we saw the bottomless ghost-hole.

Of the people who made it out alive, Professor Chen was in a precarious mental state, his mind destroyed by the shock. At the time, Julie hadn't yet learned just how intimately her own story was bound up with the Zaklaman.

CHAPTER THIRTY

Shortly after Professor Chen and Julie landed in America, the red marks showed up on their backs. The professor was in a particularly bad state, showing symptoms of a rare iron deficiency. Nothing the doctors did helped. Meanwhile, having learned from the seer's prediction that she was a Zaklaman descendant, Julie realized that this business was far more complex than she'd ever thought, and that the ghosthole was just the tip of the iceberg.

"I made an important discovery," Julie said. "The writing on the dragon fossil that no one could read is exactly the same as the strange marks on our backs. These strange symbols supposedly indicate the location of the eye of the divine. Now we just have to get our hands on it. Otherwise all of us—you, Kai,

Professor Chen, and I—will die agonizing deaths. Professor Chen, being older, is already starting to suffer."

"What a story," I told her. "I can't believe your grandfather was the Partridge. I'm trying to let it sink in."

"It is pretty incredible. I hope you're not scared," said Julie. "Because I need your help finding the location of the eye of the divine."

"What!" I cried. "Of course I'm not scared. And I'm not going to just stand by while you and the professor are in danger. While all four of us are." I stood from the park bench and started to walk off.

"Where are you going?" Julie called after me.

I turned around. "We've been talking all afternoon, and it's getting late. Kai and Gold Tooth are still waiting for us at the market. I should help pack up the stall." I gestured for her to follow me. "We can go find Professor Qiu in Shaanxi tomorrow. He has to reveal what he knows."

Julie sighed. "Impulsive as always." She got up and we headed out the way we'd come. "It's never going to be as simple as that," she went on. "Why do you think Professor Qiu is so tight-lipped? Don't you think he might be afraid for his own safety?"

"Could be," I admitted. "Or maybe someone in power is putting pressure on him to be silent. You Americans don't understand certain things about Chinese society."

Julie shook her head, confused. "Like what?"

"Let me give you an example. Let's say a powerful figure announces that one plus one equals three. Then along comes Professor Qiu to prove that one plus one adds up to two. Because the guy who spoke first is more powerful, he's not going to want to be contradicted. Professor Qiu might have deciphered the dragon bone writing and discovered something that didn't fit with the present social order, so his bosses would have told him to keep his mouth shut. That might be why he was behaving so strangely."

Now that I knew what was at stake, I was more determined than ever to shake the truth out of the professor. I'd be saving myself *and* paying back Julie for the time she'd saved my life.

"Let's go get Kai and Gold Tooth," I now said to her. "We need their help. We'll plan our next move over dinner."

Back at Pan Market, we found the other two wrapping up a deal selling some jade headbands. These were poor specimens, but business had been so good these few days that we were now scraping the bottom of the barrel, and we would soon need to make another trip to Shaanxi to replenish.

I helped pack up, and then we headed to a restaurant. Once we were seated, Julie filled the others in on the startling tale she had told me and announced that I was going to help her find the eye of the divine.

Gold Tooth's eyes were wide. "I think it would be better to just stay here and enjoy a few more good years," he said. "Business is booming! If you go reverse dipping instead, well, you never know how things will turn out. Those tombs are full of dumplings."

"But, Gold Tooth," Kai said, "we'd need to reverse dip anyway. How else are we going to get more stock to sell? Don't worry, we won't make you go with us. If there really are dumplings, count on me to deal with them."

The older man grinned, flashing his gold tooth. "Tough guy! Everyone knows you're a real hard case."

Kai nodded, then frowned. "Wait, are you making fun of me?"

"Not at all," said Gold Tooth smoothly.

Seeing Julie silent and frowning, I knew she was worrying about Professor Chen. "All right, guys, let's get down to business," I said. "And, Kai, this is a nice restaurant, so don't sit with your legs up like that."

"It's comfortable," Kai said. But he lowered his feet, which were resting on the chair, his knees bent upward.

"All right, we need a plan. How are we going to get this eye of the divine?" I continued.

Kai perked up. I was pretty sure he was excited to go reverse dipping again, and he didn't care about finding the eye as long as we got to break into tombs and steal treasure. Gold Tooth's eyes were sparkling too—any antiques we brought back would sell for a pretty penny. And with his black-market connections, he'd be able to get us whatever we needed for our expedition.

The four of us talked for a while before finally deciding that our first step would have to be deciphering the dragon bone. The next morning, Julie and I would go find Professor Qiu and pry the meaning of those symbols out of him. Meanwhile, Kai and Gold Tooth would stay in Beijing and make the necessary preparations.

Julie handed me the gold-hunting charm left behind by World's End. I was thrilled—it made me feel like a proper reverse dipper. It seemed the fates had bound us as a trio of reverse dippers.

Julie also brought back some of the gold-hunting apparatus left behind by her grandfather: a steel umbrella, a corpse rope, flying-tiger claws, a whirlwind digger, seeking-dragon smoke, a wind-cloud sack, corpse incense, corpse gloves, northern pearls, a yin-yang mirror, and water-fire shoes. There was also a bag of various gold-hunting remedies for poison and various afflictions.

These were the things that gold hunters had relied on for centuries, and now we had access to them too. Many of them I'd heard of but had never actually set eyes on.

With these traditional implements, plus the modern tools Kai and Gold Tooth would pack—shovels, flashlights, gas masks, binoculars—we'd be prepared for anything. Still, when we'd failed in the past, it was usually because we'd underestimated our opponents. That's how it is with reverse dipping—experience and courage are much more important than any amount of equipment. And we had the experience, though none actually counted as reverse dipping. The excursion with Kai at Wild Man Valley was to a deserted military installation; the Jingjue City expedition with Julie, Professor Chen, and Kai was technically an archaeological dig; and the Dragon Ridge tomb was empty. Still, they had been arduous experiences, and we'd learned a lot from them.

Even so, we were talking about people's final resting places, which meant a lot to the ancients. Any tomb we entered would be full of defenses—we'd have to be careful.

Our discussion over, we parted and headed to our respective lodgings. The next morning, Julie and I caught a flight to Xi'an, and from there we took a train to Professor Qiu's archaeological camp at Gulan. There, we were told that an accident had shut down the site, and Professor Qiu had left abruptly.

CHAPTER THIRTY-ONE

LUCKILY, MR. LIU TOLD US THAT PROFESSOR QIU HAD LEFT for Stone Tablet Village, not far from Gulan, half a day ago. He counseled us to take a guide, as the landscape was confusing. With that, he hollered into the street, and a boy of ten or so with a shaved head came running to us. Mr. Liu introduced him as his great-nephew, who came regularly to Gulan for his school vacations.

"Erxiao, enough playing," he told the boy. "Be good and take my friends to Stone Tablet. They're looking for that archaeologist, Professor Qiu."

Erxiao was covered with dirt and had a runny nose. He nodded happily and skipped ahead to lead the way.

Stone Tablet was indeed difficult to get to, passing over

uneven ground and narrow pathways that were as twisted as sheep intestines. Erxiao cheerfully told us it wasn't far off, just on the high peak up ahead.

Julie couldn't stand looking at this filthy child, and she finally got out her handkerchief to wipe his nose. "Your name is Erxiao? What's your surname?"

The kid dabbed at his nose. "Wang. I'm called Wang Erxiao."

"Hello, Wang Erxiao. I hope you're not leading us into a trap," I joked.

"What's a trap?" the boy asked, staring at me.

Julie smiled. "An innocent lamb. How refreshing," she said.

"You're pretty," Erxiao told her.

I playfully swatted Erxiao on the head. "You've got good taste. But you're too young to look at women. Kids these days . . . if they're not hooligans, they're lovesick."

Before I'd finished speaking, a tall man with a white bandanna around his head appeared around the corner. "Stay where you are!" he said, brandishing a heavy wooden club. "Did you say you're hooligans?"

I jumped, not having expected anyone to be out here in the wilderness. "Hey, lower your weapon. We're all friends here. No need to cause trouble."

The man looked me up and down, waving the club aggressively the whole time. "You're the one causing trouble. You can't enter this area. It's been sealed off by local soldiers."

I didn't know if the guy was a soldier himself, but I doubted any would be armed with wooden clubs. Just as I was about to get into a proper fight with him, Erxiao ran forward. Fortunately, the man broke into a grin. It turned out that he and

Erxiao knew each other from the village, and just like that, the man put away his club.

The man spoke with a thick country accent. It took me a long time before I could finally understand what he was trying to tell us.

It turned out that Stone Tablet Village—which got its name from a nearby ten-foot-high stone tablet from some past dynasty—used to have the only maker of coffins for miles around. He'd started out as a carpenter, and one day, he happened to be constructing a coffin when he took a dinner break before applying the usual eighteen layers of lacquer to the wood. After drinking a few glasses of beer, he began reflecting on how bad business was lately. The coffin was the first order he'd had in more than two weeks. In a temper, he thumped the side of the coffin and sighed, then fell into a drunken slumber on the lid.

That night, he had a dream: the coffin was filled with a large clump of ice—ice so cold that he began shivering violently, as if he'd fallen into a frosted cave. Suddenly, someone thumped urgently on the door of his home, waking him up. He opened the door to find someone in need of another coffin. One of the villagers had died in the night.

It was rare for two jobs to follow so closely together. The carpenter was overjoyed, but out of respect, he plastered a mournful look on his face. As he made a show of grief, he waved his arms and happened to hit the nearly finished coffin. The neighbor handed over a deposit and left him to get on with the new order.

The sun wasn't fully overhead when his work was interrupted again. There had been another death and another coffin was needed. It seemed odd. There were only a handful of deaths in the village every year, and now there had been two in a matter of hours.

The coffin maker thought something must be wrong, then recalled his dream of the night before. He wondered if he could have caused these deaths by hitting the coffin? To find out, he slapped the half-finished coffin again. Before nightfall, there had been a third death.

He was both anxious and delighted—anxious because he had no idea what was going on, and delighted because he'd never need to worry about his business again. He was on the road to riches. It didn't matter to him that people he knew were dying. Soon he was doing so well he could barely keep up with demand.

His workshop was now completely devoted to making coffins. He discovered another secret: the harder he hit the special coffin, which he ended up keeping for himself, the farther away the death would be. That was when he decided to buy up all the nearby coffin businesses. Now that he had a monopoly, he just had to hit the side of that half-finished coffin and the money would start rolling in.

He didn't dare do this too often—who knew what was really going on?

The secret never left his lips, but secrets have a way of being discovered. Eventually, the villagers grew suspicious and started whispering about what he was up to. There was no proof, of course, so they could hardly report him to the police, but everyone started looking at him as if he were the god of death himself, and they stayed as far from him as they could. He never found a woman willing to marry him.

Not long before our visit, the coffin maker had died at home. By the time his body was discovered, it already stank to high heaven. His shop was empty—he'd sold all his coffins. The only one left was the half-finished one. The villagers had heard the rumors and were all terrified, but the village council had to take action. After all, they couldn't very well leave him to rot in his own house; it was summer, and a body might spread disease. Several brave villagers carried the corpse over to the unfinished coffin that remained.

When they shifted the coffin into position, they saw that it had been resting over a crack in the ground. It looked like a deep crevice, and when some of the men stuck their hands in, they felt an icy wind. Curious, they pried up the floor tiles around the area, revealing a cave beneath the floor.

The leader of the local brigade volunteered to go investigate. They lowered him in a basket, but a short while later, he was frantically tugging at the rope to be hauled back up again. When he surfaced, he was quaking with fear. It took a while for him to calm down and tell the others about the brick-lined room he had seen belowground. The room had a stone bed, on which was a stone box covered in strange writing.

He had opened the box to find that it contained six red-jade animals, strange beasts he couldn't identify. Searching the room, he noticed another level going below, but it was pitch-dark, and he'd been too frightened to go any deeper.

The soldiers followed proper procedure and reported the incident right away. Professor Qiu and his team were called to investigate.

The village was abuzz with excitement and rumors. Every-one wanted to see exactly what was going on. To maintain order, the professor told the soldiers to keep gawkers well away from the workshop and the underground cave. He didn't know what was down there and wasn't about to risk it getting damaged. The soldiers set up a checkpoint at the village entrance, which is why Julie and I got stopped.

"Sir," I said, knowing I'd have to come up with a reason for him to let us pass, "Ms. Yang and I are close associates of Professor Qiu. We have urgent information for him. Can you please help us get to him?"

The soldier looked at us warily, clearly suspicious. But before he could decide anything, a woman rushed up from the village.

"Professor Qiu is dead! The professor's dead!" she shouted.

CHAPTER THIRTY-TWO

JULIE AND I STARED AT ONE ANOTHER, OUR BRAINS BUZZING.

The woman proceeded to tell the soldier what had happened. Professor Qiu and another archaeologist had been lowered into the cave in a basket. After more than an hour, the soldiers shouted down but got no reply. Worried there had been an accident, the soldiers determined they should investigate, but certain this was the road to death, if not hell itself, no one volunteered to go underground. The soldier at this checkpoint, who happened to be the brigade leader, was the same one who'd gone into the cave earlier, so the village elder sent the woman to fetch him.

Sensing an opportunity, Julie shot me a glance. "Professor Qiu may not be dead," she said. "He may just need help."

"That's right," I said, knowing it was up to Julie and me to get the two men back.

I grabbed the soldier's hand. "Sir, it's an honor to shake your hand. You were the first hero to brave the dangers of the cave. Now it's our turn." The soldier puffed up visibly at my words, and I continued on. "I know what these caves are like. You've already been down into its freezing depths once. And since Professor Qiu is a friend of ours, Ms. Yang and I will go down again on your behalf. That way, we'll get to save an old friend and follow your brave example."

He smiled but shook his head. "It's not that I don't want to let you in," he replied. "It's just that we've been given orders. No strangers are to be allowed. Sorry."

I was getting angry. I'd tried bribery and flattery, and neither had worked. Now I was going to play dirty. I grabbed the end of the soldier's wooden club and scowled at him. "Listen, Ms. Yang is a special representative from America. If you get in our way, she'll get in touch with her embassy, and next thing you know, your brigade will be disbanded. You think you're so important? Look at her—she's getting impatient. I can see it in her face. I'm only telling you all this for your own good, because you seem like a nice guy. Now will you let us in?"

The soldier was clearly having second thoughts. After a moment, he meekly led the way.

I gave Mr. Liu's great-nephew a couple of yuan and told him to return to Gulan and buy himself a treat.

Julie and I didn't dare delay. We hurried after the soldier into Stone Tablet Village, which was in a little basin surrounded by higher ground. This was an excellent place to be situated—in dry weather, the pressure was different enough in the valley that it rained anyway, and when the Yellow River flooded, the hills kept the water out. The population was five or six hundred, and as we looked down at their houses, everything appeared neat and orderly.

Not far ahead we spotted the giant stone tablet, the writing on it long worn away. At its foot was a headless beast of some sort. Even as Julie and I rushed by on our way to rescue Professor Qiu, we couldn't help stopping to take a closer look, but there was no way to tell its origin.

"It doesn't seem to be a tombstone," Julie said. "Have you seen anything like it before?"

"Never!"

I looked around as I kept walking. This was a quiet spot with mild weather, perfect for a village, yet the surrounding hills were jagged and disorderly, not suitable for burials. I didn't think there'd be an ancient tomb here. Even if there was, it surely wouldn't belong to an aristocrat. But the soldier had said the first level of this underground cave had brick-lined walls and a stone bed. What lay below it?

All our hopes were resting on Professor Qiu. There could be a dragon's nest down there and we'd still have to get him out. Julie and I hurried on.

The soldier led us to a workshop on the east side of the village. An inscription hung over the door, and a swarm of villagers were gathered near the shop, gawking at the fuss. Even if they were eager to see what was happening, I doubted any of them would dare step through that door. Everyone was afraid of ghosts, discussing fervently whether this cave led to the dragon palace beneath the Yellow River, and whether this disturbance would anger the Dragon King and prompt him to flood the valley—or, if the cave was a portal to hell, whether it was better to seal it tight at night to keep hungry spirits from creeping up from the underworld. A man who turned out to be the local elementary schoolteacher had an even more persuasive theory: "All of you are wrong. This is all just superstition. Listen, didn't they say there's cold air coming up from the opening? Obviously the hole leads to the South Pole. Ice is going to start falling through from the other side of the world, and it'll drown all you idiots."

As the wheels turned in every villager's brain, Julie and I followed the soldier into the workshop, where he introduced us to the village elder and his fellow brigade members. He announced that Julie and I would be going into the hole.

The village elder hugged me tightly. "You are welcome. We hope you will find the two archaeologists alive. If it weren't for all the stories about the coffin maker and his strange power, the villagers would be less afraid. Even our local soldiers aren't trained to carry out such a mission."

I understood what he was saying—he wanted to push all the responsibility onto me. I wasn't going to waste time arguing, so I brushed past him and looked at the underground cave. The fissure was wide, and it was dark in there. I didn't have any equipment with me and didn't see how Julie and I were going to do this by ourselves. We needed help.

Including the leader of the soldiers, there were eight men now standing here with their clubs, rifles, and blazing torches. I stood before them and said, "Please listen! Two of our colleagues are in trouble. I know you are anxious about what lurks below, but we need your help. This is probably some ancient ruin, not a pathway to hell. And you won't be working for free—I'm offering you a hundred yuan each, plus an extra hundred if you get the archaeologists out. Are you on board?"

The soldiers had been unwilling to risk their lives, but upon hearing that they might earn two hundred yuan each, they perked up. Standing straight, faces growing determined, they answered yes resoundingly.

Money had won the day. I got them to bring all the rifles they had, while the village elder got us some candles and flashlights. Everyone also got a whistle made from local tree bark.

Julie nudged me. "Don't forget, there are at least two levels we need to descend, but what if it goes even farther down than that? Professor Qiu might have ventured deep, and who knows what he encountered. Let's cover our mouths and noses with damp towels and make sure we have torches with us. If the torches go out, we have to leave at once."

I nodded in agreement, then told everyone to follow Julie's instructions. Three soldiers were left at the surface to raise and lower the basket, while the village elder and his council would guard the front door, not letting any other villagers in.

When everything seemed ready and I was just about to be lowered, a commotion started at the door. A blind man barged in. He wore dark glasses, had a scraggly beard, and was clutching a tattered old book and brandishing a bamboo walking stick. "Who's in charge here?" he hollered. "I need to talk to whoever's in charge."

"Didn't I tell you to keep everyone out?" I shouted at the village elder. "How did he get in? Send him away. We're wasting time."

The blind man hurled himself into the room and lashed out in the direction of my voice, whacking me with his stick.

"What a rude young man! I'll forgive you, though, as I'm here to save your life."

The village elder rushed over to me. "Mr. Hu, this is a famous fortune-teller in our province," he said to me. "Last year, my wife was bewitched by a fox spirit, and this gentleman lifted the spell and saved her life. You should listen to what he has to say. He's never wrong."

"I don't have time for this!" I roared. "I thought they'd gotten rid of all you village charlatans. Get out of my way."

The blind man's lips twisted into a sneer. "I was once the personal seer for the commander in chief of Jiangxi, back before you were ever born," he railed at me. "I'm not going to stand by while you get innocent people to risk their lives for nothing. Be warned, if I told you what awaited you in that hole, you would be quaking."

I was ready to shove him into the hole myself, but he seemed to have the respect of the villagers, and I didn't want to offend anyone. "Go on, then, tell me," I snapped. "If I don't get frightened, will you stay out of my way?"

"I can't reveal what awaits you below, but if you enter this cave, you must bring me with you. Without my guidance, you'll go in vertical but come out horizontal."

Julie had been listening quietly, but now she stepped boldly up to the blind man. "Do you think there's an ancient tomb down there, and that if we bring you with us you'll be able to help yourself to a treasure or two? If you say another word, I'll have you chased out of here."

The blind man was startled, and he lowered his voice. "Ah, so the young lady is in the profession. Could you both be gold hunters? All right, seeing as we're all in the same business, I won't keep you in the dark any longer. I was known in the field, long ago. Lost my sight reverse dipping in Yunnan. Now I'm old, wandering these villages and telling fortunes to feed myself. Why not bring me along? Share the wealth? I'll just use it to buy myself a coffin."

Julie looked like she didn't know whether to laugh or cry. She glanced at me, and I shook my head. This guy was probably more trouble than he was worth, and besides, this cave didn't look like an ancient tomb. Even if it was, why should we cut him in?

Though he couldn't see us, the blind man seemed to know exactly what we were thinking. "I have a copy of *Duozi's Visual Map*. It's yours if you share the treasure with me," he told us.

"I've heard of this document," I said. "A map of meridians. I believe there's only one copy in the world. If you really have such a precious item, why not sell it instead of begging us to let you tag along? Do you think we're idiots? It's probably a bad egg." That's gold-hunting slang for counterfeit treasure.

"No matter what, I'm older than you. You ought to treat me with more respect. Do you want all these people to think you don't know how to behave? Ever since ancient times, feng shui has been a closely held secret. No one but a true member of the gold-hunting order should be allowed to look at these mysteries. How could I just hand this knowledge over to a civilian? Make your decision."

We had delayed far too long already. "Fine, whatever you say. Even if there aren't any grave goods down there, I'll buy your *Duozi's Visual Map* with my own money. But you can't come down with us. Help me out here instead, and say something to these soldiers to calm their nerves and give them courage."

The blind man obligingly called the soldiers over. "Gentlemen, this is no ordinary cave," he told them. "Back in the day, when First Emperor Qin was visiting, he found the pill of immortality in this underground cavern. It was he who put up the stone tablet outside your village. Later on, the Western Chu warlord Xiang Yu and Emperor Liu Bang of Han both used this cave as a refuge in wartime. They were successful, for they absorbed the energies of the cave. Brothers, I say you have the strength of tigers. Get to the bottom of the mysterious cave and your lives will soar hereafter."

This seemed enough to galvanize the men. I cut off the blind fortune-teller before he could say anything too ridiculous, and we started our descent: me and the leader of the soldiers in the first basket, then the next four men, and finally Julie.

CHAPTER THIRTY-THREE

THE LEADER AND I EACH HELD A LIT TORCH AND A RIFLE. Looking up, I saw the opening twenty or so meters above us. It looked like a natural formation, with no sign of human interference. We were in a broad tunnel, about seven meters high and ten meters wide, paved with long stone slabs. The walls were covered in beads of moisture, and cold and dampness penetrated my bones.

Gulan was generally a dry area, so for the soil to be damp only twenty meters down must have had something to do with Stone Tablet Village's unusual geography. Because it was in a valley, and the rainy season was so long, more water accumulated here than in the surrounding areas. If there had ever been an ancient tomb here, it would probably have been ruined long ago.

We could see the contours of our surroundings clearly. In addition to the fissure we'd descended into, there were also numerous cracks opening off the tunnel, as if this were an earthquake zone. Luckily, though the passageway was simply constructed, it also looked extremely sturdy, with no sign that it might collapse.

The leader pointed up ahead, saying that was where he'd seen the stone platform with the box on it. The village council was holding on to it for safekeeping.

"What happened when you went farther in?" I asked.

The leader shook his head. "There was another hole in the floor. It looked deep, and when I shined my flashlight in, I couldn't see anything at all. The wind that rose out of it gave me goose bumps. I didn't dare look, just grabbed the stone box and ran. Oh yes, I heard water down there."

As all seven of us made our way to the stone-lined room, we called Professor Qiu's name. There were distant echoes and the dripping of water, but no other stirrings.

The stone-lined room was about the size of a regular apartment and was made from stacked rock rounds. The entrance was a semicircular opening with no door, and although it was obviously human-made, there was a natural grace about it. I asked Julie if she could tell what the room had been used for, but she didn't know. We went through the round opening and found nothing inside but the stone bed.

It was a neatly shaped smooth platform that didn't look like the typical resting place in a tomb. We examined it from every angle but couldn't work out what it was for. In front of it was a square hole opening onto a forty-five-degree tunnel deep enough that when I shined my flashlight in, I couldn't see the bottom. It was possible to walk down the slope, and we wondered if that was where Professor Qiu had gone. I called down to him a few times, but there was no answer.

I led the way, leaving two of the soldiers behind to guard the entrance, just in case. As we descended the stone-paved passage, we could hear water flowing somewhere beneath us. Suddenly, I was worried that Professor Qiu had fallen in and drowned. I quickened my steps. When we got to the bottom, we found ourselves in a human-made cavern, with a pool in the center. The water seemed black in our flashlight beams, too deep to see what lay beneath. Several metal loops had been fixed to the ceiling, from which thick chains dangled into the water. These were made of some strange black material that didn't appear to be metal, but I couldn't tell what else it might be. When we tried to have a closer look, some of the chains suddenly twitched violently, sending ripples across the placid pool.

The five of us remaining—Julie, the leader, two soldiers and I—all stepped back at the unexpected movement. There was no wind here, so what had made the heavy chains move?

I glanced at Julie, but she shrugged and shook her head at me. It seemed clear that we had to take the risk of raising whatever it was to the surface, in case it had something to do with Professor Qiu's whereabouts.

The soldiers were starting to get uneasy. These were tough rural folk who would have faced an armed platoon without qualms, but thousands of years' worth of superstition were deeply rooted in them, and the chains made them unsettled.

"Mr. H-Hu," the leader stammered. "What if there's some sort of . . . monster down there? If we disturb it, it might come eat our whole village."

The two soldiers nodded in agreement. "Yes, yes, maybe it's the Yellow River monster," one of them said. "If we set it free, there'll be another disaster."

While they spoke, I frantically scanned the cave for something to convince them it was safe. If they got spooked and ran away, Julie and I wouldn't be able to do much on our own.

I was absolutely certain there wasn't a tomb down here. I knew my feng shui, and Stone Tablet Village lay in a valley. While the surroundings were certainly beautiful, there was also too much water underground, and no one in their right mind would want to be buried here.

Besides, I was familiar with tombs from all periods, and neither the tunnel nor the stone room looked like a burial chamber. If anything, the stone platform looked like an altar— the sort used to arrange grave goods on.

Looking around the cavern, I couldn't see any other way out. This was the end of the road. Professor Qiu and his colleague had definitely come down here, so where were they? In the water? I felt one of the chains—it was in fact metal, coated with some strange substance that absorbed light and prevented rust.

The chains were still shaking a little. The movement didn't look like the result of an underwater current—a living thing was probably causing it. Could there be some giant turtle, or even a dragon, held captive down there? Of course, I couldn't say anything to the soldiers about my thoughts. Then I remembered the blind fortune-teller and, like him, decided to fight superstition with superstition. The most urgent thing was to haul up whatever was down there and see if it helped us find Professor Qiu. So, with a resolute expression, I turned to the soldiers. "Listen, everyone, this is a test of our spirit. Blood may flow and heads may roll, but we have to pull up those chains."

The leader stepped forward. "Mr. Hu, it's the Yellow River monster down there. You're asking us to cause big trouble. We won't do it."

I wasn't too sure about the wisdom of this move either, but I kept my face full of confidence. "Don't you remember what our friend the fortune-teller said?" I made my voice boom in an attempt at authority. "That blind man, the reincarnation of Zhuge Liang, has five hundred past lives and eight thousand years of knowledge. He said this is a celestial cave, and I know he's right. In my studies of antiquity, I've seen descriptions of such places. Deep within this pool is a heavenly furnace where the magic pills of immortality are forged. If we can acquire such a marvel, then according to international law, we should . . . we should . . ."

Julie saved me. "According to international law, whoever first discovers such an object enjoys naming rights," she chimed in.

"Yes, precisely! Do you know what naming rights are?" I pointed at one of the soldiers. "Let's say you, soldier Li Dazhuang. If you were willing, we could name the pill of immortality the Dazhuang pill. And when our nation's factories begin manufacturing this medicine and distributing it for the benefit of all, everyone will know of your contribution. And of course, the five of us will be the first to take these pills. I can guarantee that."

The soldiers looked at each other, clearly convinced. The combined force of superstition and national glory, not to mention the lure of immortality, was all it took to sway them. There was one other worry, though: if this was a celestial furnace, why were the chains moving?

I tried to bluff through that. "As for the chains, they're moving because . . . because the pills have so much energy in them. A true life force."

Everyone nodded; they seemed to think this made sense. Certain now that this was a celestial furnace and not the river monster, they started rolling up their sleeves.

"Tianyi, are you sure?" Julie asked me softly. "There might really be a living creature down there."

"Trust me. I wouldn't play around with our safety. Look at all the situations I've gotten us out of. Judging by the feng shui of this area, I can guarantee there's no ancient tomb down here, so we don't need to worry about dumplings. And this is a peaceful valley, not some deep forest, so there isn't some fierce animal lurking in the water. Even if there is, it's chained, and we have rifles. But if it's Professor Qiu down there, would you want to delay a second longer? And it might be him—we don't know."

"It's not that I don't trust you," said Julie, "but you don't make it easy. So what are you going to say to these village men when they're done hauling up the chains and there's no celestial furnace or magic pills?"

I sighed. "I have no clue. But I'm hoping you'll help me out."

The men were ready now, and the leader shouted at me to get into place. Julie and I stuck our torches into the ground near the water's edge and stood with our rifles cocked and ready.

"Go ahead!" I shouted.

The three soldiers pulled the chains in unison, as if pulling buckets from a well. It looked like the mechanism was so well designed that not much effort was needed.

My palms were sweating, and Julie looked fearful too as those chains creaked their way up. More than ten meters of links passed before our eyes. Then, with an enormous splash, something dark and heavy broke the surface.

"Praise the ancestors!" the leader exclaimed. "You were right, Mr. Hu! That's the celestial furnace of immortality!"

CHAPTER THIRTY-FOUR

THE CHAINS ROSE A COUPLE OF FEET MORE, AND NOW A HUGE black object was dangling above the surface. In the hazy light of the torches, we couldn't quite see what it was, only that it was round and crudely fashioned, similar to a water tank. This definitely wasn't any sort of animal.

None of us had actually seen a celestial furnace—could this be one? Had my nonsense somehow been the right guess? There are stranger coincidences in the world. I got Julie to point her flashlight at the object and picked up a torch as I went closer to investigate.

The soldiers were fixing the chains in place so the thing would stay suspended over the water. The pool was no more than three meters across—really more like a large well than a pool—so we were able to reach out and touch the thing.

At closer range, we could see that there were mystical carvings all over the container, which was covered with tiny holes. Julie and I couldn't guess what it was for. It was hard to tell even what period it was from. And what secret could it hold that it needed to be held by so many chains?

A heavy cone-shaped lid sat atop the container, fastened by six latches. Water had been draining through the little holes as we watched. Although this thing was shaped like a water tank, it seemed to have the opposite function.

By this time, even someone as slow as the leader could tell this was no celestial furnace. "Mr. Hu, do you know, this reminds me of the leaky old urn that sits in my garden."

"That's not possible," I said. "Does your urn have so many intricate carvings? Look at that design—this has to be an ancient artifact. Now you'll just have to wait for the government's cultural bureau to bestow a finder's reward on your brigade."

"I think I know what this is," Julie said. "It's a torture implement."

"You mean the sort of thing where you stick your prisoner inside, dunk him into the water, then pull him up again so the water drains out, just before he has time to drown? I've seen those in movies. But why bother with fine carvings on a torture device? Anyway, no point in guessing. Let's just open it and see what comes out. For all we know, it might actually hold immortality pills."

"Is that a good idea, Mr. Hu? What if there's a demon inside?"

"How many times do I have to tell you—there couldn't possibly be anything like that in this place. Don't be so spooked."

Seeing that they weren't going to talk me out of it, the soldiers gave me a leg up so I could reach the top of the strange object. I grabbed hold of one of the sturdy chains and ran a hand over the surface of the tank. Sure enough, it was painted metal, much more solid than a normal ceramic urn. What on earth could this be holding? I decided to open the lid just a crack, ready to clamp it down again if anything inside moved.

Although they'd been underwater, the latches weren't rusty in the least but clicked open easily. I'd gotten five of them open when the strange container wobbled, as if something in it was thrashing about. Taken off guard, I grabbed a chain. Whatever it was flung itself against the sides.

Julie and the soldiers screamed the professor's name, telling him to stay calm. But the noise continued, and no voice answered. I threw the final latch open. Still holding on to the chains for balance, I kicked the lid off.

The inside of the container was inky black. The others held up their torches, but that just blinded me and made it harder to see inside. I bent over, intending to ask Julie to toss a flashlight to me, but as my face neared the opening, I caught a whiff of a stench so foul it made me gag.

Covering my nose, I peered into the darkness. A pale human hand rose toward me. "Professor Qiu?" I yelped, reaching to pull him out.

As soon as my hand closed around it, I knew something was wrong. This hand was cold and hard—not a living person's hand. The realization dawned a second too late, though, because I'd already started pulling reflexively before I realized this hand was just bones, and an entire skeleton was attached to it.

Even in this dim light, I could see the stark white skeleton clearly, glistening with water droplets. I screamed and took a step back, sliding off the container and falling headfirst into the pool.

The water was bone-piercingly cold and went straight up my nostrils with a sharp jab of pain. Luckily, Kai and I had often gone swimming in the sea as children, and the water felt like second nature to me. I felt no fear at all as I kept my eyes open, though there was no light, and searched for my way up to the surface. I was dizzy from the fall, and with darkness all around, I had no sense of direction. There was no sound. If I couldn't figure out which way was up, I was going to die down here.

Just as I was giving up hope, there was a burst of light— someone was swimming toward me with a waterproof flashlight. As the figure came closer, I saw that it was Julie.

I grabbed her outstretched hand. Her other hand held a rope, and at her signal, the soldiers hauled us back, gasping, to the surface. "Tianyi, that was so close," Julie said, panting, her face pale. "If I'd been just a few seconds later . . ."

Another strange noise came from the suspended container, as if someone was pounding the sides for help. Our heads snapped up as we wondered, could there be a ghost in there?

"Don't worry, I'll go take another look," I said to Julie. "If I fall in again, I'll need you to give me mouth-to-mouth."

She rolled her eyes at me and pointed at the soldiers. "Sure, I bet those guys will be happy to."

"Why so harsh?" I smiled. "I'd do the same for you, and yet—"

"You know what?" she interrupted. "You and Kai, you've never cared about life or death. A situation like this, and you're still joking around. Why not be serious? What did you see up there, anyway, that made you fall in?"

I blinked, not wanting to tell the truth in case she thought I'd been too easily scared. "When I opened the lid, I saw some sort of trap. So I calmly flipped backward to avoid it, and that's how I fell in."

"Forget I asked. I might as well go look for myself." And with that, Julie scraped her wet hair back and piled it into a loose bun, then got the soldiers to give her a boost up to the container, which was still emitting peculiar sounds. The men were definitely jittery and seemed certain a monster was going to hurl itself out at any moment. I warned them not to fire and tossed a flashlight up to Julie, yelling that there was a skeleton inside. With that warning, hopefully she wouldn't be startled into falling like I had.

She stayed up there quite a while, rooting around inside the container. When she jumped down, she was brandishing a jade bracelet. We all stared at it, completely clueless. After my time in Pan Market, I'd developed a good enough eye for antiques that I could tell at a glance this was fake, worth a couple of yuan at most. Was the skeleton that of a woman? How long had she been in there? Had her corpse been put into the container, or had she been alive when she went into the water? None of this made any sense.

"Tianyi, guess what was making that racket?" Julie asked.

"The skeleton. It must be possessed."

"Nice imagination." She laughed. "No, it wasn't a bone demon. I had a good look. There are three skeletons, all adults, and a couple of dozen strange fish, two or three feet long. They seem unusually strong—even with all the water gone, they're still thrashing around. That's what's making the noise and causing the chains to rattle."

"That's strange. Are they special flesh-eating fish?"

"Don't know."

The leader butted in. "Mr. Hu, I've been staring at this bracelet, trying to remember where I've seen it before. I think it belonged to a woman in our village. She was married many years ago in another town. A few months back, she came for a visit, showing off this bracelet, bragging that she got it in Guangdong for a few thousand yuan. All the other wives were jealous and went home to demand expensive jewelry from their husbands too."

I could guess where this was going and urged him to finish the story.

"The woman left without saying goodbye, and we all thought she must have had an argument with her parents and run off home to her husband. But now it seems she was attacked and ended up in this pot."

Before I could reply, we heard footsteps approaching down the passage. I thought it was the two soldiers we'd left on the level above coming to see if we were all right, but instead Professor Qiu emerged. A man followed him.

I ran over to them. "Professor Qiu, you're alive! You almost scared us to death. I've come all this way to see you. Then I thought you'd been eaten by fish. Where did you just appear from?"

The professor smiled, as if he'd been expecting to see us. I quickly explained the situation.

Taking a closer look around the cave, Professor Qiu said, "This tank is an awful device—I've seen something like it in Yunnan. But this isn't a matter for archaeologists anymore. I'm going to call the police. Everyone, let's go. Be careful not to disturb the scene of the crime. We can talk more when we've gotten out of here."

With that, everyone obediently trooped back the way we'd come.

The village elder was delighted to see us all unharmed. I gave the soldiers the cash we'd promised them, and although they were disappointed not to have tasted the pills of immortality, the money was a nice boost.

After instructing the village council to call the police, the professor took Julie and me to dinner. I had many questions about what happened in the cave, and I asked them all on the way. Professor Qiu explained that he'd gone into the cave with his assistant, and he too had seen the chains descending into the pool. They hadn't tried to raise the container, though. Going back the way they'd come, they found a hidden passageway at the top of the first tunnel, leading to a space with a lot of stone tablets.

The hidden tunnel ran parallel to the one we knew about, only lower down. Because it was out of our line of sight, we hadn't seen it. The professor only happened to notice it on his way back, when his flashlight dipped. He'd led his assistant down that way, examining the stone tablets, only to find that because this passage was lower, there was much more water damage. Part of the roof had collapsed behind them, leaving them trapped.

Luckily, the professor and his assistant were eventually

able to move aside the debris and climb out. When they got back to the surface, they saw the two soldiers standing guard, and when we didn't show up after a while, they came looking for us.

As far as he could tell, the tunnels dated back to the Qin dynasty. There were others in the area, from expeditions led by the first emperor's alchemists. There wasn't much archaeological significance to them, apart from the stone tablets, which would be valuable to scholars.

"What about the red-jade animals found inside the stone box?" I asked. "And that strange dunking tank. Do they date back to the Qin dynasty as well?" Professor Qiu shook his head. "The stone box and that underground chamber, including the chains and container, all came much later. While I was in Gulan, I heard that people around here would go missing every few years, but I didn't put two and two together. I'm no detective, but I've formed a theory about what might have happened here. It's not a national secret, so I'm happy to share it with you."

CHAPTER THIRTY-FIVE

Julie and I listened intently as Professor Qiu told us his theory.

"Before the Dian kingdom of Yunnan fell to the Western Han, there was already a great deal of unrest within the province, and in fact part of it had seceded. This community lived in the Congshan Hills, cut off from the rest of the world, until they were gradually erased from history, appearing only in a few obscure records.

"This tribe that left the ancient Dian kingdom naturally formed their own distinctive way of life. One of their unusual customs was to drown captives in underwater tanks and leave them there as fish food. These fish gained a great deal of strength from feasting daily on human flesh. The tribe believed this strength passed on to them when they subsequently killed the fish for their fish soup. The skeletons, meanwhile, were removed from the tank on the night of a full moon and ceremonially burned as an offering to the six jade beasts.

"Impossible to say how someone from Stone Tablet Village had got hold of this device, but by spreading rumors about the underground cave, they managed to create such dread that none of the villagers would go anywhere near it. Whoever this person was, they kept the secret until now. Was it the coffin maker? Was it someone else? That will have to wait for the police investigation."

Such was Professor Qiu's theory. Unfortunately, he finished speaking just as we were about to tuck into some braised fish, and I had to put down my chopsticks. "You're like the Asian Sherlock Holmes," I said, feeling a little nauseated.

"It's because I've seen a tank like that before, when I was in Yunnan," Professor Qiu said, clearly in a better mood this time around than at our last encounter. "It's originally from Southeast Asia—though I never expected this barbaric practice to still be going on now. And do you remember me saying Professor Chen once saved my life? That also happened in Yunnan."

"Hmm. Actually, Professor Chen is the reason Julie and I came to find you. What happened in Yunnan?" I asked. Professor Qiu sighed. "It's a story I'm ashamed of, but as it's been so many years, I might as well tell you. Professor Chen and I were sent to Yunnan for reeducation—a form of punishment that was meant to correct our thinking. Chen is more than ten years older than me, and I think he felt he needed to take care of me. I wasn't as well behaved as I should have been, and I got involved with a local widow. I don't think I need to tell you what a problem that would have been, given the strict morality of the time."

The professor continued. "I couldn't stand the pressure and criticism, and I was ready to hang myself. I was standing with my head through the noose, when Chen rushed in just then and cut me down. If he hadn't been there, I wouldn't be alive now."

I knew this was our opportunity. The professor was in an expansive mood, reminiscing about the past. I jumped in to say that Professor Chen's illness had gotten much worse, and Julie brought out the enlarged photograph of the strange writing on the dragon bone. We put it in front of the professor and said we were begging him, for the sake of his old friend Chen, to break his silence and tell us what this meant.

Right away, his face went pale. He hesitated for a while, chewing on his lower lip, before he finally said, "May I take this away and study it? Any information I share with you must be kept confidential. When we're all back in Gulan, the two of you come see me in my hotel."

Worried that he might change his mind, I said we'd hang on to the photo for now, then fixed a time to see him in Gulan the next day.

Right after dinner, Julie and I set off for Gulan. We'd barely left the village when we were stopped by the blind fortune-teller, who was trying once again to sell me his map. I'd almost forgotten about him. As for his map, I knew it was just a regular feng shui map that wouldn't be of much use. Everything on it was already in my books. Besides, the real thing would have had some value as an ancient artifact, but you could tell at a glance this was a cheap fake.

"Why don't you try your luck with someone who doesn't know any better?" I suggested.

"I want this to go to someone who truly understands it," he insisted.

"Anyone who truly understands it will know you have a counterfeit copy. Maybe you should just keep it for yourself."

Seeing that I was on to him, he put the map away and started begging us to bring him to Beijing, where he might be able to make some money telling fortunes.

He seemed so pathetic that I started to feel sorry for him. After some discussion, Julie and I decided that we could definitely help him and would bring him back with us and find him somewhere to live near Pan Market. Gold Tooth could look after him, and with that glib tongue of his, he might even be good for business. I warned him not to tell any more of his crazy fortunes, though, in case he got us accused of spreading public disorder.

He nodded hastily. "That makes sense. I'll hold my tongue. When we get to the capital, I'll know how to behave."

And so we brought him along to the Gulan hotel with us.

The next afternoon saw us waiting anxiously for Professor Qiu's return. Leaving the fortune-teller in his room, we met the professor at his hotel reception lounge.

He once again made us promise to keep any information he revealed to ourselves. "About the dragon bone—I didn't want to say this yesterday, because I was still concerned about giving away the secret," he said, "but I spent all night thinking about my friend Old Chen, and I think I have to speak up."

"I don't understand," I said. "What are you so scared of?

This is from thousands of years ago—what's there to keep secret?"

"It's not that it has to be kept secret; it's that the world might not be ready for this. The documents I have are highly classified. These strange dragon bone texts speak of incidents that would shock most people, things that are found nowhere in the historical record. We broke the code some time ago, but it's been so many years, I don't know if I can fully explain what it says. It's complicated—there are a lot of gaps in these manuscripts, and that creates the possibility of a deviation from the original. Getting a single word wrong might change the meaning entirely—"

"You told us all this professional stuff before," I interrupted, "and I still don't understand what it has to do with us. We just want to know about the northern pearl. Could you just look at Julie's photograph and tell us if that's mentioned anywhere?"

Professor Qiu took the enlargement and stared at it for quite a while. "I'm telling you this for Old Chen's sake. You were asking about the northern pearl. That's a subject I know quite a bit about. It was probably some sort of symbolic item used in rituals, and it resembles the human eye. The first recorded instances of its existence come from the Western Zhou. As for the original manufacturer, and what material it was made of, we still don't have that information. This text you're showing me is similar to others I've seen. I don't dare say this refers to the northern pearl, but I can state with confidence that this symbol, the one that looks a little like an eye, a little like a whirlpool, is the ancient word for 'phoenix.' What you see here is a description from the Western Zhou of the phoenix calling out over the mountains."

My mind filled with questions. "Phoenix? But that's just an animal that the ancients made up. Are you telling me they actually exist?"

"That's hard to say. These dragon bone texts were heavily encrypted to keep the knowledge from regular folk and generally contained national secrets—so I believe them absolutely. Though, you're right, phoenixes don't actually exist. So this could be a double code—a secret within a secret."

"So you think the word 'phoenix' is code for something else?" Julie asked.

"Not quite." Professor Qiu smiled. "In the past, the phoenix stood for good fortune, and over the centuries, various religions have co-opted that meaning. So that's one possible reading, though we don't know for sure what the symbolism was in this particular set of dragon bones. I'm just hypothesizing based on other manuscripts I've seen, and also from the context of this piece."

I nodded. "That fits, because the northern pearl was also known by another name: phoenix gall. I don't know where this name comes from, or what this sort of jade, shaped like an eye, has to do with the mythical creature. Professor, are there any references in this picture to an ancient tomb, or any other clues about the place?"

"None. I'm not keeping anything from you. I'll roughly translate the whole thing, and you'll see it just describes the phoenix crying out over the mountains, nothing else."

Julie and I looked at each other, feeling like we'd been

plunged back into the fog. We'd been so sure that this photograph would tell us something about where to find the northern pearl, but this was completely unhelpful. I got the professor to write out his translation anyway, and sure enough, there was no mention of its location. I read it several times to make sure I hadn't missed anything, but it seemed the trail was broken again.

Starting the search would be like finding a needle at the bottom of the ocean. I gritted my teeth in frustration, and a vein started throbbing in my head. Next to me, Julie was trembling a little, tears pooling in her eyes.

Seeing how despondent we were, Professor Qiu pulled out a photograph of his own and placed it on the table. "Don't despair. I took this picture yesterday. Look—if you were to go into the old forests of Yunnan, you might find something there."

The photo was of the six blood-red jade beasts, all of them strange, not quite like lions and tigers, some feathered, some one-eyed, all ferocious. They were striped with quicksilver, and although the handiwork was exquisite, you couldn't look at them without getting chills.

When I thought these had been in the possession of the coffin maker, I shuddered all over. "Professor, this box came from Stone Tablet Village. It's the stone box that was found beneath the coffin maker's workshop, right?"

"Yes. I thought you might find it useful, so I had my assistant take a photo. Look closely and see if you can spot the clue."

Julie had turned away from the hideous creatures, but hearing this, she immediately picked up the image and stared at it closely. "Professor, the beast with the single eye . . . an eye so big, so out of all proportion . . . it looks like the northern pearl."

"That's exactly what I thought," said the professor. "So you see, there's still hope."

We were thrilled for a moment, but then hesitated. The ancient Dian kingdom of Yunnan was all the way across the country from southern Xinjiang, so what did it have to do with the northern pearl? Unless, of course, this elusive artifact had been there all these years, hidden away in the tomb of some Dian monarch.

CHAPTER THIRTY-SIX

ACCORDING TO LEGEND, THERE WAS A BLACK-MAGIC CULT IN the ancient Dian kingdom. They were eventually driven into exile and chose to live deep in the mountains. Their leader was called King Xian—one of the many self-proclaimed monarchs in China's history. The six red-jade beasts were used in their rituals, representing north, south, east, west, heaven, and earth. King Xian would take a hallucinatory drug, putting himself in a trance state, and the jade animals would be placed on separate altars to create a magnetic field, forming a satanic totem that could penetrate directly into his consciousness.

The jade pieces used by King Xian would have been several times larger than the ones we found. These miniature versions were likely used by a witch doctor in his realm. As for how they fell into the hands of the coffin maker and how he came to master this branch of magic, we had no way of knowing. Perhaps he was a grave robber and had found them buried somewhere. Perhaps he was a descendant of the witch doctor who'd once owned them.

Professor Qiu's theory made a lot of sense and gave us a glimmer of hope. But when we asked where King Xian's tomb was likely to be, he had no idea. The king's devotion to the dark arts meant it would be remote and well hidden, so our chances of finding it after so many years were slim.

In any case, Professor Qiu advised us not to go tomb robbing. There were many other things we could do, he said—science was so advanced these days, perhaps there was a technological solution? We shouldn't be too fixated on the northern pearl. We shouldn't rely too much on the beliefs of ancient times. Back then, people didn't have a complete understanding of the natural world, and many of their beliefs were conjured out of thin air. Thunderstorms and snow were seen as magical occurrences. He promised to let us know if he came across any other clues.

I thanked him. "You don't need to worry—we're not going to break into his grave," I told him. "Besides, even if we wanted to, how would we find it?"

He nodded. "That's all right, then. I hate grave robbers more than anyone else in the world. Although it's true that archaeologists and grave robbers both seek out artifacts, the latter tend to cause damage. The country and the people must—"

I stood to go. I didn't want to hear the professor ramble on. Julie and I thanked him and returned to our hotel.

Our plan was to head back to Xi'an after lunch and then

to Beijing. Julie seemed preoccupied about something, and she didn't eat much. The blind fortune-teller was silent for a change. And I kept staring at the photograph of those six jade animals.

Every lead we'd followed had turned into a dead end. Our only option now was to head to Yunnan in search of King Xian's tomb. If we were lucky, we'd get our hands on the phoenix gall itself. If not, hopefully we'd at least come away with another clue or two.

But what hope did we have of finding it? All we knew was that it was in Yunnan, probably in the Lancang River delta. But the Lancang is a long river—it continues down into Southeast Asia, where it becomes the Mekong—and we could hardly go along it mile by mile, tearing up the soil.

"Aren't you always bragging about what a feng shui expert you are?" said Julie. "So we'll go to the river, you'll look up at the stars, and you'll tell us where it is. Yes?"

I smiled bitterly. "If only it were so simple. I can be certain on flat land, but Yunnan is covered in hills, and in addition to the Lancang, two other rivers slice across it. There are mountain ranges running right through it, crisscrossing the land. It's far too complex to get any kind of feng shui reading."

"You actually sound despairing, for once," said Julie.

"I'm not despairing, just uncertain. I have confidence, though—that never leaves me. Let's go back to Beijing, talk to the others, and maybe search for more clues farther afield."

The blind man suddenly piped up. "If the two of you are planning a reverse dip in Yunnan, let me advise you now to give up. It was in Yunnan that I came to grief, trying to break into

King Xian's tomb. The traps were deadlier than any I've ever seen. I left behind six of my companions, dead, along with my sight. I'm shivering to think of it now."

His words were like a thunderclap. "What did you say?" I said. "You found King Xian's tomb in Yunnan? If you tell a single lie, you can forget about coming to Beijing."

"How could I lie about a thing like that? I reverse dipped the Dian king's tomb on Li Family Mountain, but I got there too late, and all the artifacts were gone. All I found in the burial chamber was a thighbone and half a map of the ancient Dian kingdom carved into human skin. I hate to leave empty-handed, so I helped myself to the map. Back in Suzhou, I got a restoration expert to clean it with acetic acid. After sixteen washes, it was finally clear enough to read. And it marked the way to King Xian's tomb."

Julie looked disbelieving. "King Xian led his followers into the hills, far from Dian kingdom," she said. "They were cut off from their former home. How could this map have ended up in the Dian king's grave? You'd better not be bluffing us."

"King Xian made sure he'd be buried in a place with good feng shui, but one that couldn't be reverse dipped. Every leader's greatest fear is having their eternal rest disturbed. After he died, though, one of his followers wanted to return to Dian kingdom, so he offered the secret of the location to the Dian king, insisting that he could choose his new leader an equally good place. This was recorded on human skin. But in the end, the Dian king's tomb wasn't nearly as well hidden, which is how I got my hands on this map."

The blind man pulled something from a pocket and

unfolded it: the map. It had been restored but was still fairly blurry. We could only just make out the outlines of mountains and rivers.

"I carry this around with me, though I wouldn't normally show it to anyone. I hope you believe me now. And I have a warning—you see the bit marked Insect Valley, with a blank patch there? Strange things lurk in that area. If you tried to go in there, you'd almost certainly not get out."

Suddenly, he removed his dark glasses. Our hearts thudded at the sight of his face: where his eyes ought to have been were cavernous sockets, with thick crimson veins like withered vines trailing from the empty holes. Even the eyelids were gone.

He sighed as he put his glasses back on. "Even after these many years, I can still remember every second of that trip, my last reverse dip. If anything could be called terrifying, it would be that!"

I knew that the fortune-teller made his living spinning lies, but something about the way he told this story made me think every word of it was true. Yet what was it about that place that made it so special? I'd never heard of a feng shui spot so secret no one could find it without a map. How powerful was King Xian's tomb in Insect Valley?

Then I remembered Professor Qiu's warning: that King Xian was devoted to the dark arts and hadn't been an ordinary mortal. He fed his subjects to fish so that he could live longer, a practice that had apparently survived thousands of years. It was hard for a regular person to imagine such depths of evil.

Trying to find out more, Julie explained about the drowning tank and how the professor had said it was probably a relic from Yunnan. The blind man snorted, tugging at his beard. "Who is this Professor Qiu?" he said. "'Professor' sounds so grand. What does he profess? What does he know? He's afraid to admit he doesn't know, so he makes something up and misleads you."

"What are you saying?" I asked. "You think Professor Qiu is wrong?"

"As far as I know, King Xian's magic powers come from down south, from the region that is Myanmar today. He practiced a form of ancient Teng magic that's still in use, though in a very diluted form."

"Back in the day, I went with six others deep into the Yunnan hills. Before setting out, we asked around the nearby villages, trying to understand what we were in for. There is a strange tank that is part of Teng magic: it only works if you drown someone in it. The inscriptions on the outside are a spell that imprisons the soul in the body even after death. There's no greater cruelty. When the fish swim in through the holes and feast on the flesh, they also eat the soul of the departed. The body is reduced to bare bones in no time at all, and the fish grow to a length of three feet in a couple of weeks. Soup made from these fish is incomparably delicious. There's no greater taste."

I had to put down my chopsticks. "The way you're talking about it, I'm guessing you've tasted this soup yourself?"

"No way. If I had, I wouldn't be alive now. After the fish in the tank are grown, they're no longer fish, but creatures known as Teng. These Teng contain the vengeful spirits of the dead, which are a form of lethal poison that kills without leaving symptoms—the victims die with smiles on their faces as they recall the delicious flavor of the soup."

Julie wrinkled her brow. "So that was the coffin maker's secret. Whenever business was bad, he used Teng magic to kill people and increase demand for his coffins. I guess King Xian can't have been a good person either."

"The coffin maker knew a little Teng magic, but only a very little—you can't compare him to King Xian."

"Can you tell us more?" Julie pressed him. "What happened to you in King Xian's grave? If you can give us useful information, I'll consider getting Tianyi to let you have one of his antiques."

"I don't want your antiques!" snapped the fortune-teller. "But you asked nicely, so I'll tell you. This is a painful memory, though. . . ."

Back in Suzhou, the fortune-teller told us, he got the human-skin map restored, then deciphered the location of King Xian's tomb. He was overjoyed—his reverse dips so far had not been successful, but this was certain to be a real coup. He assembled a number of old hands at the trade, from all the different schools—gold hunters and mountain movers among them. After looking at the map and discussing the matter, they decided that the best way to take on this job would be to dig their way into the tomb.

The most experienced among them thought King Xian's tomb wouldn't be too large, because his empire hadn't been too powerful. The map showed it was in a valley and followed the natural contours of the land. In that period, the Dian nation kings were buried with bronze carriages and horses, terracotta warriors, all sorts of treasures. As the saying goes, the starving camel is still bigger than the horse, so they thought King Xian's grave would still contain its share of good things."

Even from that blurry map, they could see that the tomb was located on a tributary of the Lancang River called Snake Creek, which wound its way through a snowy peak called Dragon Mountain, though the locals had nicknamed it Sorrow Mound. It was 3,300 meters above sea level.

The creek meandered down into a river valley, which was filled with mist year round. There were a lot of bugs there, so it acquired the name Insect Valley. Hardly anyone lived around there. The landscape was lovely, and the air often filled with vibrantly colored butterflies. The white fog that descended could be deadly, though, so few people dared venture in. It was said that this was a "Teng cloud," summoned by the late King Xian to keep his tomb safe. Only when a storm cleared the air was it safe to enter—otherwise the demon mist might engulf you.

Beyond this valley was a vast waterfall, referred to in feng shui terms as a water dragon. The human-skin map said this place was chosen by the king's witch doctors, and the mist was called the "water dragon's sickness." Under its spell, your vision would blur, you'd start to feel faint, and bit by bit your body would shut down.

The great thing about this spot, apart from its excellent feng shui, was that this place was so dangerous, hardly anyone dared to go in.

The fortune-teller and his colleagues knew this wouldn't be an easy job, but they were determined to give it a go, their judgment clouded by the thought of all the treasure they might find. After crossing the snow-covered mountain, they waited more than ten days above Insect Valley until finally dark clouds formed and the rains came. The mist was torn apart by harsh winds, and they were able to rush through the storm into the deadly valley. They were halfway down when, abruptly, the wind and rain stopped, and the sun beamed down again. White fog rose all around them.

Scattering in all directions, they tried frantically to find a path to safety. The mist would have stopped their hearts if they'd taken a single breath.

The fortune-teller made use of his training to hold his breath as he sprinted for his life. He managed to get out, but the poisonous air destroyed his eyes. Luckily, he stumbled upon their local guide, who'd been waiting for them at the entrance to the valley. The fortune-teller had to gouge out his own eyes to prevent the poison from entering his bloodstream, and that was how he managed to survive.

Julie and I listened closely to this story, and we both felt that the reason the expedition had failed was simple lack of preparation. It wouldn't have been hard to take precautions against this deadly mist, but they'd simply blundered in.

"It's rare to see such dense clouds of poison," Julie said. "Maybe it's something to do with the location and native plants that give off toxins. In any case, a gas mask or antidote should be able to prevent the poison from affecting us. I don't see why this would have anything to do with Teng magic."

"Not so," said the blind man. "If it's that simple, why has no living person ever made it into King Xian's tomb? As for what the fog is made of, you can read about it on the back of the map."

Julie turned over the scrap of human parchment, and we

saw clusters of words and pictures. It seemed from this that there were four other burial sites surrounding the main tomb, and also various ministers buried nearby. Quite a stately setting, for a second-rate king.

There was also a record of the king's own description of his grave: "When I die, bury me in dragon king mist. My soul will be immortal, and the dragon sickness will protect me. Unless the sky crashes down, no outsider will find me."

"So if the sky doesn't fall down, we'll never get into his grave?" I muttered. "But what does that mean? In ancient times, didn't they believe that shooting stars were a sign that the sky was about to collapse? Could it be referring to that? Maybe we need to wait for a particular time in order to break into the tomb?"

The blind man shook his head. "Can't be. I've been studying this riddle for years, and I still don't have any idea what it could refer to. This king must have trampled on many lives during his reign, and surely his enemies would have tried to break into his tomb afterward. There must be something about the place that made it impossible—more than the danger of the valley, the tomb itself must be full of deadly traps. I'm warning you now, stay away from King Xian's grave."

We'd made up our minds, though, and nothing would dissuade us from going to Yunnan. We had to see the place for ourselves, before deciding whether or not to venture in. Julie bought the map from the blind man, and then we went to pack our things. Soon we'd be back in Beijing, and after reuniting with Kai, we'd make our way to Yunnan, where we'd hopefully find the answers we were looking for, in the heart of dragon sickness, in the ancient tomb of King Xian.

ABOUT THE AUTHOR

Born in Tianjin in 1978, the year China's reforms began, **Tianxia Bachang** (the pen name of Zhang Muye) is a child of the new China. His careers have been many and varied, a winding path of self-discovery that would never have been open to his parents' generation. An avid gamer, he has chosen his online avatar as his pen name, and his stories have been bestsellers within the gaming community. *The Dragon Ridge Tombs* is Tianxia Bachang's second book to be translated into English; the first was *The City of Sand*.

ABOUT THE TRANSLATOR

Jeremy Tiang has translated more than ten books from Chinese, including novels by Zhang Yueran, Wang Jinkang, Yeng Pway Ngon, and Chan Ho-Kei, and has been awarded a PEN/Heim Grant, an NEA Literary Translation Fellowship, and a Henry Luce Foundation Fellowship. He also writes and translates plays. Jeremy Tiang lives in Brooklyn, New York.